PRAISE FOR
THE MAN WHO FELL IN LOVE WITH HIS WIFE

'A very skilful practitioner of a genre hitherto dominated by Nick Hornby and Tony Parsons . . . With its irreverent and original religious twist, this novel should secure his position in that particular literary gang . . . literary comfort food – a smooth hot chocolate' *Time Out*

'A fast and entertaining read . . . It all has a Richard Curtis-esque veneer . . . It has Colin Firth written all over it . . . His writing is just the right mixture of tongue-in-cheek meets heartwarming and he makes you laugh . . . it works because it's real' *Sunday Express*

'Slick, cool and fast-paced, this novel jogs smartly along with the zeitgeist of the twenty-first century' *Newbooksmag*

'An inspired creation . . . A perfect gem of warmth and humour with a charming twist, it is highly addictive and worthy of mass recommendation' *The Bookseller*

'For those of you who loved Father Dempsey in Paul Burke's debut novel, *Father Frank*, this follow up is a gift from heaven' *OK!*

'Laughs a-plenty as former Father Frank Dempsey copes with being a dad' *Daily Mirror*

PAUL BURKE

The Man Who Fell In Love With His Wife

HODDER

First published in Great Britain in 2004 by Hodder and Stoughton
A division of Hodder Headline
First published in paperback in Great Britain in 2005 by
Hodder & Stoughton

A Hodder & Stoughton Paperback

3 5 7 9 10 8 6 4 2

A CIP catalogue record for this title is
available from the British Library

ISBN 0 340 82818 8

Typeset in Monotype Sabon by
Palimpsest Book Production Limited, Polmont, Stirlingshire

Printed and bound in Great Britain by
Mackays of Chatham Ltd, Chatham, Kent

Hodder Headline's policy is to use papers that are natural, renewable
and recyclable products and made from wood grown in sustainable forests.
The logging and manufacturing processes are expected to conform to the
environmental regulations of the country of origin

Hodder and Stoughton Ltd
A division of Hodder Headline
338 Euston Road
London NW1 3BH

To Dee Beechinor

ACKNOWLEDGEMENTS

Eternal gratitude, as ever, for the unique skills of Philippa Pride for making me do it three times when I never thought I could do it once. And to Sara Kinsella for making me do it better. Special thanks to Sidney Platt – 100 not out and an inspiration to us all. Drinks are surely owed to Steve Hayden, Sophie Ritchie and Gerry Bryant who were more help than they'll ever realise. Thanks also to Jack and Eleanor whose material needs are a constant incentive and finally, of course, to the wife with whom the man fell in love.

1

Although Sarah was his first wife, Frank Dempsey had been married before. His first match, however, had been less than ideal. Although he'd always seemed so happy, so utterly fulfilled, he'd secretly felt the pain of gnawing uncertainty since the day he'd walked down the aisle.

He remembered the ceremony only too well, smiling his way through a hundred hugs and handshakes, all the time thinking, Oh, God, what have I done?

Some sort of answer didn't seem too much to expect since it was God to whom Frank had just pledged his life. By becoming a Catholic priest, he had 'married' the Catholic Church, and signed up for a life of chastity and self-denial. Just like an ordinary marriage then, he'd tried jokingly to console himself, making a desperate attempt to look on the bright side. At least he didn't have to wear a ring. Not like Sister Amelia who, along with all the other nuns from the Convent of the Holy Family across the road, sported a gold band on the third finger of her left hand. A symbol of her marriage to God, apparently, but what sort of marriage did the poor woman have? She had never seen her 'husband', she didn't even know what He looked like. She'd spoken to Him thousands of times, but He'd never once deigned to reply. He'd never taken her out, bought her a present or shown her the slightest smidgen of affection. She'd never been able to introduce Him to her friends. 'Where is He?' they might ask.

'Oh, He's everywhere,' would be her reply. Well, He'd need to be with all those other wives in convents all over the world.

Not surprisingly, Frank wasn't entirely convinced that Sister Amelia's beloved spouse really existed. Oh, there had allegedly been sightings and miracles from time to time, but not for a while. Oddly enough, not since the invention of cameras and videos. Frank had therefore come to regard God in the same way he regarded space aliens. He couldn't say for certain that they didn't exist but his scepticism was best expressed in one simple question: why was it that these little creatures only seemed to turn up on remote prairies in Fyfe, Alabama? Why not in the middle of Oxford Street? And didn't the same question apply to Jesus? One quick comeback gig in Hyde Park would prove conclusively that He was the man. Believers by the billion could then watch open-mouthed via satellite as he ran through the old back catalogue – healing a few lepers, doing that brilliant routine with the loaves and fishes and, as an encore, taking a gentle stroll down the middle of the Serpentine.

Frank never did see Jesus or the Virgin Mary in the West End of London, but it was there that he finally found his faith. He saw an apparition whose existence, unlike comparable sightings at Fatima and Lourdes, was irrefutable. She was divine. Dark hair, chocolate-brown eyes, and a figure to die for. From the moment Father Frank Dempsey's covetous gaze fell upon Sarah Marshall, he knew that his vow of celibacy was on a life-support machine. Once it became clear that his love was reciprocated, an invisible doctor had come in, coughed politely and switched it off.

Released from his first entanglement, Frank found himself once again at the altar, this time with a far more compatible partner. He treated his second set of vows far more seriously than he'd ever treated the first. The hundreds of friends and relatives who had crammed into St Thomas's Church in Wealdstone watched in delight as Father Lynam asked the standard question, 'Do you, Francis John Dempsey, take Sarah Louise Marshall to be your lawful wedded wife?'

Frank, however, heard it rather differently: 'Do you, Francis John Dempsey, agree to swap Holy Orders for Holy Matrimony and, in so doing, turn your back on a life you thought you'd have to endure for ever? Do you bid farewell to the Spartan presbytery in Wealdstone that you share with two lonely, celibate men to go and live in a funky flat in Fulham with a gorgeous woman who finds you every bit as sexy as you find her? Do you forsake an ascetic and isolating existence to experience physical and emotional fulfilment just when you thought you never would? Do you finally want to stop living a lie and start reaping your rewards on earth rather than waiting till you get to heaven, which, let's face it, may not even exist?

There was only ever going to be one answer: 'I do.'

When Father Lynam turned to Sarah, she heard exactly what he said: 'Do you, Sarah Louise Marshall, take Francis John Dempsey to be your lawful wedded husband?'

However, on the bride's side of the church, they heard it rather differently: 'Do you, Sarah Louise Marshall, agree to marry this penniless, unemployed ex-Catholic priest who, at forty, is ten years older than you? Granted, he's handsome, witty and intelligent, but do you really think he's ideally placed to make a success of his life and your marriage? Do you realise that, because you're the one with the successful career in advertising, you'll have to pay all the bills? Do you really know what you're doing?'

And Sarah's reply was as emphatic as Frank's: 'I do.'

2

Most people, even those who don't drink it, love the smell of freshly ground coffee, and as this heavenly aroma alarm-clocked its way up Frank's nostrils and gently coaxed him from his slumbers, it made him feel happier than he had ever felt in his life. Not because it was being ground in the adjacent chic, brushed-steel kitchen by the heart-stoppingly sexy woman in a short robe who was now his wife, but because the smell of freshly ground coffee was the smell of freedom. The smell that allowed him to be honest and finally admit: 'I, Frank Dempsey, have never liked tea.'

It would be easier for a priest to admit to his parishioners that he didn't believe in God than to put his hands up and say he didn't believe in tea. He couldn't begin to count the cups he had been forced to swill down in the course of his work. To refuse a 'cuppa tay' in an Irish-Catholic household was tantamount to owning up to being a lifelong admirer of the Black and Tans. His hosts would never have understood. They would have stopped, teapot tilted, and looked at him askance. 'What do you mean, you don't like tea?'

Suspicion would be aroused, some sort of tacit trust would be broken, and getting them to do as he asked would be almost impossible.

Luckily, he'd hit upon a wonderful idea. At his next parish, he would say he was allergic to the vile beverage, just as he'd always told people he was allergic to cats when they'd tried to dump their sly, spiteful killing-machines on his lap. Allergic to tea? Brilliant. Except, of course, there never had been a 'next parish' and now there never would be.

Led by his sense of smell, Frank's other senses flickered into life and lifted him out of bed. He'd never liked lying in. Alone, in a hard single bed with a crucifix above the headboard, why would he have wanted to? Even now, swamped in the opulence of a king-size duvet, head floating serenely on luxurious goose-down pillows, he felt no desire to lie there on his own once his eyes were open. He never wanted to watch TV in bed or have breakfast in bed – he'd spent too many years as a hospital chaplain, watching sick people do just that.

No, in Frank's opinion, bed was for sleeping and one other activity, the joy of which he was rediscovering. To start with, it hadn't been a great success. Expectations were too high. Twenty years of chastity are hardly the best preparation for your wedding night, and Frank's resulting performance was rather like that of a man trying to play snooker with a length of rope. It wasn't long, however, before the rope tautened and those twenty un-fulfilled years were forgotten in one glorious moment.

He got up and walked through to the kitchen, tenderly embraced his wife from behind, and nuzzled his face into the nape of her neck. It had been a fabulous night. The rope had been taut on more than one occasion and was heading that way again.

'Mmm,' said Sarah, with a sultry giggle. 'Much as I'd love to, I'm late for work already. And, anyway, we *have* got the rest of our lives.'

The thought of this filled Frank with delight and despair. Yes, he was deliriously happy, set free from his vow of celibacy to marry a girl who had turned out to be perfect beyond his wildest dreams. However, as far as his life was concerned, the referee had just blown for half-time. In many ways, he had played well in the first forty-five minutes but, as he walked down the tunnel, he knew that his second-half performance would have to be magnificent. He'd have to play in a way he had never played before. And he had no idea how he was going to do that.

3

Basically.

Sarah, despite her natural tolerance and happy disposition, had developed an aversion to the word 'basically'. It had joined other words and phrases – namely 'All righty', 'Pardon my French' and 'Well, I never did', which she found as irritating as tinfoil on a filling. Perhaps it was over-exposure to Mike Babcock, an ex-client whose vocabulary was unhealthily dependent on it, that had sown the seeds of her abhorrence.

Mike was cortically incapable of speaking for more than twelve seconds without saying that word. '*Basically*, what we need to do is . . .'; 'What I'm *basically* saying, is . . .'; 'So, *basically*, we were all in the pub . . .' There was also something rather patronising about the way people like Mike used it. Weren't they implying that they were having to reduce what they were saying to 'basics' so that you, you buffoon, could understand it?

Sarah, however, allowed herself a secret, silent use of the B-word when she came to the conclusion that, though newly married, her life was basically unchanged. She lived in the same sunny basement flat, drove the same car and sat at the same desk at the same London advertising agency where she had sat since leaving university.

On this grey January morning, despite the traffic on the Fulham Road, which had made her wonder whether she might have been quicker on crutches, she had surfed in to work on a warm wave of post-nuptial thrall.

First day back. First day with her name under D instead of M on the agency phone list. Sarah Dempsey. She was getting used to it now. She rather liked it. Christ, it could have been a lot worse. Her new husband might have been called Frank Pratt, Frank Hoare or, with his Irish provenance, Frank O'Looney. She'd rejected that faintly ridiculous show of 'equality' that leads some couples to the self-conscious creation of clumsy double-barrelled surnames. She had no desire to rechristen herself and her husband Marshall-Dempsey so they could spend the rest of their lives sounding like a firm of solicitors.

She'd perfected her new 'Sarah Dempsey' signature and was very happy with the result. It was completely illegible. She'd designed it that way. As you get older and more enigmatic, surely your signature should follow suit.

On with the laptop – log in: *smarshall*. No joy. Whoops, of course, try again: *sdempsey*. Password? This was unchanged. Craig in IT had once told her that most passwords were fairly easy to work out – almost invariably the name of a loved one. Sarah loved shoes but had made her password a little more oblique: *aglet*. Very few people even knew it was a word. But Sarah, perusing an old copy of the *Reader's Digest* one day in a dentist's waiting room, had discovered that an aglet was that bit on the end of your shoelace.

With its infuriatingly cheery jingle, Windows XP trilled into life, and sdempsey began to plough her way through the 346 unread e-mails, 99 per cent of which would be of no interest to 99 per cent of their recipients:

Double room to let in Tooting. Close to tube. Non-smoker preferred.

Gold earring found in ladies' loo. Contact Claire on ext 4213.

Hi, y'all, after three crazy years in Accounts, I'm leaving for pastures new, so if any of you old reprobates fancy an ale and a fare-thee-well, I'll be in the Rat & Parrot from 5.30 on Friday.
Cheers, Timbo.

Quietly relieved to have missed 'Timbo' and the rest of the finance department downing a couple of quick ones before heading off to catch their six thirty trains to Essex and Kent, Sarah sorted the wheat from the chaff. Among the unwanted missives were quite a few congratulatory messages along the lines of 'Welcome back, how was it?'; You're a dark horse, aren't you? We must catch up and you can tell me all about it.' Sarah knew that the following month's worth of lunchtimes would involve sitting in various bars and restaurants 'telling people all about it' and answering their questions, the most popular of which would be 'Why him? A Catholic priest?'

Any woman who had met Frank, and had seen his short, dark George Clooney hair, his relaxed, intelligent charm, his piercing blue eyes and slow-release smile, never needed to ask that question. To those who hadn't, Sarah could only respond with a cavalcade of clichés: seasoned old campaigners like 'I just knew he was the one'; 'When you know, you know' and 'We were drawn together like magnets' tumbled out before she could stop them. Worst of all, whenever she was asked about the vow of celibacy that hadn't really made him the most eligible of men, out came 'Love will conquer all.'

'So what was it that really attracted you to him?' was the usual supplementary enquiry.

From his extraordinary quiver of qualities, Sarah chose to concentrate on the one arrow that had so quickly pierced her heart. 'His confidence,' she would reply. 'His rock-solid confidence' which, for Sarah, had a potency on a par with powdered rhino horn. She went on to distinguish confidence from selfishness, and explain that if confidence ever swelled into arrogance, the bubble burst, the magic vamoosed and the aphrodisiac lost its power.

'Did you always think that you'd marry him?' was another she was asked on several occasions.

'God, no,' would be her truthful reply, 'I tried my best not to but . . . well . . . [insert cliché here].'

She carried on deleting her way through her in-box until she came to the one e-mail she had been hoping for.

From: vanessa.williams335@hotmail.com Subject: Client meeting.

Sarah knew exactly what it was going to say:

Client is coming in at lunchtime to discuss how best to move the Supershine brand on strategically in response to changes in the hair-care market. I've booked the conference room from 1.00 and would welcome your input. Please let me know whether you can/cannot attend.

Sarah and Nessie, her former flatmate, had been sending each other this e-mail for years, rather like those people who appear on *Home Truths*, chuckling with John Peel about how they've been sending the same birthday card back and forth to each other since 1953. There was no client meeting, there was no client. Nessie didn't even work in advertising: she was an opera singer. The 'conference room' was the lunchtime bustle of Amalfi, a popular Italian trattoria round the corner and the 'meeting' was held whenever any gossip required their immediate attention. Today, naturally, it was the sudden replacement of Marshall with Dempsey.

Sarah had a healthy appetite but loved lunching with Nessie because her best friend's formidable esurience made her feel anorexic. She was only three minutes late but Nessie had already devoured a basket of ciabatta, and was dunking the final crust into a pool of olive oil the size of Lake Como. 'Darling,' she boomed from the bottom of her professionally trained diaphragm, 'how are you?'

'Never better,' beamed Sarah, and she meant it.

'And how's Crocodile Dundee?' This was how Nessie regarded Frank, a charismatic man who had quit the only life he'd ever known to marry the woman he loved.

'Oh, he's coping . . . I think.'

'Coping with your Imelda tendencies?' asked Nessie, teasing.

'Said the kettle to the pot.'

Both Sarah and Nessie maintained a hopeless addiction to

shoes, which ensured that they received Christmas cards from their grateful friends at Emma Hope and Jimmy Choo. Nessie loved buying any form of footwear because she knew she could swallow an entire ciabatta bakery and her shoe size would not be affected. For Sarah, it was a variation on the same theme. Her five and a half was the one size she never needed to maintain or reduce. They both had a sizeable collection, but neither could compete with Nessie's friend Sue Haddleton, whose thirty-seven pairs were meticulously stored in their original boxes, each with a Polaroid of its contents neatly taped to the outside. Sue was the Imelda's Imelda.

'No, but come on,' said Nessie, 'this is a man who had forsaken all his worldly goods and chattels. Then he marries someone whose Selfridges' bill would exceed the gross national product of most third-world countries. Must have been a bit of a shock for him – for both of you.'

Sarah laughed. 'Listen,' she said, pointing an accusatory bread-stick at her friend, 'you could lay out every pair of shoes, every item of clothing, every lotion, potion and expensive bottle of perfume that I possess and its combined value would still be only a fraction of what he must have spent on records, seven-inch singles, twelve-inch singles, albums. Your old room has turned into the Virgin Megastore.'

'Well, didn't he work as a DJ before he was a priest?'

'Yeah, but that was years ago. He must have at least three or four hundred new CDs as well. I've never asked him where he got them. In fact, there are a lot of things I've never asked him.'

'Well,' laughed Nessie, eyes widening as the waiter placed a gargantuan plate of linguine in front of her, 'you don't really know him, do you?'

'Well, that's the weird thing. From the day I first met him, I felt like I'd known him all my life.' Oh, Christ, she thought, another cliché. 'And the nice thing is, I'm still getting to know him. It's a bit like an arranged marriage. I sometimes feel like an Asian girl from Burnley who's just married this stranger from a village in Pakistan and it seems to be working out really well.'

'Arranged marriages often do,' said Nessie. 'Far greater success rate than we have. Except, of course, yours was probably the most unarranged marriage I've ever heard of. No one else had any part in it. No one else knew anything about it. Ah, your wedding was so romantic. Mind you, I did think you were up the duff.' She paused. 'You're not, are you?'

'No, I am not,' said Sarah. 'Anyway. How are things? Rehearsals going okay?'

'Yeah, fine. It's *La Bohème*. I've done it before. Guido, the director, is very good but he's a bit of an old woman. Still, nice to be in London for a change.'

With Epicurean speed and dexterity, Nessie wound about half a mile of pasta round her fork then continued, 'How are you managing for money? It's just not true, is it, that two can live as cheaply as one? And, all right, you were always very good about the rent but the pittance I paid you did sort of keep you in shoes, didn't it?'

'Yeah, you're right, but don't worry. He didn't turn up totally skint. They had a massive whip-round for him at his last parish. It came to nearly twelve grand and he handed the whole lot to me. Says he can't be trusted with cash. Apparently, as a priest, he was preprogrammed to give it to the needy and old habits die hard.'

'But what's he going to do to earn more?' said Nessie, with a grin that was four parts amusement and one part concern. 'That twelve grand will just leak out of you.'

'Well, he's writing his book so, hopefully, just as that money runs out, he'll get a huge advance.'

Nessie had no doubts about Frank's ability. 'And he will, you know. He's so clever, so funny – and what a story.'

'Anyway,' said Sarah, 'what about your love-life? How's Robert?'

'Rob-*air*,' replied Nessie, affecting a French accent, 'is still French. As far as I know.'

'As far as you know?'

'Yes. We've gone our separate ways.'

'Oh,' said Sarah, disappointed, 'I thought he was nice.'

'Ah,' said Nessie. 'But you weren't sure, were you?'

'Well, I only met him a couple of times.'

'But you wouldn't have been able to tell. I must stop going out with foreign men, no matter how gorgeous they are, because it's so hard to gauge what they're really like.'

Sarah was confused. 'What do you mean?'

'Well, with an English bloke, as soon as he opens his mouth, you'll know whether he's bright, thick, public-school, a bit of rough or whatever, but with foreigners something gets lost in translation. Robert was just French so it took me six months to realise he was a bit of a dork. Still, plenty more fish in the sea.'

And there would be. Nessie could always reel in the catch of her choice. She laughed in the face of other girls' 'eating issues', their 'Carb days', detox regimes, Hay diets, only-eating-in-daylight diets, their 'No veg for me, thanks, I'm on Atkins' diets. Nessie felt that diets, like unicycles, were wonderful things for other people to go on. With her comely, plumptious figure, which might have been drawn by Beryl Cook, she couldn't fathom these wearisome weight-watchers, with their odd combination of vanity and self-loathing.

'Do you fancy really skinny men?' Nessie would ask her more twig-like acquaintances, through a faceful of tiramisu.

'No,' would be their invariable reply.

'Then what the hell makes you think that they fancy really skinny girls? Darling, I'm living proof that they don't.'

Now she glanced at her watch. 'Christ, I'm late. Second time this week. Guido's going to throw another hissy fit.'

Sarah called for the bill and made the first tiny dent in Frank's twelve grand.

'Oh, darling, thank you,' said her friend, and kissed each of Sarah's cheeks. 'You will come to the opening night, won't you?'

'Of course,' said Sarah. She always did, although she had often thought that opera, like olives, was something people only pretended to like.

'So, it's going well, then?' said Nessie, as she turned towards the door.

'Yeah,' said Sarah. 'So far, so good. I'm really, really happy.' She paused. 'Basically.'

4

Frank thought it would be easy.

He thought most things were easy. Not because he was a multi-talented genius but because he wasn't. He had learned at an early age to avoid anything that caused him difficulty. As a result, he couldn't play bridge, backgammon or the bassoon. He had never picked up a golf club or a foreign language; neither could he cook, paint or sew on a button. He'd never understood the poetry of Baudelaire or the purpose of trigonometry. And although his father was a bricklayer, the building gene had not been passed down. Frank was so pitiably inept at practical chores that he turned green at the very mention of self-assembly furniture.

But writing? Almost every human being in the Western world can write something. It's not like being a cellist, a plasterer or a gynaecologist – these disciplines take talent, application and years of training. Tell most people to write a story and they'll come up with something. Tell them to rewire a house and see how far they get.

It was this rather obvious appraisal of writing that had led Frank, like others before him, to believe he could do it. For most aspiring authors, it's the swift realisation that they can't that sends them scurrying back to their day jobs. For an ex-Catholic priest who was now married, that wasn't an option.

What on earth was he going to do? Despite his intelligence and charisma, he had no tangible talents, and no man has ever put down as his occupation 'really nice bloke'. He'd become a priest because he couldn't think of anything else to do. And, more than twenty years later, he still couldn't.

He'd thought briefly about becoming a teacher. Very briefly. He suddenly remembered how classrooms had changed since the last time he'd been in one. He remembered that teachers were no longer allowed to discipline unruly pupils. It would be a nightmare. He'd also be dealing with the first generation of parents who hadn't been disciplined either, so there'd be the constant threat of a smack in the mouth from some fat, tattooed yob in a shell suit. Or, worse still, from her husband.

At the moment, he had no other plan that might net him a collection of contemporary banknotes. His twelve-grand cushion, though still plump and comfortable, would soon start to lose its stuffing, so he was doing his best to knuckle down.

However, like countless others, he found the hardest part of writing to be the application of bum to seat. He looked for any excuse to divert him from what he was supposed to be doing. He only wished he'd been born practical: then he could have found endless shelves to put up and walls to dry-line.

Sitting down and thinking wasn't really his métier. His great gift had always been his ability to communicate. What had set Father Frank Dempsey apart from other priests were his eloquent and amusing sermons, which had always guaranteed that both pews and collection plates were overflowing. He was a natural raconteur who could entertain people *ad infinitum* with stories from childhood and priesthood. This ability had been one of the things that had drawn Sarah to him and ensured that her fascination with him would never fade. She could hardly be blamed for assuming that a man so verbally adroit would be able to transfer that talent to the page.

But she was wrong.

What she didn't know was that Frank seldom wrote anything down. If he did, he always forgot whatever it was he was supposed to remember. The pocket diary sent to him every year by the *Catholic Herald* would spend twelve undisturbed months in a drawer: if he put an appointment in it, he would be letting his memory off the hook and handing over responsibility to a little black book, which he would then lose, forget, and then forget he'd lost. Far better to keep everything in his head where it could never go AWOL.

He'd never written a sermon in his life, taking his cue instead from Billy Connolly, another gifted maverick with little use for paper or pen. During his live shows, the Big Yin apparently had someone standing in the wings, holding up the occasional sign saying, 'The Pope' or 'Pub crawl in Glasgow', and that was all he needed to go into twenty minutes of freewheeling brilliance.

Frank's sermons were similarly unrehearsed. All he had in his head when he closed the Gospel was a starting- and finishing-point, leaving him that huge bit in the middle to extemporise. It was this that the congregation, no matter how bleary-eyed or hung-over, would always heave themselves out of bed to hear. They were fabulous flights of fancy in which Frank employed a spellbinding, almost Churchillian range of rhetorical techniques.

Unlike Churchill, though, Frank had the concentration span of a gnat and the self-discipline of a smack addict. He was undone by the lonely process of writing. He was wholly unprepared for the soul-destroying silence, the solitude and lack of interaction. He was a gregarious man whose life had revolved around his parish and the people in it. His days had always been spent among them, either at mass, at the parish centre or enjoying warm, Irish hospitality in any one of a hundred households. He had never been a loner, never wasted a moment in contemplative prayer. He saw little point in trying to commune with someone who was never going to reply.

Odd, then, that during one of his many long, dull, unproductive stretches, he found himself waiting for a muse, one of the nine mythical daughters of Zeus who were each blessed with the power to release creative inspiration. Of course, the idle idol was nowhere to be seen and Frank wasn't surprised: he'd spent the previous twenty years waiting at a metaphysical bus stop for God to come along in a big red double-decker with 'The Meaning of Life' displayed on the front. That particular deity had never shown up so why should this one be any different?

He needed the muse to unseize his brain. It was like a petrol tank with a kilo of sugar in it – before the introduction of lockable petrol caps, this had been a routine prank in the Kilburn of Frank's youth: as soon as the key was turned in the ignition, the sugar jammed every mechanical part and the car needed a new engine.

Frank sat cursing the cursor that flickered tauntingly on his blank screen, then took a broader view of what he was doing. He was writing an autobiography entitled *To Be Frank*. A clunking great pun, but it was still the most natural title for the memoirs of anyone called Frank. He was writing it because Sarah had said he should. It was a fascinating tale, she'd told him, the priest who didn't believe in God. Frank, though always seduced by compliments, had his misgivings. 'Thing is,' he'd protested, 'I won't be bringing in any money.'

'Yet,' she'd assured him.

'But who's going to buy it?'

'Lots of people. Trust me, I read a lot of books. At least, I did until I met you. And that's what convinced me.'

'Convinced you of what?'

'That your story, the way you put it over, will sell by the truck-load.'

'Yeah, but—'

'Look,' she said, 'just think of yourself as an actor or a musician, they don't always earn regular money, but if they're talented someone will always want to pay for that talent. You're so talented that the money will eventually come rolling in.'

'Eventually?'

'It'll take as long as it takes. There's no pressure.'

And that was Frank's problem: the fact that there was no pressure was the greatest pressure of all. And Sarah's blind faith, like that of his ex-parishioners, was something he couldn't bear to betray.

Suddenly he found himself haunted by a book of which he'd seen at least fifty copies, piled high in a remainder bookshop. Its title was something like *Kerry Dixon – My Story*, the autobiography of an ex-Chelsea striker. Kerry had been pretty good in his eighties heyday, but he wasn't a superstar like Beckham or Best and his story was less than riveting. Yet someone had persuaded him that it was worth telling – when, judging by that towering stack of unsold copies, it clearly wasn't.

Still no sign of the muse, so Frank tried going out for a walk. Flaubert had found his flow by walking through a quiet avenue of trees, so Frank decided to find his by strolling alone through Bishops Park. Unfortunately, as he strolled past the children's play area, he felt like one of those strange men his mother had always told him never to talk to. Especially since he was now muttering incoherently, in the search for a spark of creativity. He remembered something his old friend Father Lynam had been fond of saying: 'Man creates nothing, Frank. God created everything. Man merely rearranges it.'

Frank, with all the words in the English language at his disposal, was powerless to rearrange them into a truly original order. The only thing he could think of rearranging was his hair. A haircut was always good for passing the time, but as Frank contemplated his third in as many days, he realised that unless he wanted to go for the 'Ageing Rent Boy' look, his next appointment would have to wait. Perhaps a full set of highlights, extensions or dreadlocks would be a better way to wile away an hour or two.

Then, in a move that would have shocked his old PE teacher, Frank Dempsey decided to go to the gym. After all, PE had been easier than writing essays so it must be a hell of a lot easier than writing a book.

Arriving at the Go For It! Health & Fitness Centre, he realised that PE was no longer as simple as it used to be. There was now a bewildering number of ways for him to get red, sweaty and repulsive. As Kelly from the Go For It! Reception Team explained, Frank could try spinning, ice-climbing or roller-soccer. When she offered him a 'Swiss ball workout', he couldn't bring himself to ask her what this might entail.

He opted for the gym because at least he knew what it was, and hauled himself on to the treadmill. He looked in vain for a 'dawdle' or 'saunter' setting, and began to pound reluctantly along. He wasn't sure whether to be appalled or amused by the walls of mirrors that showed him how ridiculous he looked from a variety of angles, trotting along but going nowhere trying to run away from the book he had promised to write. Yet even when he raised his trot to a canter and his canter to a gallop, the book was galloping along behind him. When he slowed down and got off, so did the book. It followed him over to the free weights area where he took one look at the aptly named dumb-bells and went off to have a shower. The book followed him there too, politely passing him the soap and shampoo, before accompanying him home.

He put his key in the door-lock, hoping that the muse might have let herself in and be sitting by the computer, waiting to help him, but she wasn't. The flat, complete with blank computer screen, was exactly as he'd left it. Frank slumped on the sofa, opened his mind and let it wander. Perhaps, relaxed and receptive, it would be struck by inspiration.

After a couple of minutes, he found it was struck instead by any useless thought that wanted to come in. People he thought he'd forgotten suddenly rose from the past, with Siobhan O'Mahoney first in the parade. A pale, freckly, green-eyed girl with hair the colour of Lucozade, she had sat next to Frank at St Joseph's RC primary school and could easily have been crowned 'Miss Genetically Unfortunate 1970'. Frank wondered what had happened to her. Was she married? Kids? And how about her mum who used to work in the wool shop on Kilburn High Road?

Then an evil spirit broke in and started to shovel coins into the juke-box from hell. It contained hymns, 'Alleluia, sing to Jesus', bits of Latin – *Pater Noster qui es in caeli* . . . and a horrible selection of seventies pop songs that went round and round on a random and eternal loop: 'Billy Don't Be A Hero', 'Ooh Wakka-do Wakka-day' and, worst of all, 'Remember You're A Womble'.

Having mentally produced a big stick and chased his tormentors back to Wimbledon Common, Frank would reflect, breathless and sweating, on why his mind had become weak enough to welcome the Wombles. As he regained his composure, he began to realise that, for a writer, his ego was the wrong way round. Writers are often shy, unassuming people whose quiet, almost timorous demeanours disguise egos the size of Jupiter. They really believe they have something significant to say and are driven by an intense desire to say it. Frank, though naturally confident, almost cocky, had a core to his character that was surprisingly humble. Cloaked in his vestments, he could perform, and his lack of faith had meant that every Sunday had been a theatrical performance. It was only ever an act. The altar had been his stage and his flock the audience. Now he felt like Superman divested of his powers – just an ordinary man of forty with no beliefs and nothing to say.

On paper, he had done nothing extraordinary. What made him extraordinary was that he had been a priest who had never believed in God. That was the crux of his story, but it was the bit he was unwilling to tell. In doing so, he would be denouncing the beliefs of his ex-parishioners, beliefs he had nurtured and encouraged. In a tacky reversal of an ancient sacrament, he would be confessing to them and asking their forgiveness, admitting that he had been travelling on a false passport since the day he was ordained. Why disappoint and upset all those nice, if gullible people?

Still no muse. For the first time in his life, Frank felt lonely. Lonely enough to consider going salsa dancing or recording a humorous outgoing message on his answering machine. His mind turned to Kettle Chips. He was tempted to lie on the sofa in his underpants, eating a jumbo-sized bag, while he watched all the nuts-and-sluts TV programmes that littered the daytime schedules.

He was now counting the minutes until Sarah came home from work. He felt like one of those 'hovering husbands' who were photographed hovering behind their famous wives, their own careers stalled. Neither could he face becoming a 'hoovering husband' – unemployed and unemployable, taking care of domestic matters while his wife was out winning the bread.

He was filled with horror at the thought of Sarah one day describing him as her 'rock'. A 'rock' was what a 'sweet' bloke becomes when he finally gets a girlfriend. Frank had no desire to be anyone's 'rock'. Solid, dependable, dreary and grey; only there to be leaned on or climbed over.

He had never realised how much he'd miss the camaraderie of his parish, how his soul would ache with uselessness. He hadn't fully appreciated how the purpose of his own life had been to improve other people's. How every day his endeavours had made a difference to someone. Far from rejoining the real world, he now felt disconnected from it. He'd lost his place, his sense of purpose, his *raison d'être*. Any status he may have had, any pride in his work had vanished, and no matter how many times he clicked his fingers and said 'abracadabra', he couldn't make it come back.

What he was now doing made no difference to a living soul. His 'book' had not been commissioned. Nobody was out there waiting for it. His level of commitment and industry was of no consequence to anyone. And that was when his ego finally kicked in. He had become accustomed to the respect and adoration of everyone who knew him, and couldn't bear to have that supply cut off. The silent, deeply conceited world of the writer wasn't for him.

Perhaps the muse had inspired him after all – he knew now what he was going to do. Like many courses of action that seem like the coward's way out, this one would require courage. He dreaded having to face Sarah, but he'd have to – and he'd need every rhetorical trick he'd ever employed.

Pacing nervously up and down the room, he practised his lines: 'Darling, I'm so sorry. There's no easy way to say this. I cannot do what you want me to do. I can never be what you want me to be.'

Pause.

'I'm going to have to go back to the day job.'

5

Tom Jones had married young. And despite his legendary libido, he had been married to the same woman since he was sixteen. Their courting had apparently been done via a phone-box at the end of Tom's street. Such was his sentimental attachment to it that when red phone-boxes all over Britain were phased out, he had bought that particular one and had it shipped out to his California mansion.

It's something that very few people can do. Even the most uxorious man would probably be unable to acquire the place where he had first met his wife – clubs, bars and other such venues can't be picked up and carried off by those whose relationships had begun there.

Frank, however, had done a Tom Jones. He'd met Sarah in a taxi and he could keep it for ever because it was his taxi. It had been left to him by a deceased parishioner and his 'day job', apart from being a priest, had been as a part-time taxi driver. He'd used the cab to raise funds. When a passenger had climbed into the back Frank had made it clear that he was not a licensed cab driver but a Roman Catholic priest – the dog-collar was a bit of a giveaway. He would take passengers wherever they wanted to go in return for a donation, which they could drop into a steel box bolted to the floor of the cab. It extended the principle of giving people a lift and letting them chip in for petrol, and generated a huge amount of cash for charities all over the world. Sarah had got into the taxi one lunchtime and, in effect, had never got out. She had made Frank promise that he would never get rid of the rendezvous for all their early dates – not that either of them had realised they were 'dates' at the time. Since she was a little girl, Sarah had wondered who her husband would be. She knew he was out there somewhere but who was he? Even when she and Frank were together in the taxi, Sarah never suspected that 'he' was right under her nose. Since he was a celibate Catholic priest, this was understandable.

It had been a wonderful old-fashioned courtship because neither of them realised it was a courtship. Everything they shared was covert, illicit and exciting: the pleasure of each innocent drink, each innocuous meal and each harmless stroll in the park was heightened by the fact that it wasn't strictly allowed. The merest brush of his hand against hers was charged with more sexuality than the uninhibited passion of a couple unencumbered by Holy Orders. For almost a year they'd been living inside a Barbara Cartland novel.

Now the dream was over and Frank was forcing himself to wake up. He needed to feel part of the human race. He needed to emerge from his basement bunker and get out into the real world. And there were few places on earth more real than Bethnal Green.

6

Frank had spent three years living and working in the East End of London. Most of his parishioners had lived in 'social housing'; a grotesque misnomer, since these squalid, crime-ridden estates contained some of the most antisocial housing in the Western world. Often he dreaded making house calls. Although he loved the families he visited, he was thankful he was a priest and not a doctor with a bag full of drugs just begging to be stolen.

However, on this dark January afternoon, he was delighted to be returning to Three Colts Lane, London E2, underneath the arches near Bethnal Green station. Each arch housed a garage or bodyshop dedicated solely to the maintenance and repair of London taxis.

Since the area was in the heart of what had once been the Kray twins' 'manor', Frank always got a slightly ooky feeling when he went there: back then, under the arches, it hadn't been just taxi doors and panels that were beaten and filled in. He spotted his own vehicle, fully serviced and MOT'd, parked outside Effy Baker's arch.

Effy (real name Leslie) had earned his sobriquet through his constant use of a profanity beginning with F. Frank had first met him when his exhaust had fallen off after he had gone over a particularly vicious speed bump just off Whitechapel Road. Roaring like a Lancaster bomber, its stricken exhaust dragging a trail of sparks behind it, the taxi had limped along Three Colts Lane to Effy Baker's arch where proprietor had greeted driver with, 'Fuck off, I'm busy,' without even looking round. Effy, a burly, gravel-voiced man in his late fifties, had assumed that his new client was one of his old ones. On seeing that the man at the wheel was a benign-looking clergyman, he was mortified.

'Oh, Christ, I mean, Jesus, no, I mean, Gawd – I'm so sorry, Vicar, I thought you was . . . Well, how come you're drivin' a black cab?'

'It was left to me by a parishioner and, rather than sell it, I thought I'd use it to raise funds.'

'Funds?' said Effy, intrigued. 'What for?'

'To keep my church and parish going – St Thomas's in Wealdstone.'

'Quite right, Vicar.'

'Father,' said Frank, politely. 'I'm a Catholic priest.'

'Sorry, Father, yeah, well, charity begins at home.'

'But it doesn't end there. The cash from this cab can end up with charities anywhere.'

'Good for you. I'm Effy, by the way, Effy Baker.'

'Effy?' said Frank. 'Unusual name.'

'Don't ask. Anyway, let's have a look at that exhaust of yours.'

From that moment on, Effy couldn't do enough to help – he was only too pleased to provide parts and labour free of charge to keep Father Dempsey's taxi, and therefore his whole show, on the road.

On this occasion, Frank was approaching Effy's premises slowly and quietly as he always did: he loved to catch his friend in full flow. Many of Frank's sermons had been inspired by Effy's 'discussions' with his customers. Today the man in question was a young cabbie of about thirty, who had been foolish enough to express admiration for the Kray twins.

'You're talking out of your arse, son. They were fucking horrible, the pair of 'em. Ask anyone who lived round here in those days. Ask anyone who actually *knew* them.'

'Yeah, but they only hurt their own.'

Effy snorted with disdain. 'Oh, is that right? Well, might have been true once they were in the big league, but how do you think they got started? I'll tell you how – beating up innocent people, robbing, thieving, demanding protection from all the little shop-keepers round Brick Lane. Only hurt their own? You want to have lived round here. I'm telling you – you don't know the fucking half of it.'

Unable to refute this, the young cabbie tried another much-quoted example of Kray-related mythology. 'Well, they reckon in them days, it was safe to walk the streets.'

Effy begged to differ. 'Was it fuck. Any of their lot come round and give you a clump, there was fuck-all you could do about it. You couldn't go to the Old Bill because half of them were on the firm and you never knew which half.'

The cabbie made one more attempt: 'Well, my nan reckons you could leave your front door open and nothing would get nicked.'

'Course you could because most people round here had fuck all worth nicking. But do you honestly think that if you had a few bob you could leave your door open? You've got to be joking. Not unless you were already paying protection. My old man had a car lot in Stepney. If he was here, he'd tell you what it was like. It was mob rule and you can't have that in any society. When those two finally went down, people round here were dancing in the streets. It was like VE Day. Now, of course, the Blind Beggar's a fucking tourist attraction. Imagine that! The pub where one horrible thug shoots another – a tourist attraction, selling fucking T-shirts and baseball caps. Now you got all these middle-class nonces writing books and making films about them. Glorifying what they did! I tell you, the world's gone fucking mad. Oh, sorry, Father, didn't see you there . . .'

Frank had been standing behind a pillar. He loved it when Effy got going. He was the most opinionated person he had ever met – the Man on the Clapham Omnibus, the Man in the Street, Joe Public all rolled into one pugnacious figure, expounding passionately on any subject you cared to mention. Effy Baker truly believed that he could run the country more effectively than whoever happened to be in power. 'Don't matter who you vote for,' was one of his favourite sayings, 'you still get the

PAUL BURKE

government.' But Effy's belligerence belied a sharp, analytical mind and an exceptionally kind heart. Frank liked listening to him because his views were genuinely eclectic: he was right-wing, he was left-wing, he was neither, he was both. On the left hand, he was willing to pay more tax so that the poorer members of society could be properly cared for; on the right, he favoured the return of the birch and the rope, and would have no qualms about administering them himself.

'Father Dempsey, this is – sorry, son, I'm hopeless with names.'

'Lee.'

'Lee, this is Father Dempsey.'

Lee and Frank shook hands.

'Nice to meet you, Father,' said Lee, visibly relieved that Frank's arrival had saved him from another earful. 'Anyway, I'd better slide. Cab's ready so now I've got no excuse. Cheers, Effy.'

'Yeah, tata, son, mind how you go.'

Effy turned to Frank and raised his eyebrows. 'Kids, eh?'

Frank wasn't sure whether to be flattered that Effy thought that he, unlike Lee, was a man of the world – or insulted that a man almost twenty years his senior considered him to be from the same general age group. 'Well,' said Frank, 'I suppose the reason people like Lee admire, or think they admire, the Krays is because they didn't know them. They have no concept of what it was like to have their neighbourhoods run by gangsters. They can't feel the fear that you did and I suppose we should be thankful for that. Thankful that, in that respect anyway, the world's moved on.'

Effy thought for a moment and smiled. 'You've got a point, I suppose, Father. That's the thing with you lot. You can always see the good in a situation. Sometimes I wish I was a priest.'

'No, you don't.'

'Why not?'

Frank could think of a million reasons why the very idea of Father Effy Baker would send tremors right up the Church hierarchy to the Vatican but decided to stick with the theme they

28

were developing. 'Well,' he said, 'it's a bit like the Kray twins. God may not be an evil homicidal sociopath but living in fear of Him is not unlike the way you've just described living in fear of them. Always having to abide by someone else's rules, constantly showing respect and deference that have only been earned through fear, through reputation and through the threat of reprisals. Actually, God's far worse. Upset the twins and you might have got your legs broken. Upset the Almighty and it's the roaring fires of hell.'

That was why Effy always enjoyed a visit from Frank – his unexpected way of making theological points. However, he wasn't prepared for Frank's next statement.

'That's why I gave it up.'

For maybe the first time in living memory, Effy was stuck for words. 'I mean, hang on, but . . . y— you did fucking what?'

'Gave it up. You no longer have to call me "Father" and you can say "fuck" as often as you like.'

'Fucking hell!'

'That's better.'

'But why?'

'I met the girl of my dreams – dreams I hadn't even had and hadn't realised I could have. Now we're man and wife.'

'Fuck me!' said Effy. 'You don't hang about, do you?' He thought for a moment, then continued: 'Still, it was bound to happen.'

It was Frank's turn to be surprised. 'What do you mean, bound to happen?'

'Good-looking fella like you? Law of averages. Of all the fares you ever get, sooner or later you're going to meet one you fancy and who fancies you, priest or no priest. So many cabbies have met their future wives in the course of their work – mind you, not half as many as have met their bits on the side. If you've got an eye for the birds you couldn't be in a better job.'

Frank was intrigued. 'Why's that?'

'Well, for a start women have always been attracted to cab drivers. Don't matter what they say, most women want a man who knows what he's doing, knows where he's going and that's where the black cab driver scores heavily. Most cabbies can talk the hind leg off a donkey, goes with the territory. Of course, once he's found himself some extra-curricular, he's got a vehicle that was practically designed for it. And, naturally, a cabbie's flexible working hours are ideal. "Sorry, love," he says to his wife, "I'm stuck at the airport." He's accountable to nobody, so he can meet his bit of skirt any time, any place.'

Frank had to admit that it was this freedom, unique for a Catholic priest, that had allowed his relationship with Sarah to blossom.

'So, what are you going to do, then?' said Effy. 'You going back to cabbing?'

'Just for a while,' said Frank, 'till I get myself sorted.'

'If I had a quid for every time I've heard that one,' said Effy, with a throaty chuckle. 'Now, you be careful. You're a married man now. I know I'm a bit past it, too many miles on the clock, but I wouldn't be able to trust myself. That's why I fix taxis rather than drive them.'

'Lead us not into temptation,' said Frank, getting out his wallet.

Effy fixed him with a mischievous grin, handed over the keys, then waved his hand, waived his payment and said, 'Amen.'

7

Certain parts of London do not exist. Bond Street, for instance, Petticoat Lane and Lower Regent Street. Scour the *A–Z* from Abbess Close to Zoffany Street, and you won't find any of them. Frank had driven many people to the place they knew as Petticoat Lane, which is actually called Middlesex Street. He couldn't count the times he'd taken a fare to New Bond Street or Old Bond Street, but never to Bond Street. Obviously he knew where passengers meant when they asked for Lower Regent Street – the bit between Piccadilly and Pall Mall – but its name was still plain Regent Street.

Having said goodbye to Effy, Frank was heading for another place that didn't exist: West Kilburn. It used to exist but, like Maurice Micklewhite and Reginald Dwight, West Kilburn had decided that it would be better off with a new name, so this scruffy, unprepossessing part of town had rebranded itself as Maida Vale.

Frank's success as a part-time fund-raising cabbie had taken him by surprise. He hadn't realised how far successive governments and local authorities had allowed London's public-transport system to decline. He hadn't had time to notice that the tube had fallen into dangerous decay and that the privatised overground trains and buses were now run for profit rather than passengers. Londoners could no longer depend on public transport to get them where they wanted to be when they needed to be there, and the sight of a black cab driven by an obliging priest who would pass on their fares to charity was like manna from heaven. The cab was never empty. Frank could have filled it twenty-four hours a day. For at least three days each week, he had to make a conscious effort to stay out of the driving seat to avoid neglecting his pastoral duties.

Hence the disappearance of West Kilburn. Affluent people had once rolled in from the leafy suburbs to their desks in the West End or the City on trains and buses that had run like clockwork. This was no longer the case. Human beings were now being transported in and out of London in conditions that were legally unfit for cattle. A great premium had therefore been placed on houses and flats within close proximity to the centre of town. Scuzzy areas like Hackney, Kennington and Ladbroke Grove, where previously the middle classes would never have ventured, had been colonised by those no longer willing to risk asphyxiation in the subterranean depths of the London Underground. Eventually they had found their way to Kilburn, the poor and predominantly Irish part of London where Frank had been born and bred.

Kilburn – even its name was now under threat. Most of its more recent arrivals preferred to say that they lived in Maida Vale, Queens Park or West Hampstead.

Frank parked the taxi outside what had once been Barclays Bank – West Kilburn branch. It was now the Maida Vale Brasserie, but Frank had been into it once in its former incarnation for his one and only job interview. To become a priest, he'd had to satisfy a selection panel of his suitability before he could begin his vocational training; once ordained, he was never interviewed for a job, just dispatched to whichever parish the bishop had decided to send him. His interview with Mr Pendlebury, the branch manager at West Kilburn, had been instrumental in propelling him towards the priesthood. He had emerged from it having already taken his first vow: He vowed that as long as he lived he would never subject himself to the boredom, predictability, fiscal prudence and humdrum drudgery offered by a career in Mr Pendlebury's little fiefdom. Especially when the only oft-quoted benefit of banking was that it was a secure occupation, a job for life.

Now remembering how many 'jobs for life' had been lost as branches like Mr Pendlebury's were replaced by call centres in India, Frank couldn't help thinking, Oh, really? Had he taken the job with Mr Pendlebury, he'd probably have been on the dole by now. He might have been crossing the street to 267 Shirland Road in search of employment – which, ironically, was what he was now doing, having given up his own 'job for life'.

The door was answered by big, rubicund Irishman in his late sixties, who embraced Frank like a long-lost son. 'Frankie,' he said, 'we've been expecting you.'

8

'Keep the pledge, wear the pin and say the prayer.' So read the motto that had been framed and hung in the hallway into which Frank had just stepped. It had been there for as long as he could remember, for this was a house he had visited regularly since he was a small boy. It belonged to the man who had just embraced him, Joe Hennessey, known to everyone as 'Joe the Taxi'.

Joe was an old friend of Frank's father and a typical Kilburn Irishman of the old school: thick-set, warm-hearted, badly dressed and devoutly Catholic, Joe also had the compulsory penchant for the Dubliners and Jim Reeves. However, he differed from most of his fellow parishioners in one crucial respect: as a lifelong member of the Pioneers, not a drop of alcohol had ever passed Joe Hennessey's lips.

In a country renowned for its love affair with liquor, there was bound to be a voluble minority who opposed it, and the Pioneer Total Abstinence Association had been part of Irish life for over a hundred years. The movement was founded in 1898 in response to the havoc that alcohol abuse was wreaking on Irish society. So far, so good: all very commendable. However, it wasn't quite as simple as that. With the Catholic Church, it never is. And although the Pioneers were dry, they were soaked in a particularly virulent strain of Catholicism. The organisation was devoted to the Sacred Heart of Jesus – a weird notion with which Frank, as an ex-priest, was only too familiar.

It was all coming back to him. Apparently, some time in the seventeenth century, Jesus had appeared to a St Margaret Mary Alacoque. Or so she said. Or so someone allegedly said she said. She was a little girl who shunned any sort of pleasure: she preferred silence and 'corporal mortfication' to playing with other children. So when, still bleeding from self-inflicted wounds, she told people that Jesus had pulled out his heart and shown it to her and, what was more, had demanded that feast days be devoted to this blood-smeared piece of his anatomy, should they have believed her or taken her to see a child psychologist? The peasants of medieval France believed every word the poor, disturbed girl had told them, and hundreds of years later, as Frank could see, the legend of the Sacred Heart was alive and pumping in West Kilburn.

He had often asked himself how anyone could possibly believe this nonsense, and the answer, as with most things Catholic, involved a deal – in this case, a veiled threat: unless you promised to worship the so-called Sacred Heart, you might jeopardise your place in heaven. In return, a number of rash promises were made: in return for unquestioning devotion, the Heart would make 'tepid souls become fervent'; if your soul was already fervent, it would 'quickly mount to high perfection'; and, of course, the Heart would 'bless every place where its image is espoused and honoured'.

So, 267 Shirland Road, a big old four-storey house with the offices of Sacred Heart Cabs in the basement, was well and truly blessed. An imposing picture of Jesus – long hair, beard and big red heart glowing rather comically outside his chest, his finger pointing at it just in case we hadn't noticed – looked down on Frank from above the mantelpiece as he walked into the sitting room. The black and white shot of John F. Kennedy, that other pictorial staple of devout Catholic households, had to be content with a place on the sideboard. Joe Hennessey welcomed him in – Frank had always been amused by the irony of a man who had never touched alcohol having to share his name with a brand of Cognac, but had never had the temerity to mention it.

Neither had he publicly questioned the veracity of the Sacred Heart of Jesus story or any of the other tales on which the tenets of the Catholic Church were based. If people like Joe wanted to believe them, fine: they weren't doing any harm. And Joe was doing an awful lot of good – Sacred Heart Cabs had been delivering people safely to their destinations for more than forty years.

When Joe had first arrived on the Dun Laoghaire boat in the mid-fifties, he had become, like countless other Irish immigrants, one of 'McAlpine's Fusiliers', labouring on building sites all over London. His guaranteed sobriety meant that he always drove the van. When the foreman chose his men from those who had lined up outside Camden Town tube station at six in the morning, looking for work, it was Joe who drove them to the site. It was Joe who drove them to the pub on a Friday night so that they could do exactly what he had pledged not to do and blow their wage packets on booze. One night, as he waited, yet again, until closing time to stack their comatose bodies into the back of the old Bedford and drive them to their digs, he decided that the life of a Fusilier was no life for a Pioneer.

Joe had never picked up a trade. He had wanted to train as a plumber but every foreman he had ever worked for had found him far too useful as a driver. He wondered now why he'd want to spend his life with his hand up other people's U-bends or in a bone-rattling old van when he could spend it driving a car around the city that was now his home.

From under a loose floorboard in his grotty room in Paddington, Joe removed all the cash he had amassed by not drinking. He took it down to Warren Street and drove back in a second-hand Morris Oxford. With the prayer of the Pioneers stuck to the dashboard, the first Sacred Heart Cab took to the streets. Word got round, and Joe got busy. Before long, he had a platoon of young Pioneers desperate to escape the Irish labourer's life in London, which seemed to revolve entirely around alcohol. Abstinence was a natural qualification for a cab driver, and passengers always felt safe when they discovered that their driver had taken the pledge and was wearing the pin to prove it.

With such a brilliant business idea, Joe could have franchised it and been a multi-millionaire years ago but that was where his devotion to the Sacred Heart of Jesus was a wonderful thing. He had set up covenants to various Catholic charities and a percentage of any fares paid to Sacred Heart Cabs was always sent to those in need. So what if the Pioneers' good work was being carried out primarily to smooth their own passage to heaven? At least the work was being done. What was more, Joe had always provided employment to people who wanted it. As long as their vehicles and their knowledge of London were sound, as long as they pledged to abstain from alcohol (at least when they were working), they could always earn good money as Sacred Heart Cabs drivers.

At sixty-eight, Joe was no longer seen at the wheel of a cab but he was still very much in the driving seat of his business. His two sons, Kieran and Sean, worked with him but Joe was still The Controller.

Kieran had been in Frank's class at school and, although he was a Junior Pioneer, had displayed a less than temperate attitude to alcohol. On more than one occasion, Frank had carried him home from parties because he was too drunk to walk, often singing a medley of 'Danny Boy' and 'Anarchy In The UK'.

At Frank's house, Kieran would be dumped unconscious on the sofa, and left to sleep it off. A call would be made to the Hennesseys to say that their son was at Frank's and would be home in the morning. Since the Dempseys were a good Catholic family, Joe raised no objection. However, it happened once too often. Frank remembered trying in vain to wake Kieran from his drunken stupor to tell him that a Sacred Heart Cab was on its way round to pick him up.

'I thought it was you.' Joe's smiling, pin-wearing wife Breda had entered the front room, carrying a tray of tea. Having produced eight children, Breda, a small, bustling partridge of a woman, had been aptly named: she put down the tray, gave Frank a warm hug and said, 'Sure it's lovely to see you, Frankie.'

Frank knew what was coming next and braced himself.

'Cuppa tay, Frank?'

'Er . . . no, thank you.'

Joe and Breda looked at him as though he had committed a mortal sin.

'You won't believe this,' he chuckled, and tried out his latest lie, 'but I've developed this allergy. It brings me out in a rash and, according to the specialist, it's tea.'

Frank's hosts were now looking at him as though he'd just been diagnosed with prostate cancer. 'Oh, that's awful,' said Breda. 'You poor, poor thing. How can anyone be expected to manage without tea?'

She shook her head in dismay. 'Can I get you anything else?'

Since alcohol was banned in the Hennessey household, and Frank was unlikely to be offered an elderflower *pressé* or the smoothie of the day, he thought it best to decline. 'No thanks. I keep a big bottle of Ballygowan in the cab.'

'Well, I suppose you have to,' said Breda. 'No tea! That's terrible.'

'Well, you know how it is here, Frank,' said Joe, cueing up his favourite hoary old joke. 'We're not just teetotal, we're *tea*total. Isn't that right, Breda?'

Frank acknowledged Joe's hilarious pun with a light smile. 'So, how's it all going?' he asked. 'Plenty of work? Plenty of drivers?'

'Oh, more than ever,' said Joe, with a grateful glance towards the Sacred Heart of Jesus.

'Room for one more?'

'Always room for you, Frankie. Isn't that right, Breda? I was only saying the other day that if you wanted to carry on cabbing till you got yourself sorted, you'd be more than welcome. I was going to ring you but I thought you might have other plans.'

'Not at the moment, Joe, so just tell me where you want me to go.'

'Ah, this is grand. Nice bunch of lads working for us at the moment. Isn't that right, Breda?'

Frank smiled to himself, seeing that Joe hadn't lost one of his most famous foibles. His conversation was always peppered with 'Isn't that right, Breda?' yet he never paused for his wife to answer and took no notice of her even when she did.

'Yes, quite a few Muslims now,' said Joe proudly.

Frank was surprised by this new interdenominational policy until he remembered Joe's first criterion for any Sacred Heart driver. Then it made perfect sense.

'Women too. A lot of women feel safer with a female driver. Isn't that right, Breda?'

Breda nodded. 'And how's that lovely wife of yours?' she asked. 'I've never seen such a beautiful bride. Jesus, that was a turn-up for the books.'

Frank's ear was tuned to pick up even the slightest note of disapproval but there was none. He had been expecting at least a little hostility from older, more traditional Catholics for reneging on his vows, but, to his surprise and relief, he was yet to find any. His own parents, in particular, had been delighted, rather than distraught. His father, the most stoical and traditional of men, with the gruff emotional repression so typical of his age, creed and class, had actually wept with joy. He had even admitted, through his tears, that, although he had nothing but the greatest admiration and respect for priests, he'd never wanted his own son to become one.

The Hennesseys were similarly forgiving. Joe took a sip from his huge mug of tea, and embarked upon a soliloquy that Frank had heard him deliver many times before. 'As you know, Frank,' he began, 'the whole basis of the Pioneer movement is love and compassion for those suffering from alcohol or drug abuse.'

Oh, Christ, here we go, thought Frank, mentally noting the inclusion of the new word 'drug': the Pioneers had updated themselves for the twenty-first century.

'We express that love through lifelong sacrifice and commitment,' said Joe, then changed tack in a way that Frank hadn't anticipated. 'But that love pales into insignificance when compared to the love a man feels for his wife.'

This time he looked across at the woman he'd adored for forty-five years. 'Isn't that right, Breda?'

9

Frank had watched *Sleepless in Seattle* alone – Sleepless in Kilburn had had no wish to watch a schmaltzy film in the company of Father Curran, another confirmed bachelor. He remembered thinking it was the sort of film that only an unromantic person might consider romantic. He liked the soundtrack, though, especially Gene Autry singing 'Back In The Saddle Again'. This apposite track was playing as Frank drove over to St John's Wood to pick up his first fare as a Sacred Heart Cabs driver. He loved having the right track for the right moment, so the singing cowboy was followed by Big Youth's skanking reggae version of 'Hit The Road Jack', Sniff 'n' the Tears' 'Driver's Seat' and 'Route 66' from the Stones' first album.

He knew all about ipods, itunes, and downloading five thousand tracks from the Internet then carrying them around in an MP3 player the size of a matchbox but he had no interest in doing so. His passion was collecting records. Their physical presence was as important to him as the music they contained. And in case he might want to listen to them in the cab, he spent hours transferring them individually on to a hand-tooled C90.

Accompanied by at least a dozen C90s, he was out and about – Kilburn, Camden, Kentish Town, Putney, Peckham, Penge. For the first time since he had rejoined secular society, he felt he was doing something useful. Whizzing past the headquarters of the Handmaidens of the Sacred Heart, just north of Regent's Park, in the knowledge that a small percentage of his takings would go towards helping them, Frank experienced the warm glow of virtue, which had been missing since he'd hung up his vestments. He looked at the notes and coins that his passengers gave him as though he had never seen money before. In his time as a priest, hundreds of thousands of pounds had passed through his hands to someone, somewhere whose need was greater than his. These notes and coins were different. He'd earned them; he could keep and spend them however he liked.

As a child, he'd had the First Beatitude drummed into him: 'Blessed are the poor for the kingdom of Heaven is theirs.' As an adult, he knew that there was nothing remotely 'blessed' about being poor. And, anyway, he didn't want the kingdom of heaven – he'd rather have fun on earth. He'd never been bothered about life after death. Devoting himself instead to life *before* death, he sped off towards Baker Street.

He glanced in his rear-view mirror, and realised that, for the first time in weeks, the book was not following him. He'd been expecting to feel like Dennis Weaver in *Duel*, unable to escape his tormentor, but instead he was Roger Daltrey in *Tommy*, his sense of vision restored, cartwheeling through a field singing 'I'm Free'.

He'd been wrong to think he could write a book. He'd only agreed to it to try to make some money. And that was a sure-fire way for any author to ensure that he doesn't – you should never write a book because someone else says you should: the desire to do it has to come from yourself and Frank couldn't imagine it coming from him. That had obviously been Kerry Dixon's mistake – that, and wearing those ridiculously tight shorts.

Maybe he'd better phone Sarah and tell her about his life-changing day. No, she might be in a meeting. She'd call his mobile soon enough. And she did.

'Hi, it's me,' she said, then asked the question invariably put by anyone calling a mobile. 'Where are you?'

'Um, Dorset Square. Hold on a sec . . . Yeah, that's it, number thirty-nine. Okay? Right, that's six fifty, please. Oh, thank you, very kind. Yep, mind how you go . . . Hang on, darling, let me pull over . . . Right. Hello?'

Clearly Sarah knew the answer to her second question, but she asked it anyway: 'What are you doing?'

Frank hadn't changed since his schooldays. He might have been forty years old. He might have gained a theology degree from Christ Church. He might once have been a mature, successful and respected parish priest, but he was still doing what he'd always done: he'd been out having fun instead of doing his homework.

His articulacy deserted him, just as it always had when Mr Bracewell asked him for the non-existent homework that had been eaten by a non-existent dog.

'Um . . . listen,' he said to his wife, who was all ears, 'I can explain.'

10

Frank had never liked staying in. The little terraced house where he'd grown up had been less than luxurious. There was an awful lot of lino and the rare patches of carpet were either bobbly or bald. The washing-machine was three streets away at the Coin-Op launderette in Donaldson Road, yet Frank was happy to cart two black bin-liners of laundry there because it meant going out. He wasn't alone: Kilburn teenagers were only too willing to do their family's washing because it meant a two-hour sojourn at the Coin-Op. There, in the warm, Persil-permeated privacy, the boys could smoke, swear and try to hypnotise themselves as the garments rotated in the huge steel drums.

Frank was happy to go anywhere. From an early age, he'd earned pocket money running errands for certain neighbours. He had cycled all over Kilburn and Cricklewood taking little notes from one house to another, until one day his dad saw him leaving a particular house in Dyne Road. Without explaining why, he called an immediate halt to this activity. It was years before Frank discovered that the houses he'd been visiting were safe-houses and that he had, in fact, been running errands for the IRA.

The priesthood had intensified his dislike of staying in. Evenings with the half-pissed Father Reilly were not Frank's idea of fun. Yes, he had an affection for the old boy – in the same way he might have for a pungent old Labrador – but he had nothing in common with his ageing colleague and no desire to sit drinking Paddy with him watching *Panorama* on a fuzzy black and white TV.

Now, for the first time in his life, he looked forward to staying in. His home was a gorgeous flat in Fulham. He loved it there, with its abundance of light and space, the white walls, the dashes of low-key colour, even the astonishing number of shoes in the wardrobe, that made him wonder if he'd married a centipede. He loved the stripped floors, huge Heal's sofas and the kitchen, which was full of unfamiliar accoutrements – the garlic press, couscoussier, mouli-julienne and Swiss-made mandoline that symbolised the journey he had made. Along with his vows, he had also let go of the plates of fatty meat and overcooked veg prepared by Mrs Ruane, the presbytery housekeeper.

Frank had only endured those meals if he had stayed in for the evening. More often than not, he and his taxi had pulled up outside one of a dozen takeaways where his custom was welcome and payment waived. He always knew where to get good food and tonight was no exception. He had brought home a couple of huge halal kebabs and a bottle of Moroccan Merlot.

'It was like being at school. Trapped, unable to go out until I'd finished my homework', he explained 'I was starting to hate it here. I just had to get out.'

'I know what you mean,' said Sarah. 'Do you think we ought to move? I don't want you to feel like a lodger. Perhaps it would be better if we started afresh in a place we've chosen together.'

Frank had bitten off more than he could chew. Literally. He was trying desperately to swallow a huge mouthful of grilled lamb, salad, pitta bread and piquant garlic sauce so that he could stop her pedalling off down this route.

'Yeah,' she continued. 'Somewhere you'd feel more at home. Queens Park, maybe. Bits of Kilburn are quite desirable now.'

'No, no, no,' he said, finally getting his food down his gullet. 'I love it here. It's very kind of you but, oh I don't mean this to sound snotty because I have a huge fondness for Kilburn but . . .'

'But what?'

'Well, if we moved back there, I'd feel there'd been no point in growing up. I know it's no longer seen as the dump it once was but to live there as an adult would make me feel as though I might as well have left school at sixteen, got a job on a building site and married Eileen Casey.'

'Who's she?'

'First girl I ever went out with. She was very nice – I'm sure she still is – but to me she represents everything I wanted to get away from. Besides, I don't feel like a lodger. Well, no more than I ever have. I'm one of life's lodgers – I always have been, living in presbyteries I didn't own, being moved from one to another without much say in the matter. I feel less of a lodger here than I've ever felt in my life. And, anyway, it's such a great flat, I love it but, by forcing myself to stay in, I was beginning to hate it and I just couldn't allow that to happen.'

'So, have you given up on the book?'

Frank took a gulp of his wine and thought how nice it was that nobody was expecting him to turn it into the blood of Christ. 'Well, no, not exactly . . . um . . . that's not to say . . . I mean, I'm sure if I . . .'

And in trying to think up an excuse for not having written anything, for not being a writer, he had unwittingly taken the first step towards becoming one.

'Well, that's good,' said Sarah, 'because I've bought you a little present.'

Frank's eyes lit up. After all those years of never buying himself much he was always delighted to receive any sort of gift. Sarah handed him a John Lewis bag. He took it and, with unseemly haste, pulled out a Sony digital Dictaphone.

'Fantastic!' he said, knowing he'd never use it. 'The good thing about one of these is I can wander around mumbling into it and people will just think I'm on the phone. Thanks.' But he still had to explain why *To Be Frank* would never be published. 'This,' he said, waving his new gift at his new wife, 'will certainly encourage me to write something but I don't think it'll be my autobiography.'

Sarah raised her eyebrows, inviting him to continue.

'I just feel it would be, at best, a piece of self-indulgence. You know, like those awful watercolours by amateur artists. Cornish beach scenes, little boy paddling in a rock pool, woman in a patterned dress, man with rolled-up trousers holding a lobster pot.'

Sarah laughed. She'd seen those very pictures hanging on the railings behind their creators along the Bayswater Road. 'And at worst?' she asked.

'A monstrous piece of conceit,' said Frank. 'And either way, of no interest to anyone.'

Sarah still wasn't convinced. 'You don't know that.'

'Oh, yes, I do,' he replied, with the air of certainty that had always made him such a convincing cleric. 'It would be of no interest to other people because it's of no interest to me. I'm married to you now. And I think it would be wrong to try to profit from all those years I spent espousing beliefs I never believed.'

'You're being a bit hard on yourself,' said Sarah. 'You were still a wonderful priest despite – or maybe because of – your lack of faith. And that's what's so interesting.'

'But to me,' said Frank, 'it would feel as though I only became a priest so I could give it up, then publicly ridicule everything I was supposed to believe in. I just want to concentrate on my new life rather than my old one . . .'

'And?' Sarah prompted him.

'Well,' said Frank, 'I'm conscious that this is maybe not what you bargained for.'

'What do you mean?'

'That I'm not what it said on the label. You thought you might be marrying a best-selling author and you've married a mini-cab driver.'

She picked up a napkin and wiped away the piquant garlic sauce that was heading south from Frank's chin, then kissed him. 'Oh, no, I didn't,' she replied. 'I married a human being. When I first saw you, I didn't see a priest.'

'Clearly.' He grinned.

'I saw someone for whom things will always happen. What was that you said the other day? "Believe in Fate . . ."'

'. . . but lean forward where Fate can see you.'

'Well, Fate is always going to see you – you're just one of those people. I don't know where or when it's going to see you but I'm glad you're driving that taxi.'

'You're glad?' This was not the reaction Frank had been expecting: he'd been preparing for his first marital bust-up. 'Why?'

'Because,' she said, 'there's more chance of Fate seeing you when you're out and about than when you're stuck in here all day on your own, but most of all—'

'What?'

'Because you're earning some money now and I've seen the most gorgeous pair of boots in Russell and Bromley.'

11

'Today is the first day of the rest of your life,' was an example
of the ersatz motivational psychology that Frank had always
avoided in sermons or pastoral advice. It was almost as awful
as 'A stranger is a friend I haven't met yet.'

But it was the way Frank was feeling. It was the first time in
years that he didn't feel as fraudulent as a wad of snide fivers.
No longer was he a priest who didn't believe in God or a writer
who didn't believe in his work, but a husband who believed in
his wife and a man who believed in himself.

Today was the first day he'd felt good about wearing some of
his new clothes. As a priest, sartorial decisions had been made
for him: it was the black jacket over the dog-collar with the black
trousers and the black shoes. Even on the rare occasions when
he discarded the collar, he usually took the Johnny Cash option
and wore a black sweatshirt and black jeans. Today he'd decided
that his life was going to be more colourful and his clothes
should reflect this.

He recalled the rueful advice of Pat Walsh, the most henpecked
husband he had ever met: 'Never let a woman buy your clothes.
Once she buys your clothes, she's bought your soul.' Frank had
been tempted to let Sarah, a prodigious shopper with immaculate taste, choose his but Pat's words had changed his mind.

Trouble was, he had no taste – he didn't know what to buy.
Sarah advised him to go to Gap but to avoid the hooded sweat-
shirts or any garment with the word 'GAP' displayed anywhere
except the label. When he arrived home with his selection of
shirts, jumpers, jeans and chinos, Sarah was quite impressed: he
hadn't made any major errors, but she laughed when she spotted

that something in his subconscious had made him choose a black cotton V-neck and the white T-shirt. They made him look as though he'd never left the priesthood.

The trip to Gap had been a seminal moment for Frank. It had reignited his long-lost passion for the ancient ritual of swapping money for stuff. It was a pleasure he had denied himself since the day he was ordained. Every year he had always 'accidentally' let slip to his parishioners that his birthday was approaching, and when he addressed them as 'my dear brothers and sisters', he had meant it. Brothers and sisters buy you presents so, every birthday and Christmas, he had been deluged with record tokens.

Apart from that, nothing. Like his sex drive, his yearning for the frivolity of shopping had been almost, but not quite, suppressed, and now it was back with a vengeance. He had money of his own and the array of goods on which he could spend it had never looked so alluring.

He found himself coveting a George Foreman heavyweight grill pan, the new Braun hair-removal system and even a chunky nine-carat-gold sovereign ring from Elizabeth Duke at Argos.

In Sainsbury's, he had another giddy rush of sin. With a succession of housekeepers to look after him, Frank hadn't been inside a supermarket for years and in that time they'd changed beyond recognition. He wandered around, eyes wide with wonder as he filled his trolley with comestibles that he didn't know existed: balsamic vinegar, freshly baked organic bread, extra-lean mince and Snickers ice-creams. Mrs Ruane had only ever hauled the same things back to the presbytery. Bacon, cabbage and jumbo-sized boxes of teabags. It was here, more than anywhere else, that he felt he had finally left the priesthood behind. In his anonymous civilian clothes, he no longer had to be on his best behaviour. He even felt free to purloin a few seed-less grapes or a couple of sweets from the Pick 'n' Mix. As a priest, he could never risk being disgraced and defrocked over a handful of chocolate brazils.

He was seduced by the special offers: the idea of two bottles of Domestos for the price of one made him almost ill with excitement.

Standing in the checkout queue, he passed the time inventing new contemporary sins. Thou shalt not keep everybody waiting whilst thou packs up every last item before deigning to pay for them. Thou shalt not pretend thou hast not seen that great big sign saying, 'Five items or less,' whilst thou tries to shove at least twenty-eight items on to the conveyor belt before paying by Switch and asking for cash back.

At last, he could succumb to the primal urge felt by most men when they get behind the wheels of a supermarket trolley: the hunter-gatherer instincts that date back to when they lived in caves and slew herds of wild boar to bring home for their families. Returning to the flat with his cab filled with groceries was Frank's twenty-first-century equivalent.

Then it was back out into the world.

The emptiness he'd felt at the loss of his flock had been filled by a far bigger congregation. Every Londoner was now a potential parishioner and each day he met dozens. His deal with Joe Hennessey allowed him to pick up passengers off the street if they happened to hail him, which, because he drove a black taxi, they sometimes did.

Like most cabbies, Frank was a great talker but unlike many he was an equally good listener. The taxi, with its partition to separate (ex) priest and penitent, was not unlike a confessional box, and if Frank ever decided to return to the plastic piano, he could base a lot of his material on the revelations he heard as he criss-crossed the metropolis. His friendly, impartial manner encouraged a steady succession of strangers to spill an astonishing number of beans. Extramarital affairs were brazenly discussed, confidential information openly disclosed, share tips and racing certainties generously proffered. Frank's amiable disposition usually ensured that driver and passenger got along famously.

Though not always.

His least favourite passengers were those who insisted they knew a quicker way and that Frank was taking 'the scenic route' to clock up more money on the meter. Even when he pointed out that there was no meter and they had already agreed a fare for the journey, their eyes were still filled with mistrust. They were the sort of people who went through their lives assuming that everyone was out to cheat them, constantly insisting that they know better than the very people whose expertise they sought in the first place.

Rather than argue, Frank would take a deep breath, grit his teeth and take them whichever way they wanted to go. It was rarely a route he didn't know and seldom as quick as the one he would have taken.

Having directed themselves into a gridlock, they would invariably blame Frank for it, calling him either 'Driver' or 'Cabbie' to do so.

When they arrived at their appointments, they would demand a receipt, as though Frank had something to gain by not providing one. He would cheerfully oblige. As long as the cab had been hailed on the street and he couldn't be traced, he would tear one from his little pad and fill it in very, very slowly.

'Come on, come on, I *am* in a rather a hurry,' his fare would urge.

Frank would smile politely, fold the receipt and have it snatched from his hand without a word of thanks. As he drove off, he would think of his passenger trying to claim the fare back on expenses. 'One Million Pounds', according to the receipt.

12

Although Frank was happy to be driving the cab, he knew that all that sitting down might soon spread his backside out until it resembled a large bag of compost. To avoid this, he returned to the Go For It! Health and Fitness Centre.

This time, he was a little happier about 'going for it' because the book was not following him into the changing room. He smiled at the irony of paying good money to do something that, as a teenager, he'd forged notes from his mum to avoid. By then, the thrill of competitive sport had been usurped by the delights of fags, booze and girls. And yet it is the effects of those very pleasures that persuade so many men, as they find themselves being slowly encircled by the spare tyre of middle age, to return to some form of physical exercise.

Frank did not get a 'buzz' from exercise. It was just a bodily function, like going to the loo, which he carried out reluctantly for the good of his health.

He knew that the pounds he was most likely to lose would be from his wallet, which was why the parallels between the fitness industry and the Catholic Church were painfully apparent. Both were based on fear – on the principle of 'Shit, if I go regularly and I'm still like this, what on earth would happen if I didn't go at all?' People continued to worship at both altars because they were terrified of finding out. Frank too was going along for that reason but he usually felt better afterwards. Which, of course, is exactly what Catholics say after they've been to mass.

He hauled himself on to the running machine. He could never run in the street, largely because he knew he would run straight into the nearest Burger King or Dunkin' Donuts. Looking around as he pounded along, he couldn't help noticing the disproportionate number of small men straining every sinew around him. Perhaps they regarded their bodies in the way people who live in studio flats regard their homes: determined to make the most of their bijou proportions. Some of these Lilliputians, especially the prematurely bald ones with hairy chests, were lifting impressive stacks of weights, but Frank suspected they'd gladly swap their toned triceps and muscular thighs just to be four inches taller and have full heads of hair.

Breathless, flushed and horribly shiny, he staggered off to the steam room to reap the reward he felt he'd earned by spending twenty sweaty minutes on the treadmill. He fell through the door, collapsed on to the bench and let his whole body relax. This was the bit he enjoyed – the physiological confessional, where his body owned up to its sins and emitted them through the pores of his skin to be cleansed away afterwards in a cold shower. God, it was hot, which is why he found it odd that the steam room was always described as the perfect place to 'chill out'. Its all-pervading warmth reminded him of the old coin-op launderette.

The hot steam had built up so fast that it was a while before Frank realised he was not alone. He could just discern the indistinct shape of another human being, who was inhaling deeply through his nose then exhaling theatrically through his mouth. He wasn't as bad as the bloke who had sat, eyes closed and cross-legged, humming and chanting as though he was preparing for a lengthy bout of Tantric sex.

'Ah, that's better,' the other man sighed.

Frank was reminded of his Auntie Nora, who had the disconcerting habit of articulating her every thought. She'd come into the house, look at her nephew and say, 'There's Francis', and 'Francis' never knew whether or not he should respond. A polite nod and a smile usually did the trick but today, since the heavy breather was wreathed in steam and he and Frank couldn't see each other, something more was required.

'Yeah,' said Frank. 'Great, isn't it?'

'Amazing,' said the disembodied voice.

'I love the fact that I can work up a really good sweat without moving a muscle.'

'Me too,' said the voice. 'This is the only reason I renewed my membership.'

It was a distinctive voice and to Frank's ears, strangely familiar. It was old and young at the same time. Its owner was probably in his early thirties, yet the voice contained a depth and confidence that would normally have taken another fifteen years to acquire.

'Well,' the voice continued, 'I thought I'd better use this place a bit more than I did last year.'

Frank's eyes were becoming accustomed to the steam and he could now see his companion a little more clearly. Like his voice, the man was old and young at the same time. He was about thirty-two and, surprise surprise, prematurely bald. 'Why? How often did you come?'

'Well,' he said, almost apologetically, 'I did have a very busy year.'

'So how often did you come?'

'Once.'

Frank laughed. 'Once?'

'Yep. And even then I didn't do anything. I paid twelve hundred quid to have a shower. Talking of which . . .'

The man stood up. Frank still couldn't recognise him.

'That's my lot. With any luck, I'll have left half my body weight in here. See you.'

'Yeah,' said Frank. 'Cheers.'

When the man had left, Frank ran his last two words through his voice-memory banks to check it against the thousands of names and faces stored there. The search was unsuccessful.

13

Showered, dressed, with limbs aching just enough for their owner to feel a little virtuous, Frank walked out on to the street and heard that voice again: 'Twenty minutes? I've been holding on for what seems like hours and now you tell me it won't be here for twenty minutes!'

The small, fit, prematurely bald man was now both visible and irate. 'High call volume?' he exclaimed, sending the volume of his own call a bit higher. 'It's always the bloody same! Employ some more people! You don't mind taking money but you don't seem to like paying it out . . . No, no . . . I'm sorry, this has happened once too often, I'm cancelling the account . . . I'd rather walk.'

He snapped his mobile shut, saw Frank and looked a bit sheepish. The man was naturally easy-going and polite – he didn't like to get rattled. 'Bloody cab companies,' he muttered.

Frank nodded sympathetically, and it was then that his memory came up with the answer. He had never met the man but he'd heard that voice being interviewed on Five Live. He remembered the point the voice had been making. It hadn't previously occurred to Frank but since he'd heard it expressed, he had increasingly found it to be true.

'I hate to use the term "posh people" but you know what I mean,' the man in the interview had explained. 'Anyway, people like that . . . well, people like me, I suppose, are moving into areas they would never have considered before. Not just the places they live but their occupations too. For instance, I'm now running a nightclub. Friends of mine are running pubs and sand-wich bars, or working as carpenters and gardeners. You're now getting more posh pop stars. Look at Will Young and Sophie Ellis-Bextor.'

'So, why do you think this is happening?' the interviewer asked.

'For a number of reasons. New technology has meant that there aren't the opportunities any more in what you might call the traditional professions – banking, law and the City. Also, a lot of public-school-educated people, Oxbridge graduates and the like, have realised they can make just as much money and have a lot more fun doing other things. The London club scene, let me tell you, is a lot more fun than the Foreign Office.'

'So what's the next field to be colonised?'

'The football field,' the voice asserted

'Posh *footballers*?' said the interviewer, and continued, with a fair imitation of John Motson's commentary, 'And it's the Honourable Charles Tytherington-Smythe putting a lovely ball in for Lord Bathgate, who squares it for Viscount Wigram . . .'

'Oh, without a doubt. Footballers of the future will be predominantly middle class. I mean, let's face it, the fans of, say, Arsenal and Chelsea already are.'

The interviewer couldn't disagree.

'Thing is, it'll get harder and harder for ordinary kids to become footballers. Competitive sport is actively discouraged in a lot of state schools. Where I live, they hold school sports days with no winners. The kids are further disadvantaged by the fact that, rightly or wrongly, their parents live in fear of marauding paedophiles so they won't let their children go off and play in the park. What's more, hundreds of playing-fields have been sold. And, of course, if you visit any housing estate, the first sign you'll see says, "No Ball Games". The private schools, on the other hand, place great emphasis on sport, so where do you think the next generation of England players will come from?'

'Especially,' said the interviewer, 'with the amount of money that even a journeyman Premiership player can make.'

'Exactly.'

'So where, in the future, will this leave state-school children?'

Frank remembered the genuine concern in the man's voice. 'I don't know,' he replied. 'I really don't know.'

This interview had struck a chord with Frank because, at the time, he was a governor of a Catholic secondary school that had a pretty good academic and sporting reputation. Parents were desperate to get their children in and Frank had always felt guilty about rejecting those who weren't practising Catholics. Not only because he knew he was condemning their children to the dismal curriculum offered by the other schools in the borough but also because he was no more a genuine Catholic and just as much of a hypocrite as they were.

'So, do you need a cab?' he said to his new friend from the steam room.

The man looked at him. 'Well, yes, I do, as a matter of fact.'

'Well,' said Frank, jerking his head towards his taxi, 'I might just be able to help you. Where do you want to go?'

'Church Street, Paddington. I've just bought the lease on an old furniture shop.'

Ah, thought Frank. Wrong man. That forensic memory had let him down. Must be getting old.

'A furniture shop?'

'Yeah,' said the man, climbing into the back. 'I'm converting it into a sort of DJ bar.'

Bingo. It *is* him. Not getting old, after all. 'A furniture shop?' said Frank. 'Church Street – not Empire Furnishings?'

'That's right.' The man smiled. 'You know it?'

'Well, yeah. I grew up in Kilburn and everyone bought their furniture there on the never-never. Solid sign of respectability, a three-piece suite from Empire Furnishings, even if it took you twenty years to pay it off. A mate of my dad's used to arrange the HP – Jimmy Waldron, always known as Jimmy the Wardrobe. God, Empire Furnishings. I thought it had closed down years ago.'

'No. Amazingly, it hung on until about six months ago. Fantastic premises but never anyone in there. I used to think it was a front for some drugs cartel.'

'Well,' remarked Frank, only half joking, 'if you're turning it into a DJ bar, it soon will be.' He swung the taxi round and headed for Paddington.

'Thank you so much,' the man said. 'I'm Toby, by the way, Toby Swann.'

'Frank Dempsey,' said the driver, smiling into his rear-view mirror. 'Nightclub, eh?'

'Yeah, I've been involved in the club scene for a while now, but this is the first place that's actually mine.'

'I have to say,' said Frank, 'you don't strike me as the club-bing type.'

'Well, I'm not, really. After university I went straight into the Foreign Office, ended up in Hong Kong, had a blast but when they handed it back to the Chinese in 'ninety-seven, they handed me back with it. I was worried that my next posting might be somewhere like Albania so I decided I could have more fun—'

'And make more money?' asked Frank.

'And make more money,' said Toby, with a smile, 'just club-bing for a living. It's so much easier. I mean, the whole industry, if you can call it that, is still full of coke-heads who just want to party twenty-four/seven, so if you're sensible, disciplined and have a proper business plan, you can make a hill of money.'

'When are you due to open?'

'Two weeks. Provided the builders have finished.'

Frank tutted in recognition of the perennial problem, but when he looked into the mirror, expecting to see Toby's face registering builder-related worry and frustration, he saw a man without a care in the world.

'Oh, they'll be finished all right. Tell you what, if you can spare five minutes, come in and have a look.'

Frank could always spare five minutes to slake his insatiable curiosity. He had a hunch about what these builders would be like and wanted to see if he was right. As Toby introduced them, Frank knew his hunch had been spot-on.

'This is Piers,' Toby said, as Frank shook hands with the

carpenter, 'and this is Rupert.' Frank nodded at the tall, sandy-haired aristocratic-looking plumber. 'And Antony here is the electrician.'

They were the first team of public-school builders that Frank had ever encountered. Living proof of what Toby had been saying on the radio. Professional, reliable and, since they all had a little stake in the new club, it was in their interests to complete the work promptly and properly.

'Bloody good chaps,' said Toby. 'But the one thing none of them can even attempt is plastering. Luckily, after a succession of disasters, we've procured the services of the greatest plasterer I've ever seen. Come through and say hello.'

Frank was then introduced to one of the last people on earth he wanted to see.

14

It wasn't that Frank disliked Danny Power. On the contrary, he loved the big, fat Irish plasterer. He loved his warm, garrulous bonhomie, the quick vulgarity of his humour and the generosity of his spirit. However, Danny was the living, breathing embodiment of Frank's old life, of everything he was trying to escape. And so, as the big man seized him in an emotional bear-hug, full of wet plaster and friendship, Frank wondered how he would ever break free.

Danny had been the life and soul of Frank's last parish and without question the biggest, in every sense of the word, of his hundreds of fans. Frank's success as parish priest of St Thomas's, Wealdstone, had been helped in no small measure by Danny's loud, loquacious support.

He finally released Frank's head from his chest and held him by the shoulders. 'Fath – Fra – Mr Dempsey,' he bellowed. 'How the hell are you?'

'Fine, Danny,' said Frank, wiping plaster from his eyebrow. 'Just fine.'

'You two know each other?' asked Toby.

'No, I always treat complete strangers like this,' laughed Danny. 'You fuckin' eejit. Frank here was parish—'

Frank shot Danny a sharp don't-say-any-more glance, then continued, 'Yeah, I was in the same parish as Danny. I used to live in Wealdstone. Until I got married and moved away.'

All perfectly true minus one crucial detail. However, Frank's intervention had been so quick and so smooth that Toby hadn't noticed. 'Well, I expect you two have a lot of catching-up to do so, if you'll excuse me, I'll see how the other chaps are getting on,' he said. 'And, Frank, thank you so much. Look, do you have a card?'

Frank pulled a Sacred Heart Cabs card from his pocket and handed it to him. 'Just ask for Frank. Mind you, I only work during the day, not much good to a night owl like you.'

'Oh, I don't know,' said Toby thoughtfully. 'I'm sure we'll meet again.'

And, with that, the charming, courteous and prematurely bald little chap left Danny and Frank to catch up. Danny, who never needed much encouragement to abandon his trowel, suggested they do this at the Lord Admiral across the road

Oh, Christ, no, thought Frank, as he enthusiastically accepted Danny's invitation. I'm going to the pub with Danny Power, I'll never escape.

However, it was his newly awakened curiosity that led him to say, 'Cheers,' as Danny handed him a pint of Guinness. Frank wanted to know how Danny, a rich, successful sub-contractor with his own building firm, fleet of vans and huge squad of men had ended up toiling for Toby. 'Ah, it's just a little hobby,' Danny explained, swallowing half his pint in one mouthful. 'I met that Rupert a couple of months back. We were doing a job over in Hammersmith and they were renovating the house next door. Anyway, their plasterer was one unreliable little bollix. He didn't show up for the second day running and they were in a right state, desperate they were. Well, what could I do? I couldn't really say no to them.'

Frank was impressed. 'Typical of you, Dan, always ready to help out.'

'Help out?' chortled Danny, swallowing most of the last half-pint. 'Are you joking? They offered me five hundred quid for a day's work. I did them a beautiful job. They're nice fellas and they pay well, so I'm always happy to do a bit of work for them. Makes a change for me, just doing the plastering and not having to kick people's arses all day.'

He took out twenty Carrolls, removed the Cellophane, and

pulled out a cigarette in one seamless movement.

Frank looked at him. 'I thought you'd packed up,' he said.

'Giving up smoking's easy,' said Danny, with his trademark grin-and-wink. 'I've done it loads of times.'

Frank shook his head. 'You've still got your own firm, though.'

'Oh, God, yeah, but this is a nice little sideline. Anyway, how about you? I saw the card. You're workin' for Joe Hennessey. Ah, he's a good man, God love him. Still going. Must be pushing seventy.'

'Yeah. For the time being, anyway. Mind you, I'm raking it in. I get more work from Joe than I can handle.'

'But you don't work nights?'

'No, for the first time in my life I have evenings. And for the first time I have someone I want to spend them with. I can't tell you how good that feels. We go to the cinema, the theatre, out for dinner. I've missed out on so much for so long, and I'm having the time of my life.'

Thirty years, five children and an ocean of Guinness had misted Danny's memories of his own courtship but he understood how Frank was feeling, 'Ah, good man yourself. You deserve it.'

'So, how's business?'

'Well, to be honest,' said Danny, 'it's been a bit slow. I mean, I'm doing fine, like, with the work I've been doing for these fellas, but my bread-and-butter – the bigger jobs – the extensions, the conversions, the road-digging and that, we don't seem to be getting quite so much of that. I'm sure there's still plenty of work around but I get the feeling there's something funny going on. I could be wrong.'

Frank listened, knowing that Danny wouldn't be wrong, and enquired after Rose and the kids, all the time struggling with his pint of Guinness. While not finding it quite as repugnant as tea, he had never been keen on the bitter aftertaste and heavy, treacly consistency of Ireland's most celebrated export. Now, freed from the uniform that had always made him look like a pint of it, he could at last admit that he preferred ice-cold lager from a bottle, the more watery, foreign and overpriced the better.

Toby and the others were clearly in awe of Danny so the plastering could wait until the maestro was ready to return. He was getting comfortable now and Frank had a feeling that he was intending to remain so for some time. Frank was getting comfortable too. And it was this very comfort that suddenly made him uncomfortable. It would be so easy to find himself drawn back into the parochial warmth of Irish Catholic life – and the worst thing he could do.

'Dan.' He jumped up and took a final, horrible gulp of Guinness. 'I've got to pick up my next fare at St Pancras in fifteen minutes,' he lied. 'I'm going to have to love you and leave you.'

'Go on, then,' said Danny. 'After all, you've a wife to keep now. Give us your number, I'll ring you.'

Frank hesitated for one imperceptible second, then acknowledged that he had no choice but to scribble it on the back of a beer mat and hand it to his old friend.

He rushed outside, got into the cab and drove off. With the smell of plaster in his hair and the taste of Guinness in his throat, he just had to get away.

15

Sarah was so happy that she'd forgotten how unhappy she was. She was so enraptured at having met and married the man of her dreams that her disenchantment with her career had been eclipsed. Sarah was an account director, which meant ferrying ads between the agency who had created them and the clients who had commissioned them. Advertising had come a long way during Sarah's nine-year involvement – most of it downhill.

The business had changed. When Sarah had first started, the making of TV commercials was exciting and important. The majority of people in the UK only had access to two commercial television channels, so when an ad was shown, you could guarantee that millions of people would see it. In those nine years, most of those millions had hooked themselves up to cable, satellite or the Internet. The advertising business had been picked up and smashed into a thousand tiny pieces. Though now dauntingly fragmented, budgets were no bigger: there were just more and more people chasing less and less money.

Clients everywhere had become horribly cost-conscious, more obsessed than ever with the 'bottom line'. They were no longer willing to take a chance with intelligent, brave ideas. Everything had to be obvious, sales messages made repetitively clear, just in case someone somewhere didn't understand. Creativity had been jettisoned in favour of safe, bland advertising to minimise any risk to shareholders' dividends. When beans are counted and belts tightened, the advertising budget is always the first to feel the pinch since its benefits can never be precisely accounted for on a balance sheet.

Sarah believed, with good reason and research to back it up, that when times were tough and sales were suffering, there was no better chance to produce bold, original advertising and plenty of it because when things picked up the clients who'd had the sense not to cut their budgets would be the ones whose products were at the front of public consciousness. Increasingly, however, her sound commercial advice was falling on deaf, cautious or cowardly ears. She found herself expected to yield more and more to the wishes of her clients. Her more expedient colleague, Jane Steele, seemed prepared to accept this.

'After all,' Jane was rather too fond of saying, 'they're the ones who pay our salaries.'

Sarah's view was equally valid and equally invalid. 'That's rubbish,' she'd countered. 'You could just as easily say that *we* pay *their* salaries. Without our ads, they wouldn't sell their products and they'd all be out of a job.'

Regular excursions to meetings at various clients' headquarters served to remind Sarah of how fortunate she was. Her office, stylishly stark and tastefully appointed, looked out on to Golden Square. Most of her clients were marooned on soulless, windswept business parks where their cheaply partitioned cubbyholes looked out on to the M25. Sometimes she had hideously realistic nightmares about working in one of those places, with only the stringently monitored coffee-breaks to look forward to. And even then, that would mean having to insert 30p into a vending machine to have scalding-hot 'white no sugar' squirted into a horrible Styrofoam cup.

Her job was to represent the agency to the client but also the client to the agency, so every day she would find herself pulled in two directions, jumping through the same old hoops again and again. She was tired of trying to persuade nervous clients with ledgerbook mentalities to see the merits of the ads that her agency had worked so hard to produce. Or, worse, trying to tell her colleagues back at the agency that the ideas they had come up with weren't up to scratch. The best way to do this was to describe the ads as both good and original. Omitting to mention that the ones that were good were not original, and the ones that were original were not good.

These irritations, though, had been soothed by the balm of matrimonial bliss. She had a new dimension to her life, which brought her happiness, humour and harmony. Her new husband was funny, kind, thoughtful and odd. There were so many different facets to his personality. As Nessie had pointed out to her, 'Darling, you'll never need to go astray. With Frank, you could just have an affair with another side of his character.'

She never knew which side would be her reward at the end of each dreary day, but from about lunchtime she was looking forward to finding out. She had thought the hours at work would drag, but they flew by: each afternoon she could feel Frank pulling her towards him in a one-way tug of war. Harder and harder he'd tug, faster and faster she'd be pulled along until, at about six thirty, she would fall into his arms, then into his taxi to be taken wherever she wanted to go. He'd slide the partition open and she'd kneel behind it on the floor, snuggling into his shoulder, driving cheek to cheek. If Dionne Warwick's sublime version of 'This Girl's In Love With You' wasn't playing on a tape, it would be playing in her head.

Frank always seemed to know what was on, where it was on and what time it started. He'd been a priest for about nine hundred weeks so, during his tenure, he'd read about nine hundred copies of *Time Out*. He'd forced himself to do it, even though it often brought a lump to his throat and a tear to his eye when he saw the weekly listings of everything he was missing out on. He was also an avid reader of *Hello!*, *OK!* and *Heat*, and was right up to speed with the latest developments in *Coronation Street* and *EastEnders*. He tried not to miss *The West Wing*, *Will & Grace* or *Sex and the City* and was always *au fait* with the latest reality-TV shows.

When Sarah had first got to know him, she was astonished by his detailed knowledge of secular life and popular culture but, as he explained to her, she shouldn't have been. A priest cannot expect to connect with his flock if he reads nothing more than the Bible, the *Universe* and the *Catholic Herald*. If he doesn't inhabit their world, know what they know and understand their likes and dislikes, how can he hope to gain their trust and respect? How can he guide and advise them?

But now, he realised, it had been more than that. He was subconsciously making sure that he didn't lose touch because, in his heart of hearts, he had harboured the hope that he wouldn't be a priest for ever. And when he finally bounced back into the real world, he wanted to be clued-up, switched on and ready to rumble.

Sometimes they went out for a meal, sometimes they stayed in. When it was Sarah's turn to cook, she prepared the food and Frank prepared the music, dipping into his thousands of vinyl ingredients to create the perfect soundtrack. When it was his turn to cook, he would get someone else to do it for him, often driving to a secluded spot where he and Sarah could enjoy a moonlit takeaway in the back of the cab.

Sarah discovered that the more love she gave, the more she had to give, and the more she received. Before she married Frank, she'd had to choose between two old proverbs: 'Marry in haste, repent at leisure' or 'Fortune favours the brave.' She'd plunged in and followed the latter: it had been a brave decision, and fortune was favouring her now. Most of her thoughts and efforts went into this wonderful new hobby known as her marriage. Armour-plated in love and happiness, the stress of her career never seemed to make even the tiniest dent in her breastplate. Since meeting Frank, she had been running her accounts on automatic pilot. Having read an e-mail from Peter Clay, the head of account management, she wandered cheerfully into his office and closed the door behind her. 'You rang, my lord.' She smiled at her boss and old friend.

Peter seemed fidgety. 'Sarah, hi,' he said. 'Look . . . um . . . as you know, things aren't going brilliantly for the agency. It's . . . er . . . well, it's the same for the whole industry at the moment.' Evidently he was struggling to find the right words. 'Look. You're not going to like this but . . . well . . . I've been asked to draw up a list of people whom I would recommend for redundancy.'

He looked at her awkwardly and motioned towards a chair. 'I think you'd better sit down.'

16

Sarah sat down nervously and, as Peter spoke, his words seemed to come out in slow motion while Sarah's thoughts were on fast-forward.

Oh, God, it's all over – my career's in ruins and it's all Frank's fault. Since I first met him, I've taken my eye off the ball and Peter has obviously noticed. Now what are we going to do? This won't bother Frank – he couldn't give a toss about money, he's never had any. Oh, I should have known this would happen. It's all very well having a husband who drives a taxi as long as someone was bringing some money in. Oh, maybe I shouldn't blame him but . . . Clichés, clichés, I need some clichés . . . um . . . right . . . It doesn't matter, we've still got each other . . . It's only money . . . It's not the end of the world . . . They're not ringing true, though, are they? We'll have to start shopping at Kwiksave . . . buying those anonymous cans of beans for ninepence and white bread, lots of white bread . . . It *is* the end of the world . . . Come on, come on, look on it as an opportunity . . . I could do something totally different – take up sculpting or Reiki, open a teashop in the Cotswolds . . . um . . .

All these thoughts had hurtled through her mind before Peter had uttered a word. 'The first person I'm going to make redundant,' he said, slowly and carefully, 'is me.'

Sarah was relieved, astonished and upset all in one second. In fact, she was surprised by how upset she was. She'd braced herself for a life change and found herself strangely disappointed that it wasn't going to be foisted upon her. 'You?' she said. 'You're making yourself redundant?'

'Yep. You know something, I never really wanted to do this for a living.'

Sarah knew how he felt.

'I sort of fell into it after university, and it was a bit like falling into the sea. It was the eighties, there was a very strong advertising current and I got swept away. I kept promising myself I'd get out but never got round to it. Then, you know, over the course of twenty years, one job leads to another, promotions, more money. Then I got married, big mortgage, two children and, well, now I'm finally going to do what I should have done a long time ago. When I saw the nice big severance package I could walk away with, I thought, It's now or never. You're the first person I've told.'

'Well, I'm honoured,' said Sarah.

'I have to say, I was inspired by your husband. I mean, his decision to leave his profession must have been a hell of a lot harder than my decision to leave mine.'

'Well,' said Sarah, pretending to take offence, 'he did have the most wonderful incentive.'

'Yes, yes, of course,' said Peter, in case she wasn't joking, 'but you know what I mean. I never had to take a vow in church to say that I'd remain in advertising for the rest of my life, and you know how much the industry has changed. For me, the final straw was working on the launch of TopTelly. What a fucking disaster, as we all knew it would be. It was the first time in my career that I felt guilty about what I did for a living.'

'Guilty?'

'Yes. For the most part, advertising, despite what some people think, is a fairly straight and honest business. There are things out there for sale and all we're doing is letting people know about them. If we persuade people to buy a packet of soap powder or a jar of Marmite, I don't think we've done them any harm – but TopTelly was different. For the first time in my career, I knew I was guilty of the charge that's always levelled at this industry – that we're persuading people to buy things they don't want and don't need. In this case a hundred channels of absolute crap. If we'd told them it was mainly repeats, third-rate films and Preston versus Walsall in the Nationwide League, do you think anyone would have signed up?'

Sarah nodded. 'It was all rather tacky, wasn't it?'

'You can say that again. And, of course, when it all went tits up, having lost a billion pounds and hundreds of people their jobs, I had that whingeing prick Clive Holland phoning me up in tears.'

Sarah had only once met the lascivious TopTelly client, with his paint-peeling halitosis, and decided she could live quite happily without ever standing near him again. 'Why was he phoning you in tears?'

'Oh, he was being paid a fortune to preside over that shambles, and when he lost his job, he lost his trophy wife too. He was all alone at Christmas and . . .'

'You didn't!'

'I did. I had him over on Christmas Day. That was the final, final straw. I've been planning my escape since Boxing Day.'

Sarah would be sorry to see Peter go. He'd hired her from university and had been her mentor ever since. She would miss his intelligence, integrity and irrepressible sense of mischief. As head of account management, he had put together a department of extremely good people. As he unburdened more of his disaffection, Sarah remembered him disclosing the secret of running a successful department. 'It's just like having a party,' he'd explained. 'Create the right atmosphere and invite the right people.'

'So, what now?' she said. 'What are you going to do?'

His reply surprised her. 'I'm going to become a second-hand car dealer.'

'You're not!'

'I am. You know I've always loved cars.'

'Nearly as much as I love shoes.'

'Exactly. But for me, it's never been Ferraris or Aston Martins

– too obvious, too many pristine examples – I'm going to restore and sell ordinary cars from the sixties and seventies. Ford Cortinas, Triumph Heralds, that sort of thing. There's a huge demand out there. People want something a bit different that isn't going to cost them too much. As the business expands, we'll be able to take specific orders. If someone wants, say, a blue Ford Anglia like the one in the *Harry Potter* film, we'll make one to order. There are hundreds of old cars like that, rotting in garages all over the country. You can usually pick them up for next to nothing, then all you have to do is rebuild them Once we've collected a good stock, we can also hire them out for film and TV shoots.'

Sarah was pleased for him. He had it all worked out and was going to make a fortune. More importantly, he was going to enjoy every minute of it. He'd be getting his hands dirty, working with his mechanics, coming home tired but happy, calluses on his fingers, oil on his teeth, having re-created the transport of his youth. It seemed a far more innocent, pleasurable form of work, and each rescued Rover, each born-again Beetle, would remind him of more innocent, pleasurable times. 'Sounds fantastic,' she said. 'I'm going to miss you but . . .'

'But what?'

'Well, you started this conversation by saying, "You're not going to like this." What's the bit you haven't told me?'

Once again, Peter was fidgety. 'You're very perceptive,' he said, with a nervous smile.

'And you're very kind, but what's the bit you haven't told me?'

'Er . . . well . . . my replacement,' he said, apologetically, 'your new boss.'

'Yes?' said Sarah.

'Will be Jane Steele.'

17

It was an odd hiring policy but it usually worked. Every now and then Peter would bring someone in from another agency who, unlike the rest of his department, would be humourless, ambitious and unpleasant. There had been a succession of such people, who had unwittingly given a subliminal message to the rest of the department: 'This is how awful people from other agencies can be. So if you were thinking of leaving, well, I am the sort of person you could find yourself working with.'

These sedulous misfits never lasted long. They were put to work on the most soul-destroying and creatively bankrupt accounts. They would beaver away, making the most of every opportunity, trying to play politics, until they realised that their career was not going far enough fast enough and they would leave to pursue their relentless ambitions elsewhere.

All except one.

Jane Steele's arrival had coincided with the least creative and most expedient period in the agency's history, conditions in which she could flourish. At thirty-eight, she was the last of a dying breed: a woman still prepared to sacrifice almost anything for the sake of her career. Had she emerged into the workplace a few years later, she might not have been saddled with that dated eighties mindset. She might have seen the folly of squandering the best years of her life working fourteen hours a day to make other people rich. By the time she wised up, it was too late.

Over the years, whenever she'd thought about getting married and moderating the speed of the treadmill, she'd always taken the plenty-of-time-for-all-that option but now, suddenly, the boat was pulling away from the harbour and she had little hope of catching it.

She still looked great – as well she might, given the effort that went into her diet, fitness and skincare regime – but there is always something profoundly unattractive about a woman who tries too hard and takes herself too seriously. Jane had had relationships but they'd never worked out. Other people's emotions, as she'd been rather slow to discover, could not be manipulated in the same way as a career. 'Frankly,' she would tell friends derisively, over dinner at Villandry, 'he found me intimidating.' Frankly, he had probably found her boring and was now having the time of his life with someone who didn't leave him alone in bed to rush off to her seven fifteen Pilates class.

Superficially she and Sarah got on well. After Sarah's wedding, *jsteele's* was the first congratulatory e-mail to arrive in her in-box, but the sender was consumed with envy at the sight of her colleague glowing like a child from a Ready Brek commercial, visibly ablaze with contentment.

Peter Clay was clearly embarrassed about his successor. It was his one hiring that had backfired. 'You have to see it from the agency's point of view,' he said. 'She's extremely efficient, incredibly hard-working. One of life's administrators. Boy, will they be getting their money's worth.'

Suddenly it all became clear, 'So what you're saying,' said Sarah, with a smirk, 'is that Jane Steele is cheap.'

'For a head of account management in a big agency like this, an absolute – if you'll pardon the pun – steal. If they'd brought in some big gun from another agency, it would have cost them twice as much, and more, by the time they'd paid the head-hunters' commission. And the title is so important to her. Getting this job is the pinnacle of her life. She's always wanted it and, to be honest, who else would? Would you?'

'Well, I'm not really senior enough and—'

'Yeah, but even if you were,' said Peter, 'would you really want to do it and be responsible for twenty-eight people, who are always asking for more money, bigger offices or different projects to work on? Have to deal with all their gripes and problems? All that client entertaining? It sounds great, getting the best tables at the Ivy or Le Caprice, until you remember the prats you have to share them with. Honestly, I'd rather sit in a greasy spoon on my own. Jane has fuck-all else in her life. She'll absolutely love it.'

'Yeah, but—'

'You've got nothing to worry about,' said Peter briskly. 'This won't affect you. She knows how well you run your accounts, how good your relationships are with your clients. If anything, you're the one person she'll depend on for advice. Your position couldn't be better.'

Sarah wasn't convinced. She remembered Jane saying how great it would be to run a department and 'have your own train-set to play with'. Use of that phrase alone should have been a sacking offence.

And then she remembered Jane extolling the benefits of 'managing up'. 'It doesn't matter whether you love or hate your boss, you have to manage him,' Jane had explained, 'so that he becomes your resource for achievement and personal success.'

And use of that phrase should have been a hanging offence.

Sarah returned to her desk to see the little red light flashing that told her she had a voicemail message. It was Frank. The message was a bit crackly – breaking the law again, steering-wheel in one hand, mobile phone in the other. 'Hi, it's me. My turn to . . . er . . . "cook" tonight. There's this brilliant little Vietnamese takeaway in Hackney. They don't speak a word of English so you just say, "Food, two people," and take whatever they give you. It's always good – I mean, really good. Fancy it? Give us a ring, then I can swing by on the way home.'

Just his voice, so full of love, fun and enthusiasm, was enough to defuse any anxieties about Jane Steele's forthcoming appointment. Sarah had a great life and a gorgeous husband. So what if she had to go through the motions of working for that awful woman? Really, how bad could it be?

18

Beads of sweat had appeared on Frank's forehead. The Vietnamese hot and sour soup was infused with almost illegal levels of chilli so he knew he'd need another trip to the steam room in the morning to expunge its antisocial aroma. If he didn't, his passengers would be spending their entire journeys with their heads hanging out of the window, gasping for air. He also knew that it wasn't only the soup that had sent the sweat trickling on to his top lip from the bridge of his nose: it was Danny Power's proud boast that he 'knew a Paddy in every pub in London'. Each 'Paddy' knew several more and they all knew ex-Father Frank Dempsey, who was reflecting on how many of them were already in possession of his mobile number.

He thought about 'losing' his phone and changing the number but it wouldn't take Inspector Morse to figure out that a message could be left at Sacred Heart Cabs.

One of the reasons he had initially opted for the reclusive life of a writer was that it would seal him away from his ex-parishioners, allow him to forget his erstwhile holiness and become an ordinary member of society. When he had swapped laptop for taxi, he had known that he might occasionally bump into someone from his past, but he'd hoped that that someone would not be Danny Power. He looked at his mobile, lying innocently on the table next to its new pal, the Dictaphone, and wondered when its ringtones would become the tones of torment. He didn't have to wonder for long.

'Hello?'

'Er . . . hello,' said an apprehensive second-generation Irish voice at the other end. 'Is that Father, um . . .'

'This is Frank Dempsey, yes.'

'Oh, right, good . . . er . . . This is Gerry Cahill from Wealdstone, don't know if you remember me?'

Frank remembered him. Brickie by trade, nice bloke, late thirties, big QPR fan, married, two little girls, wife expecting a third, oh, God, he knew what was coming. 'Of course I remember you, Gerry. How's Kathy? Has she had the baby?'

'Yeah, two weeks ago. Little boy. Third time lucky, eh?' he said, laughing nervously. Then he swallowed. 'Um . . . Kathy and me were wondering, like . . .'

Oh, no, here we go.

'. . . since you're not a priest any more, whether you and your missus would like to be godparents. We couldn't think of anyone we'd rather have.'

If Frank's Vietnamese soup had contained some sort of truth serum, his reply would have been brutally honest: 'Well, I'm very flattered that you should ask, Gerry, but I'm sorry – I'm going to have to say no. Thing is, it would be an act of utter hypocrisy for me to stand there at the font and renounce Satan on your baby's behalf. I think the whole concept of baptism is nonsense. I do not believe in Adam and Eve or original sin. I think it's obscene even to suggest that your innocent, newborn child is a sinner and will be permanently excluded from heaven if he dies without being baptised. By agreeing to act as the baby's godfather, I would be encouraging and perpetuating this mumbojumbo. When I left the priesthood, it was partly to stop living a lie and be true to my own beliefs, or lack of them. What's more, although I am extremely fond of the people who go there, I have no desire to return to St Thomas's Church. It would be great to see you again but only if I need a wall built or you need a taxi. So, thanks but no thanks.'

However, despite the pomp and solemnity surrounding it, a Catholic baptism has, in practice, little to do with the cleansing of original sin. It's just a way of welcoming a little human being into the world and, of course, a wonderful excuse for a

Guinness-fuelled knees-up. What was more, Frank was still missing his priestly prestige, so his actual reply was rather different: 'Well, that's very kind of you, Gerry, we'd be delighted.'

He checked with Sarah and she was, indeed, delighted, mainly because it meant a nice trip to Mappin & Webb to buy a silver christening mug.

It was a sunny Sunday afternoon when the old clock tower at the end of Spencer Road told Frank that it was eight minutes to four and that he was once again in Wealdstone, the scruffy north London suburb that had been his last and favourite parish. He was uncharacteristically quiet, wondering how he would be received. Would they remember him for his good work? Would they remember how he had transformed their opinion of mass, that he'd turned it from a dreary obligation into a weekly treat? Would they remember how he'd preached without preaching, and had moved, amused and inspired them with his sermons? Would they remember how he had comforted them when they were sick, bereaved or in trouble, how his drive, energy and commitment had turned a crumbling old church hall into a thriving new parish centre? Would they remember the discos, the benefit dances, the money raised for charity? Or would they just remember the last thing he did, which was to abandon them, along with his vows?

He needn't have worried. He was mobbed as soon as he arrived at the church.

Sarah felt as though she were watching the Regent Street Christmas lights being switched on. Frank became illuminated with the friendly, easy charisma that his old parishioners adored. They were queuing up to pump his hand or kiss his cheek. Sarah was amused that no one knew quite what to call him. 'Father' was no longer appropriate, 'Mr Dempsey' too formal and 'Frank' too informal. Most people ended up calling him 'F-F-F . . .' 'F-F-F' was like Bob Geldof returning to a village in Africa to see how the money he'd helped raise through Live Aid was being put to use.

Once the formalities were over, the three hundred guests trooped into the adjacent parish centre to embark on one of those Sunday-night hoe-downs that were Frank's lasting legacy to the parish. These social events had united and strengthened a whole community and Father Brendan Donaghy, his replacement, was continuing the good work.

Father Donaghy had been unlucky in having such a hard act to follow, but fortunate to inherit such a happy, lively parish with all the pastoral groundwork done. Frank was careful not to upstage his successor, though Father Donaghy, delighted to have him back in the parish even for a few hours, was encouraging him to do just that.

'Frank,' he said quietly, 'I think you're going to have to say a few words. They're all waiting for you. They'll be disappointed if you don't. Look, I've done the Catholic bit. Just give them one of your inspirational speeches.'

Frank immediately knew how Frank Skinner must feel when approached by fans in the street, who would just gaze at him expectantly and say, 'Say something funny, Frank,' and be crestfallen if he couldn't oblige.

Before Frank had a chance to think about it, Father Donaghy had stepped up on to the stage and blown into the microphone. 'Ladies and gentlemen,' he said, 'Mr Frank Dempsey.'

A huge cheer propelled Frank on to the stage, where he began his speech as he used to begin his sermons, with silence, as his eyes swept around the room looking at every person present. Used properly, silence is a powerful rhetorical tool, so by the time Frank opened his mouth, he had the undivided attention of his audience. However, this occasion was different: he was silent not for theatrical effect but because he didn't know what to say. Fortunately, his audience was unaware of this. An awestruck hush had fallen upon every one of them. Even the baby, no longer condemned to rot in hell, seemed expectant. Frank's gaze fell upon the child and that was when he found his voice.

'Stanley,' he said to the baby. 'Stanley James Cahill. All children baptised in the Catholic Church are required to take the name of a saint, and you are no exception. I'm delighted that you have been named after St Stanislaus of Cracow, the famous eleventh-century Polish martyr.'

(*Pause while audience tries to work out whether he is being serious. Pause for a millisecond longer just to make them think that he is.*)

'The fact that Stanley is also the name of Stan Bowles, arguably the greatest player ever to wear Queens Park Rangers' blue and white hoops and your father's boyhood idol, is, of course, pure coincidence.'

(*Pause while audience laugh.*)

'But your name doesn't really matter. What is significant is that you have been welcomed into the Catholic Church and, better still, into the parish of St Thomas's in Wealdstone, and I'm here to tell you that you've really landed on your feet. Your life will be spent among some of the warmest, kindest, most generous people you could meet. People always willing to help others, people always willing to help you. Compassionate people, with a strong sense of duty and a strong sense of right and wrong.'

(*All perfectly true. Frank was skilfully avoiding words like 'God', 'original' and 'sin'.*)

'They are wonderful people, people from whom only the love of the most beautiful woman in the world could tear me away.'

(*Pause while dewy-eyed section of audience says, 'Aaaah', instantly justifying the abrogation of his vows.*)

'And because of that, I have the honour of being your godfather. That beautiful woman will remember your birthday each year because that is a promise I know I'll never be able to keep. But I do promise to be there for you if ever you need me. Danny Power has my mobile number. He'll have given it to half of London, so you shouldn't have much trouble getting hold of me.'

(Pause to allow more laughter before adopting serious face and tone to match.)

'But your life, I'm afraid, will not all be plain sailing. The world can be a cruel place, particularly in this day and age, and I worry that you'll experience more than your share of misery and heartbreak.'

(Pause while audience reflect on the veracity of what Frank is saying.)

'And when you do, even though I'm your godfather, don't come running to me.'

(Pause before moving eyes slowly from baby to his father.)

'Go and see your real father.'

(Brief pause to take them right down before lifting them up again.)

'Because he's the one who will have forced you to support QPR.'

(Final pause to accommodate huge laugh, and when laughter hits its peak, simultaneous raising of voice and glass.)

'Ladies and gentlemen, to Stanley.'

'Stanley,' came the response, in the style of 'Lord, graciously hear us', followed by spontaneous cheers and applause.

Frank stepped down from the stage, picked up the baby, held him high in the air and swung him round, then handed him back to his delighted parents. The ribbon had been cut on the party and the music, drinking and dancing began in earnest.

Frank worked his way through the throng, shaking more hands, kissing more babies and accepting invitations to dance with a string of Irish housewives.

After a while, though, he became privately afflicted by a nagging awkwardness. He looked wistfully at the bar, and thought how much he preferred his old position on the other side of it. He didn't want to be just another drunken reveller reeling round and round to Seamus Moore's 'Me Galluses And Me Gansey' in a Catholic social club. The sight of Danny Power shaking his considerable girth to 'Achy Breaky Heart' made him concerned for the achy-breaky dance-floor and suddenly he wanted to go home.

Sarah, on the other hand, whose Sunday nights hadn't been spent at hundreds of hooleys just like this, was enjoying the novelty, especially the adoration-by-proxy. She could see that his resignation from the priesthood had done nothing to diminish the almost messianic regard in which he was held. He'd done too good a job and, as they left with the sound of dozens of 'All the best nows' ringing in their ears, she realised she might have to go back to Mappin & Webb and buy a job lot of silver christening mugs.

19

It was getting ridiculous. Frank was going to end up with more godchildren than Vito Corleone. Each time he was asked, his fatal combination of kindness, guilt and vanity made him accept. Each time he agreed to take responsibility for the spiritual and moral well-being of a child whose parents he barely knew, the more he felt he was rejoining the world he had tried to leave behind.

Other sacraments joined the queue for his services. So many couples had wanted Father Dempsey to marry them but now that he couldn't, the next best thing was to invite him to say a few words at the reception. So far, he'd managed to steer clear of funerals. He didn't mind burials, as long as it wasn't raining – the poet in him preferred people to see a ray of sunshine buried in there with them. Also there was something undignified about the bereaved getting mud all over their best shoes and the hems of their trousers. Cremations, as he explained to Sarah, as he played post-prandial records for her one night, offered the greatest scope for embarrassment.

'The ashes you get aren't the remains of your loved one,' he told her. 'At the end of a busy day at the cremmy, there's a huge pile and they just scoop up an urnful and give it to you. It could be anyone in there. I mean, how could you ever tell?'

Obvious, but Sarah had never really thought about it. Death is still such a taboo that people seldom do.

'And there's always the rumour that rather than burn a brand-new coffin, they whip the body out and sell the coffin back to the undertaker.'

Sarah was appalled. 'Surely not?' she said.

'Well,' said Frank, 'that could be an urban myth but the thing about the ashes is certainly true. Also, if you're doing the service, you have to test the equipment first. I remember doing my first cremation over in Ruislip. I pushed the button, the curtains opened and in went the coffin. But no one told me I was supposed to press the button again after the curtains had closed. I didn't, and the curtains suddenly opened and the half-singed coffin came sliding back out. People didn't know whether to laugh or cry. It was a good job they hadn't whipped the body out first.

'Then there's the music.' Frank jumped up and rooted through a box of records, then pulled out a famous old single. 'This one,' he said, 'was always popular but I hated it.' The opening bars of Frank Sinatra's 'My Way' filled the room, as it had filled a thousand requiem masses. 'Listen to the words,' he said. 'There's something so arrogant about having this played at your funeral. "Hey," it says, "I'm an individual, I'm a real one-off, I always did what I wanted, I went my own way." The joke was, these people were practising Catholics who followed the herd into mass every Sunday. Hardly going your own way, is it? The other one that was getting very popular was this.' He put on Eva Cassidy's 'Somewhere Over The Rainbow', which, of course, was given added mawkish poignancy because the chanteuse herself had died of cancer and never lived to see her global fame.

'Another old favourite was this.' On went Celine Dion's 'My Heart Will Go On'. 'Always a bit ironic,' said Frank, 'since the heart inside the coffin had plainly stopped. And, of course, this . . .' Queen's Greatest Hits was inserted into the CD player. 'Track one,' said Frank, and on came 'Bohemian Rhapsody'. 'Trouble was, at one funeral near Lewisham, someone left the CD on.' He pressed the skip button. 'Track two.' On came 'Another One Bites The Dust'. 'I don't know how I kept a straight face.'

Frank was still laughing when he picked up his mobile. Sarah watched his mouth say one thing and his face say another.

'Yeah, I'd love to . . . When is it? Okay . . . St Vincent's on the Harrow Road. Right . . . Yeah, fine. Right, we'll speak nearer the time . . . Okay. Yep. Love to Bernie . . . Okay, 'bye.' With a weary sigh, he put the phone back on the table. Sarah looked at him. 'Don't ask,' he said, then told her that Kieran Hennessey had just asked him to be his son's confirmation sponsor. He hesitated for a second before going into the details, knowing just how ridiculous they were going to sound. He explained that when baptised Catholics reach 'the age of reason', they are asked to confirm their faith, rather like reconfirming a flight or a restaurant booking. Of all the holy sacraments, he went on, confirmation was, without doubt, the most pointless, the one people always forget about. 'What supposedly happens is that the Holy Spirit is given to people to make them perfect Christians and soldiers of Jesus Christ.'

Just saying this out loud reminded Frank of why he wasn't a priest any more. He took a deep breath and explained that, in a vain attempt to give it some sort of gravitas, confirmation is always administered by a bishop who starts speaking to God in front of each bewildered youth. He says something like 'Send forth upon them thy sevenfold spirit the Holy Paraclete.' He anoints them with chrism, says, 'Peace be with you,' then slaps them round the face.

But there was more, as Frank continued, in the face of his wife's incredulity. When you're confirmed, you have to take another name and, as with baptism, it has to be the name of a saint, who will look after you and guide you along the Catholic path. Frank had taken the name John – he reasoned that if he had to choose a saint to look after him, he'd choose the one who had his own ambulance brigade.

Back around 1970, Joe Hennessey had been his confirmation sponsor so Frank could hardly refuse to return the favour for Joe's grandson. It was a bit like being a godparent and, no, sponsorship did not mean that Callum Hennessey had to run into church with 'FRANK DEMPSEY' emblazoned across the front of his shirt.

20

Anyone who has ever written an advertisement will have a tragic tale to tell about the one that got away. The brilliant idea that, if only it had seen the light of day, would have brought its creator a giant pay rise and a shelf full of awards. Restrictions in budgets, time lengths and the client's imagination usually kill most wonderful ideas before they get a chance to breathe. Even if they survive such perils, the regulations governing British advertising, far more petty than in other countries, will be waiting to sound the death knell.

With leaving cards, there is no excuse, which is why they are often the most inspired pieces of work to emerge from any ad agency. Some, admittedly, are fairly lame, featuring a picture of the subject drunk at the Christmas party, accompanied by a dismally unfunny caption. Others can be rather more savage. Sarah's favourite had been given to a lazy, long-lunching copy-writer who, in almost two years, had only produced one press ad. His card was about three feet high and the front was blank, apart from a postage-stamp-sized copy of his ad. Inside, the message read, 'Thanks for all the work.'

Though cruel, at least that card had been unique – custom-made for its recipient. Surely the greatest insult for any departing member of staff is a shop-bought leaving card with a horseshoe on the front, the implicit message being, 'The place will be the same without you.'

Between meetings, Jane Steele had been sorting through various pictures of Peter Clay to find the most apposite one for his leaving card. She was going to ask one of the copywriters to come up with the oh-so-hilarious caption. She hadn't realised that Sarah, Frank, Effy Baker and Westminster Council were working on something a little more original.

'Frank? Hello, mate, it's Effy. Listen, I've got just what you're looking for. Give us the address. Eighty-three Golden Square . . . Right . . . Yeah, well, look, it's probably best if you speak to him yourself . . . His name's John Vernon . . . Hang on, I'll give you his number.'

'Mr Saunders? Hello, it's Sarah Dempsey. I spoke to you yesterday. Yeah . . . Will that be okay? Twelve o'clock, then? Great. Thanks very much.'

Jane had taken the train to Swindon. She usually drove but wanted time to go through her pictures of Peter on the way back. As the train pulled out of Slough, she found the perfect one. Peter at the end of the Christmas party, slumped motionless in a chair, head back, eyes closed, mouth open. In a flash of pure genius, the caption came to her: 'Peter listens carefully as Clive Holland explains the marketing strategy for TopTelly.'

Filled with the joy of creation, she rushed down the platform at Paddington and jumped into a cab bound for Golden Square. She'd get Darren in the studio to make up the card and tell the whole agency that it was her brilliant idea. Copywriters? Who needs them?

However, as the cab pulled up she wondered what on earth was going on. Half the agency was gathered outside around a rusty old Vauxhall Viva, which had been dumped there. They all had crayons in their hands and were signing its rotting bodywork.

'Jane,' said a colleague, handing her a crayon, 'do you want to sign Peter's leaving card?'

No, she bloody didn't, but she could hardly refuse. And her creative genius, so apparent on the fourteen thirty-five from Swindon, now seemed to have deserted her: 'Good luck, Jane XX' was the best she could manage to scrawl on the nearside front wing.

'Don't you think it's fantastic?' said another colleague, whose identity, in her seething resentment, Jane would never remember. 'It was all Sarah's idea.'

She looked across at Sarah laughing and joking in the midst of the throng. A bemused Nigerian traffic warden was now being asked to add his signature. Jane watched it all through a hazy mist that was getting greener and greener.

She was about to slink anonymously back to her desk when she noticed the photographer arrive from the *Evening Standard*. Suddenly the mist cleared and she saw an opportunity waiting to be seized. She worked her way subtly to the front of the crowd, who were now posing around the Viva's bonnet for the big picture. Afterwards, since she was at the front, she volunteered to give a brief interview to the reporter. Although she didn't actually claim credit, Jane Steele was the only person mentioned by name, and anyone reading the story the following day would assume that Peter Clay's memorable 'leaving car' had been her idea.

21

Frank was heading down the Archway Road and was, for once, alone in the cab. David Bowie had just gone, having performed a great version of 'All The Young Dudes' and Frank was unable to decide which tape to put on next. It was in this brief window of silence that he made an astounding discovery.

Maybe it was because he was driving a taxi and no longer felt the awkward rawness of redundancy, or because he was earning money and helping others that he felt relaxed and at peace with himself. Or maybe it was the physical act of driving the taxi, its perpetual motion, the familiar lunge and whine of its engine and transmission. But whatever it was, it was succeeding where all else had failed. The inspiration that had so far eluded him was forming words and sentences in his head.

He broke with tradition. Instead of listening to music, he tuned into his own head and heard the muse dictating the first paragraphs of his book. In that semi-silence, supported by the anonymous thrum of the traffic, he was able to test his words aloud, 'weighing' the sentences as he spoke, checking each one for rhythm, cadence and balance. Those that sounded good remained in his head, and those that didn't were tossed out of the window, leaving a trail of invisible litter all the way to Highbury Corner.

These were the words that had passed their first audition:

Not all forms of contraception are forbidden by the Catholic Church. Condoms, caps and coils may be outlawed but slippers have somehow escaped the wrath of the Vatican.

Walk into any devout Catholic household, especially one with four or five children, and if the husband and wife are wearing slippers, you now know the reason why. There is not a person in the world whose sexual magnetism is enhanced by furry mules or tartan zip-up booties. On the contrary, the fact that they are wearing them is a sure sign that comfort is more important than sex, and even at bedtime when the offending items are removed, that situation is unlikely to alter.

It's funny what makes a man fall in love with a woman but one of the many reasons why I knew that Sarah Marshall would be the lid to my dustbin was that, among her compendious collection of footwear, there wasn't a single slipper.

He liked the words, and the angle from which they were coming. This was a much better approach. The book could still be autobiographical, but it would be from a life-begins-at-forty perspective. It would open with his marriage to Sarah and make only fleeting references to his former life as a priest. He even had the title: *The Man Who Fell In Love With His Wife*.

What was that phrase Sarah said they used in advertising agencies? Oh, yes, USP – Unique Selling Proposition. Well, this book would have a USP. A few priests had left the Catholic Church and got married but Frank couldn't think of any who had written about it. The only comparable tale was that of the novice nun who had left the abbey in Salzburg to marry Captain von Trapp, and *The Sound of Music* went on to become the biggest grossing film of all time.

As Frank reached for the Dictaphone to record these sentences, a sudden thought shoved a cushion over the face of his embryonic literary career. He'd only been married a couple of months. Wouldn't his story be a bit like Michael Aspel leaning over a pram with a big red book and saying, 'Tonight, two-month-old baby, this is your life.' If his life really had begun at forty, then his tale was still in its first chapter. A good story needs a beginning, a middle and an end. One out of three isn't enough. And where would the story end? How would he know when he'd reached it? What if the ending wasn't so happy? What if *The Man Who Fell In Love With His Wife* became *The Man Who Got Divorced From His Wife*? What then?

Frank put down the Dictaphone and decided to concentrate on living his life rather than writing about it.

He needed something, though. The love of a wonderful woman is all very well, but when you're used to the love of thousands of people you need more. Frank was at the Old Street roundabout before he could admit this guiltily to himself.

He had to face up to the fact that, despite his popularity, he didn't have a friend in the world. Sarah didn't count. Of course she was his friend, and much, much more than that, but he didn't have any of the standard, semi-close friendships that most people enjoyed. He had, understandably, never struck up that sort of relationship with the priests and parishioners he had known over the years. Though he'd liked them, he'd had little in common with them. Their lives had been like Venn diagrams with only the Catholic bits overlapping.

But what was he looking for? Certainly not fame. He could have made himself very famous. The British public would soon have taken a taxi-driving priest to their hearts. When he then searched his soul and quit his vocation to marry a beautiful woman, he would have become a household name. Especially when his story, like that of Baroness von Trapp, was taken up by Hollywood, and he was depicted as a small boy on the big screen, running through the streets of Kilburn singing, 'The pubs are alive with the sound of brawling.'

But his story was not unique. Now and again, priests who had quit their vocations to get married made the pages of the *Sunday People*. They always seemed to be podgy, pasty, middle-aged men with wives to match: for the first time in their lives, they had not been found physically repellent by a member of the opposite sex. Since lightning was unlikely to strike twice, the opportunity, and the woman who was presenting it, had to be grabbed with both hands.

He remembered some of the other seminarians with whom he'd done his vocational training, all perfectly nice but, with their thick glasses and naïve piety, they would never have been mistaken for Brad Pitt. Most were shy young men from banal, suburban households. For them, giving up sex had been a bit like giving up Beluga caviar – no great sacrifice.

He didn't want fame as a writer. And, anyway, with a 'book' that only ran to three paragraphs and would take several years to run to much more, he was unlikely to get it. What was it he needed? It was unfair to place such a heavy burden on his new wife, who was already giving him as much love as one human being could supply. He'd had his fill of religious ceremonies, so it had to be something secular, but with no tangible talents, how would be ever get the hot buzz of public approval that he still craved?

The phone rang. It was Joe Hennessey. Pick-up at Liverpool Street station – the pick-up that would pick him up and, although he didn't yet know it, provide the answer he had been looking for.

22

As Frank was only too aware, vows are made to be broken and his vow never to work nights had always looked brittle. He had no intention of driving a taxi at night and picking up an unappealing assortment of drunks, whores, dealers and users – he didn't want to descend into a lethal depression as they violated the sunny Sacred Heart atmosphere of his cab. He worried that his sanity would quickly become loosened from its hinges and he would turn into a 'taxi driver' in the Robert de Niro mould, prowling the seamier streets of the city, terminating the low life of each lowlife in one homicidal spree.

Along with his vows of celibacy and chastity he'd taken a vow of I'm-never-going-to-work-as-a-DJ-againity. Too many spent nights playing records, like too many nights spent driving a taxi, had almost turned him off the human race for ever. Then he had seen people at their worst – their most drunken, and embarrassing.

It had started when friends asked him to drop the tunes at their weddings or twenty-firsts. 'It's all right,' they would add, without realising the corrosive insensitivity of their next remark, 'you'll know everyone.' When he heard this, Frank's heart would sink. It would make the evening about a hundred times worse. While all his mates were having a wonderful time, he would be working – an isle of sobriety in a sea of collective crapulence.

Each time this happened, he vowed that next time he'd say he had a prior engagement. Yet something within him never allowed him to tell the lie and he invariably paid the price for his honesty. He envied his friend John Torpey, who worked as a contract cleaner. John was also invited to all the weddings and parties but nobody asked him to bring his mop and bucket and clean up afterwards.

Most of Frank's old mobile gigs followed a depressingly familiar pattern. As the evening wore on and the drink took hold, the punters' inhibitions were washed further and further downstream. They would assume that because they were having a great time, Frank was too. It never occurred to them that they were only having a good time because of the hard graft he was putting in. Playing the records was the easy bit. Hauling the decks, lights and bass bins from the back of his old Escort van wasn't so much fun. Several hours later, limbs heavy, eyes stinging with smoke and fatigue, he would dismantle the system alone. Those who had been so keen to help him carry it all in were never as keen to help him carry it back out.

Worst of all, a typically Catholic confluence of pride, humility and stupidity would not allow him to charge his friends for his services. He'd always accept a 'drink' when it was folded into a wad and pressed into his hand, but he could never bring himself to ask for payment. Since, by the end of the evening, most people were too drunk to remember that 'drink', he usually ended up working for nothing.

Frank's musings on the downsides of DJ-ing had been interrupted by Joe Hennessey's call. 'Fella wants you to be his driver for a couple of days,' he'd said. 'Says he's got a lot of appointments in London and needs someone to drive him around.'

Frank was happy to be a cabbie, available to anyone, but there was a clear distinction between a cabbie and a driver. The latter term reminded him of black Ford Scorpios with leather interiors driven by men in black suits and black shades, reeking of Kouros or Paco Rabanne. With their less-than-convincing attempts at silent, menacing demeanours, they seemed to forget they were mere factotums, at the beck and call of the owners of the vulgar vehicles from which they tried to draw some sort of reflected glory.

'Who is he?'

'A Mr Swann. Asked for you by name, says he knows you.'

'Oh, him,' said Frank, pleasantly surprised. He liked Toby and saw him as a man who would never treat his driver like a serf. They had met on equal terms, practically naked with towels round their waists. Toby's great strength, as he'd already shown with Danny Power, was that he recognised talent and was prepared to pay generously for it. Frank phoned him on his mobile, agreed a daily rate and picked him up from Liverpool Street.

They got chatting. Or, rather, Toby did. Like many before him, he was intrigued by Frank Dempsey and wanted to know why, when, where and how-come. 'Bright chap like you, Frank,' he said, 'how come you're driving a mini-cab?'

Frank looked into the rear-view mirror but didn't reply, deliberately leaving Toby to fill the awkward pause.

'I mean, not that there's anything wrong with driving a cab,' he stammered. 'Christ, what I wouldn't give to know as many short-cuts and back-doubles as you do.'

Frank paused just a couple of seconds, to make sure Toby was uneasy, then said, 'It can have its drawbacks.' He grinned. 'When I'm at home and I want to go to the loo I often wonder whether I'd be quicker going along the hall or cutting through the front room then round by the kitchen.'

Toby seemed relieved that his new friend hadn't taken offence and chuckled a little too heartily.

Then Frank altered his tone and feigned seriousness. 'My past life,' he explained, 'is something I'd rather not talk about. Let's just say that I made a mistake when I was too young to know any better and I was "away" for quite a long time.'

Toby nodded. 'And now?' he asked.

'Well,' said Frank, knowing he'd hit the right note, 'I feel I've paid my dues. I'm now married to a wonderful woman and she's helping me rebuild my life.' So far Frank hadn't told a lie. He didn't want to, so another friendly but steely glance into the rear-view mirror ensured he wouldn't have to.

'No, quite,' said Toby. 'Point taken.'

For the rest of the journey they talked about music, films and their shared loathing of Manchester United and tapioca and unnecessary traffic lights.

Presently, they pulled up in Church Street and Toby pointed proudly at Empire Furnishings. 'Well,' he said, 'what do you think?'

Frank was nonplussed. 'I thought you said you opened three weeks ago.'

'We did.'

'But it still looks like a furniture shop. You've still got those G-plan suites and sideboards in the window.'

'I know.'

'Well, it doesn't really look like a club, or a DJ bar.'

'Exactly.'

Frank raised a half-impressed eyebrow. 'Well,' he smiled, 'it's different, I suppose.'

'Come in and have a look.'

For Frank, entering the old showroom was like entering a time-warp.

With one crucial difference.

23

For Frank, it was an almost sexual attraction.

He had seen them at once. Toby had unlocked the door and Frank had followed him into the cavernous old place, which still had the retro furniture and double divans placed strategically around the shop floor. It was all much as Frank remembered it from his childhood. Except for the addition of a huge bar in the middle, a parquet dance-floor and a DJ booth at the back.

And there they were: two brand-new matt black Technics 1210s. Before Frank could stop himself, he was standing behind them. He searched in vain for a couple of old twelve-inch singles to try out on the turntables. Funkadelic's 'One Nation Under A Groove' or War's 'Me And Baby Brother' would have been ideal but anything, even 'The Birdie Song', would have done.

Toby had known a lot of DJs and had seen the look in their eyes that he now saw in Frank's: the look of fanatical missionary zeal. Frank's overwhelming desire to play records, to share his musical views with others, to have his tastes and techniques validated by the almost involuntary motion of several hundred people were written all over his face.

He saw, too, the abject despair as Frank realised there were no records to play. He felt cheated, as though he had just lowered himself into the driving seat of a Lamborghini to discover it was out of petrol.

'You used to DJ?' said Toby.

'Yeah,' said Frank. 'Long time ago, before I . . . er . . .'

'Still got your records?' asked Toby.

'Thousands of them,' said Frank, with an almost touching fondness.

Toby thought for a second, then asked, 'Don't suppose you'd consider . . .'

'What?' said Frank, dropping the usual inscrutable insouciance.

'Well, coming out of retirement. What sort of music do you play?'

'Dunno. Depends what sort of people are in.'

'Congratulations, Mr Dempsey. That was the right answer.'

It was a question Toby always asked potential DJs and very few got it right. The moment they said, 'Techno,' or 'Speed garage,' or any other genre, the interview was over. What if the punters don't want that sort of music? You have to bring, play and know about all sorts of music. Some interviewees hedged their bets by replying, 'Dance,' which, in answer to 'What sort of records do you play?' is rather like saying, 'Round ones.'

All records are dance records, so what do you mean by 'dance'? Morris 'dance'? Bulgarian folk 'dance'?

Frank's reply had been right on the money, so Toby continued: 'The reason I ask is we've got most nights pretty well sorted, but there's still one night in the week I'm not happy with. The vibe isn't quite right, we need it a bit more mellow, a bit more . . . I don't know what we want but I know we haven't got it yet.'

Frank was bubbling over with excitement, but he was an old hand at letting his look disguise his feelings: he'd been doing it for most of his life. This was exactly what he needed: all the good bits about being a priest with none of the pious, theological drawbacks. The parallels between DJ and priest are uncanny. Once again, he'd be able to bring people together for the love of something they believed in. Once more he could create an atmosphere of happiness and harmony where communal emotions could be expressed and shared. In return, he'd receive the adulation fix he needed. He could return to a different, though remarkably similar stage. 'Which night are you talking about?' he asked.

'Sunday.'

Perfect, thought Frank. It would be just like old times.

Sort of.

24

Frank had been away for a very long time. Being a DJ was now a serious business, a full-time occupation. When Frank, his two decks and his rope lights were at large, there was no such thing as a full-time jock: they all had other jobs. Although trainee priest wasn't usually one of them.

He'd missed the moment when 'dancing' became 'clubbing', having jacked it in just before the DJ's meteoric elevation in status: from fat twat in Hawaiian shirt playing 'Agadoo' at the Lloyds Bank Christmas party to global megastar playing in front of ten thousand fans and getting paid more than that in euros for a couple of hours' work. He'd given it up at precisely the wrong time. Or, in some ways, precisely the right time. He'd missed the moment when technical proficiency supplanted musical knowledge. He'd missed the significance of beat-mixing, hot-mixing, slip-cueing and holding a blend. He knew nothing about cutting, scratching or doing stops and spinbacks. When he was playing, this wasn't important. Such cold, albeit skilful techniques would have turned play into work, removing all the warmth and enjoyment. By the time he'd mastered those tricks, he could have learned to be a concert pianist. And, anyway, since he'd opted to become a bead-jiggler rather than a beat-juggler, it was all academic.

He hadn't been part of the pill-crazed rave scene, the acid-house parties in muddy fields around the M25. Although undoubtedly there had been some great nights, if most of the ravers had removed their E-tinted spectacles they would have had to admit that the vast majority were awful.

He'd hadn't felt the heavy, unwelcome presence of gangsters.

Where cash, drugs and expensive equipment are involved, these horrible people are never far behind.

He hadn't witnessed the 'dance' bandwagon so readily jumped on by corpulent, corporate executives. He had never seen its back axle snap under the weight of those aboard or the sight of them falling off and scrabbling around for another bunch of suckers to exploit.

He'd been spared the advent of pallid geeks, who'd thought that DJ-ing meant spending their lives in their bedrooms perfecting a 'banging' two-hour hard-house set with no thought as to how it might go down.

He'd missed the slew of lazy 'artists' without the talent to make their own music helping themselves to the work of others, under the excuse of 'sampling', then putting it out under their own names. He'd emerged into a world where few DJs could manage more than a couple of hours. Those, like him, who would arrive at a club before it opened and play for six or seven hours until it closed were no longer plying their trade.

Frank had stepped back into a world crying out for the skills he had. Skills that, like dry-stone walling or speaking Manx, were almost extinct.

Toby knew how rare these skills were but had no idea that he'd stumbled across one of the few people in London who still had them. Frank knew he had those skills but had no idea of how rare they'd become.

25

Frank didn't know what 'vibe' Toby was looking for, but he was sure that he'd be able to provide it. There were five or six hundred singles and around fifty albums in his four 'playing-out' boxes, which were continually updated. Tunes would be promoted or relegated to and from these four and, amazingly, Frank had kept up this pointless process throughout his time as a priest, even though he'd had more chance of getting jiggy with Sister Amelia than of playing out again.

Now he was glad he had because, no matter who turned up on Sunday night, he knew he'd have tunes they'd like, including plenty they hadn't realised they were going to like.

He had driven Toby to a meeting with one of his backers at an office near London Bridge and afterwards, over a late breakfast at the Borough Café, he had spelled out how it was going to be.

'Right,' said Frank. 'To make it work, you're going to have to lose some money. Are you prepared to do that?'

'Might as well,' said Toby, with a shrug. 'I'm up to my ears in debt anyway. A bit more won't make any difference.'

'Good. Make the first Sunday like a party. Pretend it's your birthday. Invite all the people you'd like to see, especially those who are likely to tell everyone afterwards what a great time they had. Bung a load of money behind the bar, put out a few bowls of cashew nuts and leave the music to me. I guarantee that in a few weeks it'll be rammed.'

'And if it isn't?'

'Well, you'll have had a wonderful time and all you'll have lost is a few quid and some cashew nuts.'

Like thousands of others who'd had one-to-one experience of

Frank Dempsey at his most persuasive, Toby was inspired. Frank, because he always avoided things he couldn't do, was supremely confident about the things he could. And that confidence was contagious.

Toby couldn't wait for Sunday. He was a smart operator, yet he was placing a huge amount of trust in a man he hardly knew. A DJ whom he had never seen play a record, let alone operate a mixer. A man in his forties whom he believed to be an ex-con and whose entire record collection might well comprise Yorkshire brass-band music and American power ballads. But something told him that wouldn't be the case.

When Sunday night came round, Toby was resplendent – scrubbed, flossed, shampooed and conditioned. He'd bought a new Paul Smith suit for the occasion – black, three buttons, small high lapels and a snazzy purple lining. Two hundred carefully selected guests had received their invitations and, knowing the bar was free and would open at seven, were nearly all there by ten past. The bowls of cashew nuts, organic and unsalted, were on the tables around the club and the orange juice had been freshly squeezed. Toby always judged a bar or restaurant by its orange juice and was frequently surprised by the number of well-known, highly rated establishments that served the cheap stuff straight from the carton. Drinks were poured, cigarettes lit, hands shaken and cheeks kissed, but one important guest was still missing.

Frank was outside in his cab. Casually he checked his watch. Twelve minutes past seven, time to go in. He had always been meticulous about the time he arrived at a gig. He always turned up, breathless and apologetic, exactly twelve minutes late. Those twelve minutes always put his hosts into a mild state of panic: they'd just started to think he might have let them down and were hugely relieved and grateful when he hadn't. Any more than twelve minutes and you risked upsetting them, but arrive early or on time and they were never quite as appreciative as they should have been.

Frank came in backwards through the swing doors, carrying two old boxes that had once been home to little bottles of Britvic orange and now contained hundreds of seven-inch singles. Toby looked at them with a mixture of curiosity and worry. Seven-inch singles? Wasn't that like turning up with a wind-up gramophone? Frank placed the boxes inside the DJ booth, went out and returned a couple of minutes later with the twelve-inch singles and albums.

He glanced at the stylish, well-heeled crowd and thought immediately of the Vietnamese takeaway in Hackney. He never looked at the menu there: he was happy to be led by the proprietor's expertise and take whatever he was given. Tonight, he was going to be a musical waiter in much the same way. These people were going to submit to his musical taste and judgement. And, like Frank munching his crisp, fragrant spring rolls, they would not be disappointed.

The first thing they heard was classical music – the gritty eight-second snatch of Mendelssohn that preceded Rufus Thomas's 'Walking The Dog', swiftly followed by Bill Withers doing 'Who Is He And What Is He To You?', then Ann Peebles threatening to tear somebody's playhouse down, and Tom Tom Club's 'Genius of Love', before Dean Martin came swaggering in with 'Ain't That A Kick In The Head'.

The phrase 'eclectic mix', which DJs use conceitedly to describe the music they play, has become so abused that it is now almost meaningless. Frank Dempsey was one of the rare few whose music matched that description. He had no prejudices and would play any tune as long as it satisfied two criteria: the first, that it was good; the second, that it was half familiar.

Too familiar, and the crowd could be in any one of a thousand carpet-and-chrome night-spots from Newquay to Newcastle; too obscure, and they don't know what to do. There are notable exceptions, but obscure records are usually obscure for a good reason. Semi-familiarity was the key. Frank had a wealth of musical knowledge and influences on which to draw, and these were plundered to great effect. David Essex, for instance, might have become a bit naff, idolised only by bottle-blonde house-wives who lived in his surname, but Frank hadn't forgotten the moody bassline of 'Rock On'. When it followed Augustus Pablo's 'Memories Of The Ghetto', he noticed some involuntary pricking of ears and nodding of heads. As each track flowed into the next, bringing with it something complementary in terms of rhythm, mood or timbre, Frank knew the ears and heads would soon be followed by the limbs.

Eight fifteen. Still plenty of time. As much as he tried not to, Frank couldn't help comparing DJ-ing to sex. In each the art of foreplay was essential. Too many DJs pounced prematurely on their punters by playing hard, fast house records about three hours too early. They were ignoring people's basic need for the subtlety of seduction to make them shuffle off their inhibitions and shuffle on to the dance-floor. Then they were quite willing to experiment and do shameful things that they would never have considered before. Like dancing (and, God forbid, even singing along) to 'Wake Me Up Before You Go Go'.

Looking at the crowd, still at the bar, still not quite ready but, none the less, moving certain parts of their bodies without real-ising it, he thought of a more innocent analogy: nobody jumps on to a roundabout when somebody's spinning it too fast. They'll get on while it's still going slowly then build up the momentum themselves.

That momentum was still building. Frank, as always, was paying exquisite attention to both crowd and music. He knew every piece of vinyl intimately – he'd been friends with some of them for thirty years. He knew their moods and foibles, their good points, their bad points, which parties they should be invited to, and which people they could be trusted not to upset.

He controlled the crowd as easily from the DJ booth as he had from the altar. Except that he was doing it without saying a word, speaking without speaking, letting the music do it for him. Unlike his Hawaiian-shirted counterparts, he never said a word – he never had to, apart from, 'Last orders at the bar,' and 'Thank you and goodnight.'

By the time he said, 'Thank you and goodnight,' the initially shy and ice-cool crowd had danced themselves into a frenzy of funk, punk, soul and reggae. Toby had forgotten he was hosting a party, forgotten he was wearing his precious new Paul Smith suit with the purple lining. Along with almost everyone else, he had been hurling his sweaty body around to Glenn Miller's 'In The Mood', the big, brassy version from the soundtrack of *The Glenn Miller Story*, of course – far punchier than the original.

Frank finished with Ella Fitzgerald's 'Ev'ry Time We Say Goodbye', obvious but guaranteed to leave the punters in no doubt that the party was over and that he and his wooden boxes were going home.

People were congratulating Toby on the best party they had ever been to as Frank slipped quietly away. He knew that his triumphant return to the decks might lead to him earning the sort of money that, no matter what people say, is vital to the success of any relationship. The money to buy things, to go places, and to have memorable, bonding experiences together.

He realised that he was doing this for his own benefit but also for Sarah. In driving the motors of one taxi and two turntables, his attempt to become an author could be forgotten. He was delighted with the ways he was earning a living.

If only Sarah could say the same.

26

Frank had never heard of Carole Kendall, yet they had a lot in common. Most of his life had been spent as a priest and most of hers had been spent as a headhunter. Through the confessional box and the confidential 'chat', both had been privy to secrets and both, as incorrigible gossips, had found themselves tortured by their own integrity. Both had been bursting to disclose other people's sins and salaries but, to their immense credit, neither ever had.

Sarah had known Carole for years, yet she couldn't remember the first time they'd met. That was always the way with headhunters: you feel as though you've always known them, yet you can't remember how, when or where from.

Carole knew Sarah well enough to be pretty certain that she wouldn't have been delighted by Jane Steele's appointment. She knew it wouldn't make any tangible difference, but Sarah's working environment and the morale of the agency would have changed for the worse.

Collins, Davies & Pearce had always been a place where flair and originality could flourish and the talentless and ambitious were always, sooner or later, hoist by their own petard. This was no longer the case. Someone from the latter camp had been rewarded and promoted from within. For the first time transparently political tactics had been seen to pay off and that sent out the wrong signals to the rest of the agency and to the industry.

Carole knew all about the dramatic change in Sarah's home life and wondered whether she might be ready for a similar seismic shift at work. Like the skilled employment consultant she was,

Carole never tried to make people disaffected with their jobs. If they were, it would soon become apparent. She rang Sarah, went through about forty seconds of pleasantries, then suggested they met up for a coffee at Starbucks in South Molton Street. Starbucks was always Carole's venue of choice for a 'little chat' because she knew that there wasn't a sorbet's chance in hell of running into anyone from advertising.

In her view, the advertising industry, despite being the acme of capitalism, was full of people like Jane Steele who tried to pretend that it wasn't. People who, to compensate for their guilt, liked to wear their *faux*-liberal beliefs on their sleeves. While not quite red, they were of a political hue best described as 'advertising pink'. Although they spent much of their working lives promoting corporate logos, they would have read and been made to feel bad by Naomi Klein's *No Logo*. So, as well as becoming card-carrying members of New Labour, they had made a courageous political stand by boycotting Starbucks. Stopping short, naturally, of boycotting their own lucrative careers.

Over a couple of semi-skimmed lattes, Carole began with her usual opening gambit: 'So, how are you?'

Sarah might have waxed lyrical about her domestic bliss and how proud she was of her newly hip husband, but they both knew that wasn't the reason for the meeting. 'Fine,' she replied. 'Ish.'

'How's it working out with Jane Steele?'

'Well, she's playing it very low-key at the moment,' said Sarah. 'It's like she's embarrassed about being given the top job. She knows she's not good enough, and she knows that everyone else knows it too, so sooner or later she's going to make changes just so she looks like she's doing something. It's only a matter of time before we're all sent on some dreadful "team-building" day where some creep who's failed in his own career can tell us how to succeed in ours.'

Carole nodded sympathetically, took another sip of her latte and, in saying nothing, invited Sarah to say more.

'I mean, Jane hasn't done anything wrong. She might never do anything wrong and I've always got on okay with her. On the surface, at least. The problem's more with me.'

'With you?'

'Yeah. I've always had this thing that whoever I'm working for has to be better than me. I need someone I can respect, someone I can learn from, someone whose opinions are worth listening to. The moment I felt that this was no longer the case, I always said I'd move on and, well, I don't want to sound cocky, but Jane Steele is no better than I am.'

'That's putting it mildly,' said Carole.

'And although it hasn't happened yet,' said Sarah, 'I'll find it hard to do as she tells me because her way of working is very different from mine.'

'Do you fancy a move?'

'Depends where,' said Sarah. 'I wouldn't have thought, in the current climate, that there were many jobs around.'

'Well, funnily enough, there are,' said Carole. 'It's a bit like musical chairs. It just takes one person to move, then someone moves into that job and someone else moves into that one, and so it goes on. I've got something that might be just perfect for you. Bigger agency, a lot more money.'

Sarah's eyes widened: she was flattered to be considered.

'I wouldn't waste your time,' said Carole, 'with anything I didn't think would be right for you, but there is someone I really would like you to meet.'

'Who?'

'A guy called Howard Miller.'

Sarah's brow furrowed. 'Never heard of him.'

'Oh,' said Carole, 'lovely, lovely man. He'd adore you.'

'But I've never heard of him.'

'No, you wouldn't have. The job isn't in London. It's in New York.'

'New York?' said Sarah, totally thrown for a moment.

'Yes, big city, lots of tall buildings. I think it's in America.'

'Yeah, but, New York, I mean, I've never really . . . um . . . well . . .'

'Just a thought,' smiled Carole. 'You know, sometimes it's worth taking a "flyer".' She pretended to grimace at the pun she always brought in when she was trying to tempt someone to consider a move abroad.

Sarah wasn't averse to 'taking a flyer'. She'd taken one in her choice of husband and that was working out rather well. 'Which agency?'

'Miller Vassell Kerslake Schneiderman McClelland Euro SJPW.'

Sarah had always known that advertising was an immodest business. Agency founders seldom followed their own advice and found a snappy name for their product. The first interview she had ever attended was at a place called Still Price Court Twivy D'Souza. However, compared with Miller Vassell Kerslake Schneiderman McClelland Euro SJPW this was positively succinct. 'Sorry? Run that name past me again.'

'Miller Vassell Kerslake Schneiderman McClelland Euro SJPW,' said Carole. 'And don't worry, they're looking for a senior account director, not someone to operate the switchboard.'

27

Sarah was asleep by the time Frank had heaved all his records back into the flat and he didn't want to disturb her. Actually, he desperately wanted to disturb her. He was wide awake but she was fast asleep, so he thought it best not to wake her by pressing the broom-handle into the small of her back. Tired but wired, he wasn't yet ready for bed so he lay on the sofa watching some dreadful film on cable, then dropped off and woke up at three fifteen in the morning, dribbling over the cushions.

Six hours later, he was still running on that adrenaline, pounding along on the treadmill at a fair old lick as if he was training for the London Marathon. He was even keeping up with the bloke on the next machine along.

This little chap was a serious runner. Every time Frank had ever been in the gym, he'd been there too, always decked out in his Russell Athletic sportswear. Russell Athletic vest, Russell Athletic shorts, even Russell Athletic socks. Frank had often wondered why, until Toby had told him that the chap's name, rather sadly, was Russell.

The treadmill bleeped: the twenty minutes had flown by. He felt almost trim, not like the overweight, whey-faced creatures he had seen earlier, waiting submissively at the bus stop.

Having showered and dressed, he came out and was saddened to see that three of the greasy-haired, dentally challenged monuments to fast food and oven chips were still at the bus stop. He felt sorry for them, marooned and helpless; one was now taking solace in a bag of Cheesy Wotsits. This must be the first time in history when the rich were thin and the poor were fat.

He was considering performing his good deed for the day, by

pretending that he, too, was going to the Wandsworth Arndale Centre, when he was saved by the diesel wheeze of a small, over-crowded, run-for-profit bus. Its surly driver had finally arrived to cart the Weebles to Wandsworth.

Frank jumped into the cab, keen to pick up passengers and save them from the soulless indignity of travelling on buses. Desperate to earn the money to ensure that he, who hadn't stood at a bus stop since he was seventeen, would never have to stand at one again. He switched on his mobile: 'You have two new messages,' it told him.

He had to replay the first one two or three times but he still couldn't make out what the man was saying. He didn't have to. Though the words were garbled and incoherent, the message was crystal clear. Recorded the previous night, through a loud and drunken hubbub, Frank could recognise Toby's slurred elation. 'Fucking 'mazing, I mean . . . wuz jus fuckin' . . . oh, those records. I dunnowhatsay . . . call you tomorrow.'

He was as good as his word. The second message was Toby again, this time sober, lucid and awestruck. 'That was the best music I've ever heard. I think we've really got something. Can we meet up some time today? Ring me back.'

Frank's first job was to take two old Irishwomen on their monthly pilgrimage to Marks & Spencer in Marble Arch. 'It's the busiest store in the world,' they told him, proud that they were partly responsible for this. He dropped them off and agreed to meet them two hours later on the corner of Portman Square to take them, their new petticoats, cardigans and four-packs of chicken breasts home to Kilburn. That left him enough time to get up to Church Street to meet Toby at the scene of last night's triumph.

Frank never liked to see a nightclub in the morning. This sad sight reminded him of a beauty queen dragged out of bed into an unforgiving light, unrecognisable with no makeup, hair all over the place, wearing a mauve nylon housecoat. However, Empire Furnishings managed to avoid this indignity. During the day, it just looked like a furniture shop. Toby was behind the bar, mixing a couple of Virgin Marys that were almost brown with Lea & Perrins. He shook Frank's hand warmly. 'What can I say?'

Frank smiled the smile of false modesty.

'I don't want to pry,' said Toby, mindful of what he thought was Frank's criminal past, 'but where did you learn to DJ like that?'

'All over the place. Mobile work mainly. Weddings and twenty-first birthday parties, places where people haven't come to dance – you have to know how to get them to change their minds.'

Frank recalled the mobile gigs at which he'd had to work particularly hard. The Cypriot christening in Palmers Green where he'd had the bright idea of playing 'Zorba The Greek' and couldn't understand why the faces of the hitherto happy revellers had darkened and the dance-floor had suddenly emptied – until a guest informed him that they were all *Turkish* Cypriots. There had been the dreadful rugby-club parties full of three-beer queers, their inhibitions and trousers loosened by Fullers ESB, fondling each other in a matey, manly way but still fondling each other, then stumbling home to their wives and girlfriends, singing about sweet chariots. And there had been the parties in rooms above some of the roughest pubs in London where, from his vantage-point behind the decks, he could see trouble brewing like a gathering storm off the coast. And when it all went off, it had been up to him, as the only one with a microphone, to risk destruction of his precious records and equipment in the attempt to break it all up.

He still hadn't forgotten the awkward wedding in Streatham where the groom was black, the bride was white, and her father's first comment to Frank was 'I hope you ain't going to play any of that jungle-bunny music.'

Frank had had to use music to bring the opposing factions together. After a painfully slow start, the evening gradually got going. By ten thirty, the infectious rhythms had even vanquished the Enoch-loving father's innate bigotry. He ended up, jacket off and tie skew-whiff, dancing more exuberantly than anybody else in the hall. When Frank dropped 'Hot Hot Hot' on to the turntable, guess who was leading the multi-racial conga? By the time Frank had closed with 'The Last Waltz', the man was hugging his new Jamaican in-laws with real warmth and affection. If you can make a success of situations like that, a Sunday-night spot at Empire Furnishings was never going to be more than a breeze.

28

The pound signs were almost visible in Toby's eyes as Frank laid out the conditions under which he would accept a Sunday-night residency at Empire Furnishings. 'First, I don't want paying,' he explained. 'I'll take a percentage of the door and the bar, so my success depends on yours. And, second, I never want to see my name anywhere. I'm just one of the people who work here, like that Scots bloke who collects the glasses. I want total anonymity. The moment I see my name, I'm off.'

Toby was under the romantic delusion that this was because Frank, with his underworld connections, probably had some very heavy people on his case. But the only heavy person Frank was worried about was Danny Power. He shuddered to think of Danny discovering his new hobby and bringing in coachloads of ex-parishioners down for a hooley.

Toby nodded gravely, and Frank continued, 'It'll take a while for the word to get round, so you can expect next Sunday to be half empty. I suggest we put a full-up sign on the door. And get a load of your mates to form a queue outside and pretend they're desperate to get in.'

On Sunday night, at twelve minutes past seven, Frank arrived with Sarah. He had done the dress rehearsal, he was secure in his skills, he knew he wouldn't look stupid in front of the woman he adored, so he had agreed to let her come with him. He'd told her about the little scam with the bogus queue and was pleased to see that Toby had done as he had asked. 'Mind you,' he remarked to Sarah, as they tried to push their way in, 'he's gone a bit over the top.' The queue stretched all the way to the Edgware Road. Slowly it dawned on Frank that it was for real.

Inside, the nightclub was already full and Toby fell into Frank's arms virtually weeping with gratitude, making him feel guilty this time about pulling the old twelve-minutes-late trick. He kicked off straight away with Dusty Springfield's version of 'Spooky', Gotan Project's 'Santa Maria' and Jimmy Smith's 'Got My Mojo Working'. The floor began to fill and Frank knew with satisfaction that it wouldn't empty until chucking-out time, and that the bowls of organic cashew nuts would remain untouched on the bar.

Sarah watched as Frank pulled out half a dozen records at a time, leaving them sticking up diagonally from his box. 'Never think about the next record,' he explained, 'think about the next *two*. By doing that, you avoid the cardinal sin of leaving one turntable empty.'

She noticed that he always had one eye on the crowd, gleaning clues from the smallest changes in their behaviour, letting their movements suggest the next track or change in direction.

He taught her how to use the headphones, the monitors, the cue controls and the cross-fader. By nine o'clock, Sarah was playing the records, Frank just picking them out. Although it had only taken her twenty minutes to learn how to play them, she knew it would take her twenty years to learn how to choose them.

Even though Frank was pulling the strings, she felt the wild and enthusiastic response to what she was doing. Now she understood why he'd been so excited. He had never been able to let her have a go at being a priest, but this was the next best thing. Now she was privy to the mechanism that made him tick.

He was in his element, once again bringing joy to hundreds of people on the Sabbath. He'd finally found something to replace the priesthood. Or, at least, the part of it that he had missed.

Then she thought of New York, and wondered how she could even contemplate dragging him away from all this.

29

It seemed a rather facile reason for not believing in God. Especially for an ex-priest who had read theology at Oxford and had studied and appraised so many religious texts and spiritual arguments. Yet if Frank had been asked why a man with his detailed knowledge was drawn towards agnosticism his honest reply would have been, 'Because it's raining.'

He detested the way fawning, dewy-eyed Christians would praise the Lord for beautiful sun-dappled glades, spectacular sunsets over the Grand Canyon and glorious Alpine snowscapes. Yet never once did they take Him to task for raining off the cricket, waterlogging the pitch at Highbury or, more poignantly, for deliberately ruining what should have been the happiest day of someone's life.

More often than he could count, Frank had officiated at weddings in June or July when the bride and groom had thought, with some justification, that his Lordship might spread a little sunshine over the proceedings. Instead, their parades had been celestially pissed on. He sometimes wondered how many marriages had ended in the divorce courts because they had started in the rain, and how many people had had a second crack at it so they could say that the sun had shone on their wedding day.

But the soggy bridesmaids and rain-smeared photographs hardly mattered when compared to earthquakes, droughts and monsoons. Mother Nature, whoever she was, had to take the rap for those, whereas all things bright and beautiful? Well, the Lord God made them all.

Except that Frank wasn't convinced that He did, so he could

hardly hold Our Lord responsible for the cruel meteorological trick played every year on people in the south-east of England. Towards the end of March, they're usually given a taste of warm, sunny weather and every year, even though it never does, they believe it will last until the end of September.

The charade is kept up for three or four days before a cold, dark veil is drawn across the sky, the rain machine set to 'random and spiteful' and a thousand 'happiest days' are made unforgettably miserable. However, during that brief sunny respite from the gloom, Frank was trying to practise what he had always preached. As a priest, he was known for his sensitive and astute marriage-guidance counselling, even though he never felt qualified to give it. He felt more like a man with brittle-bone disease teaching people to tap-dance. He advised floundering couples to remember that they were still boyfriend and girlfriend. Before the marriage, before the mortgage, before the children, there were two people just going out together. At the root of every marriage there was a boyfriend and girlfriend. And unless that root was nurtured and nourished, everything around it would wither and die.

He had never said this to Sarah. How condescending would it be to give marriage guidance to your own wife? Instead, he always tried to nurture and nourish. His other matrimonial tenet was the definition of love. In Frank's view, it was identifying a person's needs and meeting them. However, since too many of the couples who came to him for guidance clearly believed that what their spouses needed was a smack in the mouth, he sometimes refrained from saying so.

On a seductively and unseasonally warm March evening, he thought Sarah needed a quiet drink at a nice pub by the river. He'd chosen The Crabtree, between Hammersmith and Putney bridges, because he was feeling emotional and full of love, but when that love hardened into lust, he wanted to be no more than five minutes from home. Only a couple of weeks earlier he'd been wearing a parka, scarf and gloves and, like everyone else in London, now felt a bit weird with just a T-shirt and a thin jumper to separate him from the elements.

As the first few sips of cold lager coursed through his body like a pre-med, he suddenly realised that the volley of drunken abuse he'd just heard was directed at him. 'You dirty fecker!'

Out of nowhere, the voice of Annie Cullen, a ruddy, sewer-tongued old Irishwoman, had just destroyed what would have been a perfect evening. She hadn't seen Frank since his brief spell at St Augustine's on the Fulham Palace Road where she had been a Sunday-morning stalwart, slurring out her responses at least five seconds behind the rest of the congregation. Annie, as was more than apparent, had never worn the Pioneers' pin.

'What in the name of God do you think you're doing?' she bellowed. 'And you a feckin' priest an' all.'

Everyone turned and stared as Frank gently tried to explain that he was no longer a priest and that the 'feckin' whoore' he was with was his wife.

From the shocked and reproving stares he was receiving, it was clear that no one believed him. Looking down at his attire, he could understand why. This, of course, had to be the evening he'd chosen to wear his white T-shirt and black V-neck. After sustaining a few more profane admonishments, Frank finally convinced Annie that he was telling the truth and, like drunks so often are, she was suddenly filled with histrionic remorse.

'Forgive me, Father,' she wailed, rather missing the point. 'Jesus, I'm so sorry.'

He looked at Sarah, who was steadfastly trying to persuade herself that one day she'd laugh about this. Annie had now collapsed into his arms. Holding her upright and looking into her eyes he said, 'Come on, Annie. Let's get you home.'

It was all right for Frank, partitioned off in the front of the cab. Unlike Sarah, he didn't have to share the back seat with this drunken, rancid old woman. Mercifully, the journey only lasted two minutes and Sarah couldn't help smiling at the name of the old block of flats where Annie had lived for the past forty years.

As Frank gingerly helped the old girl up the steps, Sarah could see in big letters 'The Guinness Trust Buildings'.

Somehow, the moment was lost and Sarah, understandably, did not want to return to the Crabtree and face all those people again. What was more, in Frank's haste to get Annie home, he'd taken a corner a little too quickly and Annie had pitched face and head lice first into Sarah's lovely new Joseph skirt, dribbling sick, spit and Scotch all over it. She was now itching to get home and change.

As soon as Annie got out, Sarah removed the skirt and Frank, at the sudden sight of a gorgeous half-naked woman in the back of his cab, got her home in ninety seconds flat. He leaped out, opened the front door and, having checked that the coast was clear, signalled for Sarah's beautiful bare legs to come running after him. They closed the door behind them, and Sarah put her arms round his neck and he put his round her waist. 'The other night,' she complained, 'we never had a slow dance. Can we have one now?'

Frank dived into his boxes and pulled out Aretha Franklin's 'All Night Long', but as it began, so did the ring of his mobile. Perhaps it was force of habit – too many years of dashing to the nearly dead to administer the Last Rites – but before he could stop himself, he'd answered it. 'Hello? Yes, speaking. Oh, hello. Yeah . . . okay . . . When is it? Right . . . Yeah, I know it. Look, I haven't got my diary with me at the moment. Can I call you back tomorrow? Yeah? Okay, 'bye.'

Frank put the phone down, re-embraced his dance partner, cued up Aretha again and said, 'Now, where was I?'

The phone rang again. Again, before he could stop himself, he'd answered it.

'Hello? Yes, speaking. Oh, hello. Yeah . . . okay . . . When is it? Right, yeah, I know it. Look, I haven't got my diary with me at the moment. Can I call you back tomorrow? Yeah? Okay, 'bye.'

The conversation had been identical but this time, having ended it, Frank didn't go back to Aretha. He just sat down, put his head in his hands and let out a long, weary sigh. 'Confirmation in Wembley,' he muttered, 'baptism in Beckenham. Not to mention that pissed-up old biddy. How the hell am I ever going to escape all this?'

Sarah felt a surge of sympathy. It occurred to her that religion now had little to do with theological precepts. Judging by the way these people idolised Frank, it had more to do with following the words and ideals of someone you respected and admired. That was how it was today and that was exactly how it had been two thousand years ago. Oh, shit, she'd married God.

Sitting glumly on the sofa, God didn't look particularly omnipotent, but childlike and vulnerable. 'I dunno,' he said. 'Sometimes I think we should just get away . . . I mean permanently.'

Sarah sat down next to him and took his hand between hers. 'Well,' she said slowly, 'funny you should say that . . .'

30

Frank seldom went abroad. As a priest, he'd never taken a holiday because, rather like sex, it's not so much fun on your own. He'd occasionally been sent to conferences at the Vatican, where the five-star standard of food, wine and accommodation had never failed to astound him. He'd also witnessed the selfless work of missionaries in Africa where things weren't quite so lavish, and had found it very hard to reconcile the two. Now and then, he had Ryanaired to Ireland where his parents had retired.

Trouble was, he'd never been anywhere he wanted to go, so when Sarah asked, apprehensively, if he might be interested in accompanying her to an interview in New York, he had had to be almost physically restrained from packing his suitcase. She had stuck a pin in an imaginary globe and hit the one place he had always had a burning desire to visit. Never mind that New York wasn't the capital of the USA or even the capital of the state of New York, as far as Frank was concerned it was the capital of the world. The place where whatever was going to happen happened first.

He'd grown up in the 1970s when there was a far greater chasm between the UK and the USA. In those days London was like a drab little annexe of the Soviet bloc and Frank would gaze longingly across the pond at the triple-decker hamburgers, multiplex cinemas and shopping malls, coveting the culture of late-night bars, drive-in movies and instant gratification. Even Idaho and Iowa or any of the other nondescript 'vowel states' promised more fun and excitement than Kilburn could hope to offer. Once the priesthood had imprisoned him, America – and New York City in particular – epitomised everything that his vows were denying him.

He'd longed to visit his Uncle Noel and Auntie Kath, who owned Heneghan's Bar on West 22nd Street, but realised that this was something he could never allow himself to do. The temptation offered by one big apple had been Adam's downfall and Frank felt that the other Big Apple would be his. The moment he arrived, he knew he'd immerse himself in the city's nocturnal delights. If he'd ended up in Studio 54, snorting cocaine off Margaret Trudeau's cleavage, how would he ever be able to return to holy, pastoral duties?

Fortunately the Heneghans had moved back to temptationless Tipperary where Frank felt safe to visit them.

The journey to Heathrow had him tingling with excitement, knowing that this time he was a bona-fide traveller rather than a priest-cum-cabbie who never got further than the drop-off point. In that role, he hadn't enjoyed his trips to Heathrow. The latent emptiness and envy within him had surged to the surface. Each pick-up, each drop-off reminded him that there was a big wide world out there from which he was excluded. So just checking in, venturing beyond the sign that says, 'Passengers only beyond this point', putting his hand luggage through the X-ray machine and being frisked for nail scissors made him feel, at last, that the world just might be his oyster.

It was his first trip to the States, so he thought it rather apt to be flying Virgin. He seldom noticed brands but had always retained an affection for this one. As a teenager, he would sit on a big floor cushion wearing even bigger cushioned headphones in the original Virgin Records shop in Notting Hill Gate, listening to *Tubular Bells*, his nostrils teased by the tang of 'naughty smoke'.

He felt the same sense of calm and comfort as he and Sarah were ushered into Premium Economy. He'd been dreading spending the next seven hours with his knees in his mouth but, settling into a surprisingly roomy seat, he was relieved that he wouldn't have to.

The smiling stewardess dressed in red introduced herself as Laura. Given the name of the airline, Frank had half expected her to be called Mary and to be dressed in blue with a white veil. Laura's burly male colleague did not fulfil the camp, effete air-steward stereotype in any way. It seemed an unusual choice of career for a man who looked hard enough to skate on, until Frank remembered reading that since the attacks on the World Trade Center airlines had been recruiting male cabin staff with a police or forces background. Passengers seemed reassured that it was Ray Winstone rather than Graham Norton who was handing out the complimentary peanuts.

That, however, was all that had changed. Once airborne, the pilot still came on and did his shtick. 'Ladies and gentlemen, this is Captain James Garden. We're cruising at an altitude of approximately thirty-five thousand feet. We've just passed the Bay of Biscay and are now heading out to the Iberian coastline before turning right and . . .'

Frank wondered how his passengers would react if he said, 'Hello, I'm Frank Dempsey, your driver. We're cruising at approximately thirty-five miles per hour. We've just gone through the Swiss Cottage roundabout and will be heading south along Wellington Road before beginning our descent towards your friend's flat in Maida Vale . . .'

He settled down to his first encounter with the sort of multi-channel in-flight entertainment system that you wouldn't see between Stansted and Shannon. He looked at Sarah, snoozing gently beside him, and took this as a cue to watch *Friends*, *The Office* and *Blackadder III* on the comedy channel, then developed a serious addiction to Tetris. His puerile obsession was interrupted by the polite but always slightly worrying bing-bong of the 'fasten seat belt' sign as the plane hit a tiny bit of turbulence. Sarah, never the most confident flyer, woke up and placed her hand on Frank's for reassurance. 'God,' he sighed, taking off his headphones, 'they've even got speed bumps up here.'

Sarah still looked edgy.

'Don't worry,' said Frank. 'More people are killed each year by donkeys than plane crashes. Fact.'

'It's not that,' she said

'Then what is it?'

'Well,' she said, for the ninth time, 'are you sure you want to do this?' meaning, 'Am I sure I want to do this?'

Frank gave his ninth exasperated smile. 'What? Take a free trip to New York over Easter while you go and see a man about a job?'

'But would you be happy about moving there?'

Frank looked out of the window, then back at her. 'Bit hard to say from up here.'

'But you'll be giving up—'

'Giving up what?' he said. 'A glittering career as a mini-cab driver who works one night a week in a bar?'

'It's not like that and you know it. That gig you do is fantastic and you love doing it.'

'Well, I'm sure I could love doing it in New York. It could work just as well over there. Good music is good music. Still, we'll cross that bridge when we come to it.'

'If we come to it.'

'Yeah. If we come to it.'

'But you've lived in London all your life,' said Sarah, still looking for reasons why she, not he, shouldn't go. 'You're always saying how much you love it.'

Frank's relaxed flippancy was only reassuring Sarah to a point; he knew he had to be truthful. 'But I love you even more,' he replied, 'and I'd go, in fact I'm actually going, to the ends of the earth as long as we're together.'

No smiles, no irony. This was true. He needed to say it and she needed to hear it. 'However,' he added, 'I'd draw the line at North Korea, Upper Volta or Swindon.'

New York was a different matter. The moment Frank hit the tarmac, he wanted to kiss it, John Paul II-style. Although he had never been there before, he felt like he was coming home. New York, New York – Frank felt that the name was misleading. Apart from its inhabitants being useless at football, it was nothing like York. New London would have been more apposite. New-improved-bigger-brasher-more-spectacular London, though a bit of a mouthful, would have been even better.

Frank thought back to every London parish he had ever worked in and how, without exception, its borough had been 'twinned' with some anonymous place in France or Belgium in a pointless display of European civic unity. He now wanted to tear them all down and put up one sign on all the main routes into London: 'Welcome to London. Twinned with New York'.

He loved London and had vowed he would never live anywhere else, but in the last year his vows had been dropping like ninepins so one more wouldn't make any difference. There was only one place in the world to go after London and he'd just arrived there. Like many before him, he found it all so familiar, exactly as he'd thought it would be. He hailed a yellow cab to take them to midtown Manhattan and immediately felt as though they were gliding through a movie set. He couldn't decide whether it was *Annie Hall*, *On The Town* or *When Harry Met Sally* but he was delighted to be in it. He slipped his arm round Sarah's shoulders and she snuggled in. 'Do you know,' she said, 'this is the first time you and I have been in a cab together with someone else driving it?'

It was the first time for a lot of things. The first time they had been abroad together, the first time they had taken their relationship on tour. How would it cope? Did it need to remain in its natural habitat to survive? In London, they were so close to their former lives but now, physically and spiritually, they were thousands of miles from them. They were working without a net, with only each other to rely on. The relationship suddenly felt a lot more equal. They were in this together. Their hearts had leaped as they caught their first glimpse of Manhattan's night-time skyline but neither said a word, both reflecting silently on how much they had changed each other's life in such a short time.

The taxi dropped them in Lexington Avenue on the corner of 49th Street outside the almost painfully chic W hotel. Frank still felt as if they should check in as Mr and Mrs Smith, not used to Mr and Mrs Dempsey being a legitimate married couple, perfectly entitled to sleep together.

He stepped into the lobby, marvelling at the affluence and elegance of his fellow guests, and at the sheer beauty of the Halle Berry lookalike who was checking them in.

Once upstairs, he immediately indulged in hotel-room behaviour, bouncing on the bed and flicking through the hundreds of channels on the giant, council-estate-sized TV. He wandered into the white marble bathroom with its fluffy white robes and dazzling array of Aveda toiletries. Then, suddenly overcome with he-didn't-know-what, he collapsed on to the huge bed in the gorgeous room with his gorgeous wife in the most romantic city on earth.

The shutters on his eyelids rolled down and he felt the need for an early night.

Sarah wasn't the only one who had a job interview in the morning.

31

The elevator shot from o to 39 with such alacrity that Sarah knew how circus performers felt when they were fired out of a cannon. She checked that her nose wasn't bleeding and emerged into the thirty-ninth-floor reception of Miller Vassell Kerslake Schneiderman McClelland Euro SJPW.

'Hello,' she said, with that relaxed, winning smile. 'Sarah Dempsey to see Howard Miller.'

'Okay, Ms Dempsey. If you'd just like to take a seat.' The receptionist then continued a truly impressive routine that Sarah felt was worth travelling six thousand miles just to witness: 'Thank you for calling Miller Vassell Kerslake Schneiderman McClelland Euro SJPW, you're through to Lori. How can I help you? . . . Sure. Putting you through . . . Thank you for calling Miller Vassell Kerslake Schneiderman McClelland Euro SJPW, you're through to Lori. How can I help you? . . . Sure. Putting you through . . . 'Thank you for calling Miller Vassell Kerslake Schneiderman McClelland Euro SJPW, you're through to Lori. How can I help you? . . . Sure. Putting you through . . .' Lori was astonishing, never once fluffing her lines, smudging her lip-gloss or even chipping her perfectly painted nails on the state-of-the-art switchboard.

This was how advertising was supposed to be. This was how, when she first went into it, Sarah had been led to believe it would be. Glamorous, fast-paced and thirty-nine floors above Madison Avenue. She was engrossed in the Lori show when she heard the polite voice of a Lori lookalike, saying, 'Ms Dempsey? I'm Lisa, Howard Miller's PA.'

'Oh, hello.'

'Glad you could make it. If you'd just like to follow me . . .'

Sarah followed Lisa through acres of teak, leather and plate glass, which combined to present a hugely impressive contrast to the self-conscious minimalism of her own agency. The English would feel far too guilty about such a conspicuous show of wealth. Their Basingstoke-based clients would have seethed with resentment, then used the agency's décor as an excuse to try to cut their commission. The Americans had no such hang-ups: their clients revelled in being associated with such visible commercial success.

Sarah was shown into Howard Miller's office. Naturally, like all power offices, it occupied a huge corner plot, affording dizzying double views of midtown Manhattan from any of its floor-to-ceiling windows. The man himself stood up and welcomed Sarah into his world. He was big, tanned and immaculate. Late forties, luxuriant grey hair, hand-made suit, Charvet shirt, beautiful silk tie, highly polished shoes. In America, it was all about presentation and Howard Miller was perfectly presented. 'Sarah, hi – Howard Miller.' He smiled, with perfectly capped teeth, and offered a strong, tanned, manicured hand. 'Good to meet you.'

'Good to meet you too.'

'Can I get you coffee, soda, mineral water?'

'No, thank you. I'm fine.'

'Well, Peter Clay speaks very highly of you, and so does Carole Kendall. In fact, the whole damned world speaks highly of you.'

'If only they knew,' said Sarah, not quite used to such unabashed flattery.

'Listen, let me show you the reel of some of our latest commercials. See what you think.' With the touch of a button, like something out of *Diamonds Are Forever*, Venetian blinds appeared from nowhere to cover the floor-to-ceiling windows and shut the world away. A touch of the second and third buttons activated the plasma TV and DVD player, and the cream of Miller Vassell Kerslake Schneiderman McClelland Euro SJPW's crop of commercials began to play on the screen. Clean-cut young people cavorting to jingles, handsome, rugged men driving cars across the Arizona desert, and perfect families sharing communal orgasms over Mom's apple pie. The extravagance of the production values only highlighted the lack of creativity. Howard smiled proudly, while Sarah almost ruptured her spleen trying to laugh at what might or might not have been the 'comedy' moments.

Ten commercials, each lasting thirty seconds, but those five minutes felt like five years. The reel finished, the blinds were sent back into their ceiling recesses, and midtown Manhattan sparkled back into view.

'So, what do you think?'

Sarah didn't know what to say. She didn't want to be rude to this nice, urbane man. It would be like saying to a friend, 'Your new house is hideous,' or 'Your baby looks like Steven Berkoff.'

'Well,' she said, choosing her words carefully, 'I think there might be room for improvement.'

She almost jumped out of her skin when Howard threw out a huge, hearty laugh. 'Room for improvement? How's that for classic British understatement? Sarah, they're crap. You know that, I know that. It's okay, you can come right on out and say it.'

'All right, they're crap.'

'And that's why you're here. Let me tell you where my head's at. I want to raise the creative profile of this place and the best way of achieving that, from where I'm standing, is to create a little boutique. An agency within an agency doing great work for a small number of select clients, which in turn would be a shop window for the bigger ones. You see where I'm coming from? Right now, the best ads in the world are coming out of London.'

Evidently he hadn't seen the one in which a grown man mistakes a tampon for a boiled sweet.

'I took my cue from Toyota. Huge corporation making great cars, but no matter how good those cars are, the name Toyota is not sexy. So what do they do? They create Lexus, a whole new luxury-car division, a totally new brand to pull in the more affluent customer. And it's worked. Lexus has a life of its own, people don't even associate it with Toyota, and yet that's what it is and that's where all the money goes. We're going to open an entirely separate office, someplace downtown – SoHo or TriBeCa – and pull in some exciting new clients.'

It was a great idea in principle. But so, too, were Communism, the euro and toasted-sandwich-makers. Still, as Howard said, it had worked for Toyota.

'Now I'm trying to put together a management team of young, smart, ambitious people who've spent their careers making great ads. I think this baby's going to fly and you guys will be in on the ground floor. What do you think?'

'It's very interesting,' said Sarah.

'You want to talk some more?'

'Well,' she grinned, 'I didn't come all this way just to see that reel.'

Howard let that huge hearty laugh escape again. 'Well, that's great. Come on, let's grab a bite to eat.'

Naturally 'Mr Miller' had a table at the Four Seasons, where he was known to all the waiters and to most of his fellow diners. Sarah liked him a lot, but as the conversation went on and he revealed his compendious knowledge of art, wine, music and books, she found it hard to associate this intelligent, cultured man with the garbage produced by his agency. Yes, he wanted to open this second-string 'boutique', but having seen the dismal creative standards he was used to, she wondered whether it would be possible.

There was something about Howard Miller, his perfect teeth, Hamptons' tan and exquisitely tailored suit – not to mention the sheer scale of his gargantuan thirty-ninth-floor office, the stunning décor and shark-sized lobsters being served at the Four Seasons – that left Sarah unable to take the whole experience seriously. Not that she started dancing on the tables or flicking food at the publishing plutocrats who were seated nearby – quite the opposite. She relaxed. She thought she was too young, too junior, too English to be considered for such an important job so she sat back, enjoyed the lunch, and abandoned any pretence at trying to impress her potential employer. Which, of course, was when she was at her most impressive. Howard was entranced by her wit and vivacity. Carole Kendall had told him that Sarah had recently got married but omitted to mention that her husband was an ex-Catholic priest and had been a serving one when they'd first started seeing each other.

Howard's jaw slackened and his eyes almost moistened as she told him about her fairytale romance. One half of his brain was listening, imagining the priest, the beautiful girl and the black London taxi. The other, shrewder, more commercial half was thinking about how good this girl would be in presentations – so relaxed, so bright, so charming. When the bill came, he didn't pay it, just signed it. A much bigger bill would be sent to the thirty-ninth floor at the end of the month.

'Thank you very much,' said Sarah, crumpling her napkin and putting it back on the table. 'That was wonderful.'

'My pleasure,' said Howard, and it had been. 'You really are great company and there are very few people in this town that I can, with all honesty, say that about.'

They walked out into the frantic bustle of Manhattan, which made Sarah realise retrospectively what an oasis of calm the Four Seasons had been. The sort of calm that only money can buy.

Howard clasped her hand in his. 'As I was saying,' he said, 'there's a few more candidates that I've got to meet with so I guess I'll speak with you the week after next. Anything you want to ask, just call me. I really hope we meet again soon. Have a safe journey home.'

Well, that's it, thought Sarah. What a wheeze. A weekend in New York, a funky room at the W, spectacular lunch at the Four Seasons. The job wasn't really for her, she knew that. Still, it was nice to be considered and nice of Howard Miller to go through the motions. Carole Kendall had been right. Sarah liked him a lot. What a thoroughly charming man.

She'd had no idea how long she'd be but had said she'd meet Frank back at the W around five.

I hope he's all right, she thought. Neither of them had thought to bring with them a mobile that worked in the States, so she had no idea where he was, what he was up to and how his interview had gone.

32

Frank's interview was a little less formal. He wasn't seeing anyone and he wasn't applying for a job. He was interviewing the city of New York: its streets, its people and its vibe. He needed to know if he could live there or whether leaving the only city he'd ever known would have a disastrous effect on his mind and his marriage. This was the best way to find out, an all-day walk through Manhattan, exploring the core of the Big Apple.

Which way would he turn out of the hotel? Left or right? Billy Joel or Petula Clark? Uptown or downtown? According to Billy's biggest hit, 'Uptown' was incomplete without 'Girl'. On this occasion, he was alone, so Petula won the toss.

At first, the sheer speed of the city unnerved him. He felt much as he had on his first childhood trip to Queensway ice rink, clinging to the sides while the more experienced skaters whirled around him in a daunting blur of blades and ice. Gradually he'd got his confidence, let go and joined the maelstrom. After a few tentative steps, he let go of the sides of New York and became a tiny, fast-moving cog of this huge metropolitan wheel.

He put on his invisible Discman and pressed 'play', then let the music of New York fill his head. When making his selection, he'd deliberately omitted any tune with 'New York' in the title. Those who had written them were just using its universal fame to mean any city anywhere, an all-purpose setting for sweeping generalisations about either loneliness or having a good time. Frank Sinatra's 'New York, New York' had therefore failed to make the cut, but Ella Fitzgerald's 'Manhattan', the Drifters' 'On Broadway' and Bobby Womack's 'Across 110th Street' had been included because they'd been more specific. As he headed downtown, taking in the smells, the sounds, the energy, the rhythms, the feel and foibles of this spectacular place, he could hear everything from Gershwin to Grandmaster Flash looping round and round in his head.

He wasn't going anywhere in particular. Tempted as he was by the rock 'n' roll walking tour around the East Village, he had no wish to be part of anything so structured, enjoyed by those for whom life is one long geography field trip. He preferred his own mazy, unstructured ramble through streets he felt he had known all his life.

He'd heard much about the frenetic in-your-face aggression of native New Yorkers, but having been brought up opposite a brick wall where someone had sprayed 'Kilburn Skins Kick to Kill', he found midtown Manhattan almost genteel. With neither map nor sense of direction, he still stumbled across the Empire State and Chrysler Buildings. Their scale and majesty caused his mouth to fall agape. Yes, there were tall buildings in Canary Wharf but compared with these two beauties, London's skies remained relatively unscraped. He kept walking, wandering, musing, further and further downtown.

He wanted to get lost. That would be a real treat since, as a London taxi driver, it was a feeling he seldom experienced at home. Even here, the rigid Cartesian grid structure of the Manhattan streets kept him on the straight and narrow. South of Union Square, however, they started to have names rather than numbers. This was more like it.

Crossing Houston Street, he suddenly remembered how hungry he was when the gorgeous whiff of hot brisket wafted his way out of Katz's deli. It pulled him straight through the doors, where he took his ticket, stood in line and emerged a few minutes later with a hot pastrami on rye and a bottle of Dr Brown's soda.

Eventually, lost – and happy to be so – he realised he'd been walking for five hours. He should have got himself sponsored.

Half past three – shit, he had a four o'clock appointment in Mulberry Street. Where was that? Little Italy. Where was that? Now he wished the streets were numbered rather than named. He was meeting someone for whom he didn't want to be late. Typical taxi driver and, some might say, typical man, he considered it a matter of honour not to ask for directions. However, since he had strayed along Mott Street into the middle of Chinatown and could only hear what he guessed to be Cantonese or Mandarin, he did have a valid excuse.

Five to four. Despite the New York afternoon heat and humidity, his aching limbs, and the colossal sandwich and soda that were now sloshing around inside him, he broke into a run. On the corner of Prince Street, he saw the building he was looking for. He made it with twenty seconds to spare. Four o'clock – time to go to church.

33

Frank finally stopped outside St Patrick's Old Cathedral on the corner of Prince Street. Small, Gothic and austere outside, ornate and classically proportioned inside, it was quite unlike its huge, upscale Fifth Avenue namesake. He checked the times of the masses. The next one wasn't until six – perfect, he didn't want his visit to this most religious place to be tainted with any trace of religion.

Although Frank had little time for the tenets of organised religion, he'd always loved churches and cathedrals, the older and more spectacular the better. Their cool, soothing interiors made them, in his view, second only to the steam room as places for quiet reflection. He liked to let that rich sense of history, pageantry and good old-fashioned awe seep into him. He'd always enjoyed working in churches and loved the way these ancient crucibles had given power and resonance to his words. His mind floated back to London and he recalled how the readings from the Gospels he'd given amid the magnificence of St James's in Marylebone or the Church of the Immaculate Conception in Mayfair had sounded almost true.

At four o'clock, as arranged, his old friend Father Paul Pellici walked in to meet him. Father Paul bore a striking resemblance to Tony from *The Sopranos*. No matter how priestly his attire or benign his manner, he still looked like a Mafia hood in fancy dress – one of God's goons, which, in many respects, he was. He had fond memories of the three months he'd spent seconded to St John's in Islington, where he and Frank had got to know each other. Frank had always promised to do a reciprocal stint at Father Paul's parish in Brooklyn, but both men's lives had moved on.

Father Paul was now based at the old cathedral in the heart of what was still known as Little Italy. However, in the forty-nine years since he had been born there, the neighbourhood had lost most of its Italian residents and much of its red, white and green soul. 'Frankie,' he beamed, 'great to see you, man. How ya doin'?' He was even less like a priest than Frank had been.

'Fine, thanks. You?'

'I'm good. So, you're married now, huh?'

'That's right.'

There was an awkward pause. Father Paul might have castigated his ex-colleague, upbraided him for renouncing his vows, abandoning God and all the people who depended on him for the sake of some two-bit broad. Or he might have broken down and confessed that he'd never believed in God, had been having affairs all over New Jersey and he, too, was giving up his vocation to get married. Frank wouldn't have been surprised by either reaction.

In the event, he said nothing, leaving Frank to fill the pause.

'Back in the old neighbourhood, then?' he said.

'Yep. But it's changed a lot. This old cathedral has been here for nearly two hundred years and now, for the first time in its history, we no longer say mass in Italian. English and Spanish, but not Italian.'

'Does that bother you?'

'No. It's just the way cities are, and the way they should be. The Italians don't have a right to these particular streets. They're the ones who left. Anyways, the fact that this place is called St Patrick's would suggest that you guys were here before we were. Fancy a beer?'

The two men walked round the corner to a scruffy bar called Mare Chiaro, one of the few remaining vestiges of old Italy in this increasingly chi-chi neighbourhood. Two threadbare sun-bleached flags – one American, one Italian – were crossed in harmony above the door. Inside was a sawdust floor, an old tin ceiling and a small but heavy-looking contingent of are-they-aren't-they regulars straight out of *Donnie Brasco*, sitting watching baseball at the bar.

Without being asked, Tony the barman uncapped a couple of ice-cold Morettis and handed them, with a smile, to his parish priest. Frank was expecting to be introduced but that clearly wasn't the form here. Tony's role was to provide the drinks and the ambience while his customers sat discreetly discussing business. Paul nodded Frank towards a rickety old Formica-topped card table in the corner. He then paid Dean Martin and Louis Prima to sing a few old standards from the juke-box and clinked his bottle with Frank's. 'Cheers, Frankie.'

'Cheers . . . So, how's business?' said Frank, taking a well-deserved gulp from his bottle.

'Sort of good,' said Paul, taking a slow pensive gulp from his, 'and sort of bad. Nine/eleven seemed to make people in this city a lot more aware of their own mortality. Same old story. Once they think the end could be nigh, they start cramming for their finals.'

Frank smiled. The day of judgement, he'd always thought, was the ultimate example of the old domestic threat: 'Wait till your father gets home.' He was about to share this opinion with Paul but decided not to. He didn't want to come on like a born-again Christian in reverse, flaunting his new-found heresy. Instead he asked, 'If that's the good, why has it been bad?'

'Well,' said Paul sadly, 'thanks to the *Boston Globe*, people think we're all paedophiles, so vocations have dropped through the floor. It's not quite so bad for established priests, who are already known and loved by their people, but if I was graduating now I wouldn't even consider this job. I wouldn't want the world assuming I was some kind of freak.'

'There's been a bit of it in Britain,' said Frank, 'but not on the same scale. It's a shame, because priests were given total trust and a small minority abused it. Now they're given no trust at all, yet most of them are perfectly okay.'

As a boy in Kilburn, Frank had been in constant contact with dozens of priests through church and school. He had been alone many times with almost all of them and had never once been on the wrong end of a fondling. Either these crimes were perpetrated by a tiny minority or Frank had been a monstrously unattractive child.

'How do you feel about quitting?' said Paul. 'Do you miss it?'

'Yeah, I suppose I do,' said Frank. 'You can't spend half your life doing something and not miss it.'

'But you're glad you quit?'

'Of course I am,' said Frank quietly. 'I don't think I was ever really cut out for it.'

'Me neither,' said Paul, which didn't surprise Frank, 'but I was even less cut out for the Mob.'

Looking at his bulky, brooding figure, Frank would have begged to differ.

'That's why I envy you, Frankie. You got out. I can never do that.'

'Why not?' said Frank. 'I'm not saying you should but there's no law against it. You can do whatever you want.'

'Are you kidding?' said Paul, with a dry, mirthless chuckle. 'And go into the family business? Frankie, when you come from a family like mine, there's no escape. When I was a kid, I wanted to be like my dad, my uncles, all their friends. What they did looked so harmless. I was protected – you know what I'm saying, I didn't really know what was going on. I knew it wasn't strictly legal but I still didn't *really* know. Well, one night I found out.'

He took another slug of Moretti and continued. 'You know Umberto's Clam House? Just round the corner?'

Frank had passed it on the way to the cathedral. He nodded.

'It was a long time ago,' said Paul. 'I was about nineteen. I'd taken this girl on a date. Beautiful girl from the Upper West Side. She wanted to have a meal downtown in Little Italy so I took her to Umberto's, you know, where I knew a lot of wiseguys would be hanging out.'

He paused. The memory of whatever happened that night was clearly still fresh and painful. 'Anyways, the place was full of them. It was Joey Gallo's birthday. You ever hear of Joey Gallo?'

Frank shook his head.

'Come on, Frankie, you're a music man. Bob Dylan wrote a song about him.'

In mentioning Bob Dylan, Paul had exposed one of the gaping holes in his friend's musical knowledge. Yes, Frank had a few of the old orange-labelled singles – 'Knocking On Heaven's Door', 'Like A Rolling Stone', 'Lay Lady Lay' – but that was about it. He didn't own one Dylan album and had no desire to. Many of his Oxford contemporaries had been 'into' Dylan but Frank always shied away from music that he needed to 'get into', preferring music that got into him. For that reason, Bob Dylan would remain a closed book.

'Joey was a very flash, charismatic man,' said Paul. 'Came from Brooklyn. Worked for the Gambinos. Everybody knew Crazy Joe. But he was different from the others. Very intelligent, would quote from Kafka, Balzac, Proust. But he was ruthless – killer, racketeer, loan shark, you name it. He used to keep a lion, can you believe that? A lion, in his basement, to scare his victims into paying up.'

Suddenly the Kilburn Skins who kicked to kill didn't seem so scary any more.

Paul continued, 'So, anyways, it's Joey's birthday – he's holding court at this big table in the corner. He always sat in the corner, back to the wall, facing the action, so he could see exactly what was going down. They're all drinking champagne. Joey recognises me – one of my cousins worked in his club. Sends a bottle of champagne over to the table. "Paulie," he says, "have the shrimp and clam linguine." So we order the linguine, we're drinking the champagne. This girl is loving it. I thought she was Italian, turns out she's Jewish, from a family of intellectuals, so this is a whole new world for her. She thought it was incredible.'

'Just like Bob Dylan,' said Frank. 'Another Jewish intellectual, fascinated by the same thing.'

'Exactly,' said Paul, as two fresh beers arrived unbidden at the table. 'At that moment I was on top of the world. This beautiful girl adores me, Joey Gallo has just sent champagne to my table. I could see my future. I knew what I wanted to do. I was going to be just like Joey, centre of attention, drinking champagne, hand-made suit, hand-made shoes, driving around in a new black Cadillac.'

His face darkened. 'Then, out of nowhere, four gunmen burst in and opened fire. There was pandemonium. Joey's bodyguard, Peter the Greek, pulls out a .38 and starts firing back. Blood everywhere. All over me, all over the shrimp and clam linguine. Joey staggers out on to the street, collapses on the sidewalk and dies right next to his brand-new Cadillac. I looked at the Cadillac, I looked at Joey lying dead next to it, and I thought how one had paid the price for the other and that this was not going to happen to me. Seventeen people died that night, including two innocent bystanders.'

Oh, no, thought Frank. He knew what was coming. 'And the girl?' he almost whispered,

Paul paused reflectively. 'Took a bullet in the shoulder,' he said. 'They rushed her to the hospital. I was with her in the ambulance.'

Frank, seeing his friend had drifted into a deep solemn reverie, could hardly bear to probe further. 'And what happened?'

'Oh, she was okay,' said Paul.

Frank heaved a sigh of relief.

'But, not surprisingly,' said Paul, 'she wasn't too keen on seeing me again. And that was what made me take stock of my life. It all seemed so glamorous until the moment I saw it for real. As soon as I could, I entered the seminary.'

'Some might say that was a bit extreme,' said Frank. 'Wasn't there something else you could have done?'

Paul shook his head. 'Oh, I could have done anything. Run a bar, a restaurant, a deli, worked in the construction industry, but whatever I did, I'd have been doing it for the Mob. Especially something "respectable" like becoming an accountant or an attorney. The more letters you have after your name, the more useful you are. It's like I said, when you come from a family like mine, there's no escape.'

'Except the priesthood?'

'Except the priesthood,' said Paul. 'Even more than the Irish, the Italians adore their priests, especially the mobsters. It's like they're overcompensating for the way they make a living. My story has passed into legend. Young kid witnesses the murder of Joey Gallo and receives a calling to preach the word of the Lord.'

'Well,' said Frank, 'it's sort of true.'

Paul chuckled. 'Except that the calling did not come from God. It was just the only way out of the life that was expected of me.'

Frank, whose reasons for becoming a priest had been exactly the same, if a little less colourful, knew exactly how he felt. 'And now?' he asked. 'Do you regret it?'

'Well, you can take the man out of the Mob but can you take the Mob out of the man? At the end of the day, it's in my blood. It's all about wanting respect and I have that. I'm very happy. You know how rewarding this life can be. But since that night in Umberto's, I have never been out with a woman. I've met plenty but, unlike you, I have never met one who could make my life more rewarding than it is. I haven't met a woman who made me want to throw it all away.'

The two men looked at each other, smiled, and said simultaneously, 'Yet.'

34

Good Friday was a day that Frank had both loved and loathed in his time as a priest. He'd loved it because it gave him licence to display his full range of thespian skills. It was like appearing in panto, setting his face into its annual mask of grave solemnity. Good Friday is the only day in the Catholic calendar when mass is not celebrated, though the dreary, interminable three o'clock service is far, far worse. Christ's death and crucifixion are reverently remembered while the fact that He comes springing back from the dead two days later is conveniently forgotten.

If the weeping mourners at a funeral knew that, within forty-eight hours, the deceased would be back among them, sporting only a couple of minor abrasions, would they be so upset? Would they even bother with a funeral? Yet every year millions of Catholics go through this farce for someone they didn't even know.

Every Good Friday, Frank would reduce some of them to tears of sadness and gratitude for what Our Lord had done for them. It was either this or reduce himself to tears of boredom if he didn't put on such a show. And this was the first Good Friday in years when he wouldn't have to do it. He felt like an actor, released after twenty years in a long-running soap opera, free to be his own man and to live his own life.

This day would be dedicated to pleasure. It began with sex, then the sort of revivifying power-shower to which visitors to America are not accustomed. Then he tried out some of the wickedly decadent toiletries and his face, for the first time in its life, was exfoliated, toned and moisturised

The spring sunshine lent an exuberant dazzle to Manhattan's

146

towering splendour as boyfriend and girlfriend stepped out on to the street. They just wandered, much as Frank had the day before, but at a much more languorous pace. This time, accompanied by a girl, he felt qualified to head uptown. As they strolled around Central Park, Frank was particularly taken by the gorgeous old carousel with its hand-carved horses.

'Why don't you have a go?' said Sarah, half teasing.

'I would,' said Frank, 'but a childless man in his forties riding on a carousel – it's all a bit Michael Jackson.'

Sarah then had to choose between the Guggenheim museum and Bloomingdale's. It was no contest. She justified her decision by maintaining that none of the museum's exhibits would be as stunning as the Frank Lloyd Wright building that housed them. Then, credit cards nicely warmed up, she moved on to Christian Louboutin to spend forty minutes deciding which of the many pairs of red-soled foot candy would accompany her back to London. Frank took this as his cue to wander back across to the west side of the park and, as a Beatles fan, make his pilgrimage to the Dakota Building and the Strawberry Fields memorial, all the time reflecting on the horribly accurate observation that Mark Chapman was the best thing that ever happened to John Lennon's record sales.

They wandered back towards the Empire State Building where Frank had shown remarkable restraint the previous day by not soaring straight to the top. It was something he'd been desperate to do since he was a small boy. However, since he'd waited all his life, he'd decided that another twenty-four hours wouldn't make any difference. From now on, he wanted to experience all his ambitions with Sarah and, as they stood together on top of the world, he was glad he'd waited.

One ambition followed another, and as they held hands aboard the Staten Island Ferry, gazing over at Ellis Island and the Statue of Liberty, Frank saw a poignant representation of how he was feeling. Never had he felt more liberated than he did when he hugged Sarah from behind, her head under his chin, the wind in his hair, the sun on his face and joy in his heart, as the combination of true love and New York City dissolved all miserable memories of Good Fridays past.

As they meandered downtown, they gazed at the lovely old cast-iron flat-fronted buildings in SoHo, Frank at the architecture, Sarah at the shops beneath it. When she caught sight of the new Prada store, she was almost hyperventilating. So much bigger and better stocked than the branch in Old Bond Street. Again, Frank left her to it for a good half-hour, before they headed into Little Italy.

Holding up her Prada bags, Sarah explained why she'd always preferred Italy to Spain and the difference between the two.

'It's the difference between Prada and Zara,' she said. Frank nodded. He wasn't sure who Zara was, but he got the gist. The sight of a must-have Chinese-silk handbag in the window of Amy Chan's on Mulberry Street pulled Sarah inside. As Frank stood outside, he noticed a few preppy-looking college boys of about twenty all staring with interest at the chic accessories boutique. He couldn't imagine them as keen collectors of Chinese-silk handbags, so he asked them why they were so fascinated with the shop.

'It's not the shop, man,' explained one, 'it's the building. This was the Don's HQ. Totally awesome.'

'The Don', of course, was the late John Gotti, the dapper but deadly mobster who had run New York in the eighties. Frank grinned, when he thought what Effy Baker would have to say about it. 'Well-brought-up kids hangin' round a place 'cause it used to be some fucking Mafia thug's headquarters? I tell you, the world's gone fucking mad!'

Sarah emerged with more bags – too many to carry, so, as dusk began to fall, they hailed a yellow cab to take them back to the W for more sex, more power-showers, more toner and moisturiser, which would give Frank the sort of complexion he'd always thought he'd have to be gay to acquire.

He had deliberately starved himself. He'd shunned the

enormous sandwiches, existing only on a couple of wafer-thin melt-in-the-mouth slices of pizza, then some fragrant scoops of lychee and passion fruit sorbet at the Chinatown Ice Cream Factory. He changed into one of the five new shirts he'd bought at Sean and prepared himself for a meal he'd been waiting half his life for. Having denied himself meat on Good Friday for no good reason for as long as he could remember, he'd booked a table at Peter Luger's in Brooklyn, the greatest steak-house in the world.

They walked across Brooklyn Bridge, silly not to on such a beautiful evening, and then, to make themselves even hungrier, they strolled along the Brooklyn Promenade and sat on one of the old wooden benches to watch the sun set over Manhattan. They wandered into Brooklyn Heights and that was when something inside Frank said, 'Yes.' Among the handsome brownstones, everything felt right. He'd loved Manhattan but this was where he wanted to live. Brooklyn was far more 'real'. He knew he was in a proper neighbourhood with a tangible community, something that seemed to be missing just across the East river. Their marriage, too, would be far more real in Brooklyn. All his links with the priesthood, London, Danny Power, Joe Hennessey *et al* could be severed, and they could start afresh.

Starting afresh meant eating meat on Good Friday, and at Peter Luger's, the obscenely large hunks of beef were rushed, still crackling and popping, to the tables. When Frank's arrived, he fell upon it in a symbolic act of defiance. Served with a mountain of crisp French fries, it was the best thing he'd ever tasted in his life. As he savoured its juicy, lean succulence, he realised he'd never eaten a really good steak before.

Gazing across at Sarah who, despite having sworn she would never be able to finish hers, was making a pretty good job of it, he drew a parallel between what was in his mouth and what was in his heart. He'd never experienced true love until he met her. He wanted to tell her this but decided that she might not find it terribly flattering to be compared to a plate of steak and chips.

Frank knew what he meant, though, and at that moment it was the greatest, most sincere compliment he could pay her.

At last they fell into a cab, which took them back over the bridge to a smoky little club in the East Village to hear Pat Martino play jazz guitar the way only Pat Martino can. Just after midnight, both mute with exhaustion, they hailed another cab to take them back to bed where they used up the last droplets of their energy in making love slowly and sleepily.

The New York music came back very faintly in Frank's head, Lou Reed singing 'Perfect Day'. His final thought before he succumbed to a blissful sleep was, Now that's what I call a Good Friday.

Even though it was now Saturday.

35

Sarah needed to step back – about six thousand miles – to try to regain her equanimity. She'd had a fabulous time in New York, but the hip hotel, Manhattan's cosmopolitan vibrancy, the constant opportunities for romance and retail therapy were not helping her to see things rationally. She'd fallen in love with New York City and even more so with her husband, but she needed to stand back and decide whether she wanted to live in one with the other. She was ready to fly home on Sunday, happy to miss seeing New York's famous Easter Parade.

Frank, too, was delighted to be missing it. He detested the organised, forced, rather frightening mass bonhomie of street events. The Notting Hill Carnival used to begin at the end of his road, another spectacle described as 'marvellous, joyous and wonderful' by people who'd never been to it. If they had, they wouldn't have been quite so effusive.

The Easter Parade was, admittedly, rather more innocent. It was unlikely to feature hundreds of riot police clashing with knife-wielding gangs under the Westway but he had no desire to see it. He didn't want the gorgeous secular pleasures that had so enriched his life over the last couple of days to be ruined by the sight of thousands of happy-clappy Christians parading through the streets, holding their little crosses aloft. It was one of the rare occasions that, if God had come back to earth, Frank would have felt sorry for Him. Considering the manner of His death, wouldn't a cross be the last thing He'd want to see?

So, as New York prepared to welcome thousands of Midwestern zealots, many wearing comedy bonnets, Frank and Sarah took a cab to the airport. Frank's only regret was that he wouldn't be back in time to drop the tunes at Empire Furnishings' Easter party. He'd been looking forward to playing 'The Resurrection Shuffle'.

'So, what do you think?' he asked, during one of his rare breaks from the in-flight entertainment.

'Well, it's an exciting opportunity,' said Sarah, who didn't get excited about 'opportunities'. 'Howard Miller seemed very nice but it's out of my hands. I think they're looking for someone a bit more experienced and a lot more driven.'

'But if they offer it to you?'

'Oh, I don't know. What do you think?'

'It's not about me.'

'Of course it's about you. I trust you'll be coming too,' she said. 'What will you do?'

'Well, I could easily drive a yellow cab. I don't come from New York, I don't know my way round, so I'd be perfect,' he said, with a grin. 'Also, you forget, I'm a "made guy", I have connections. If I wanted to open a club in an old furniture store, my friend Father Paul Pellici would put me in touch with the right people.' Despite the levity of his tone, Frank was quite serious.

'But is that what you want to do?' she asked.

'I don't really know,' said Frank, and he didn't really care. Whatever happened, he was going to be happy. He could live in either of the two cities he loved with the woman he adored. He'd never been one for making plans. Life, in his view, was a matter of getting roped into things. That's how it had always been for him and he'd always been very happy, and never more so than now. At the moment, Howard Miller had his hands on the rope and Frank was quite content to wait and see how hard he pulled it.

36

The following Sunday, Frank was making a few adjustments to his playing-out boxes. He'd gone very New York in his tastes and wanted to share this with his punters. He'd found Dion's 'Drip Drop' and Mink De Ville's 'Spanish Stroll' but he was desperately hunting for the Turntable Orchestra's 'You're Gonna Miss Me'. He hadn't played it for years, but when he put it on and heard the piano-laden house rhythms and four-to-the-floor beat, he knew it would go down a storm later on.

Sarah, hearing it, asked him the question she had been meaning to ask him for ages: 'Where did you get records like this?' she said. 'I mean, I know you got the oldies from robbing parish jumble sales, but what about this sort of thing?'

'This one,' he said, pointing at the treasured old twelve-inch, 'was from Auntie Jean. I used to get most of my house and hip-hop from her.'

'Auntie Jean?'

'The grand old lady of Greek Street. She used to run Groove Records in Soho. Long gone now. Auntie Jean was in her sixties even then and would often be knitting when you came into the shop, but what she didn't know about that sort of music wasn't worth knowing.'

Sarah conjured up this fantastic image of an old lady with a bus pass and a Catholic priest discussing the latest techno and garage imports.

'Also,' he continued, 'a lot of them came from second-hand and charity shops. When they saw the dog-collar, they wouldn't take any money. I got loads of odd stuff that way. I'd take anything with the words "funky", "space" or "rhythm" in the title. Always worth a punt. Which reminds me.' He pulled out Slick's 'Space Bass', another old gem he hadn't heard for years.

Toby was delighted to see him. Frank's Easter Sunday replacement had not been a great success. He'd beat-matched his tunes to perfection but spent his time looking at the decks rather than at the dance-floor and had failed to notice that fewer people than normal were venturing on to it. Many had gone home disappointed and, such is the fickle nature of London clubbers, that they would have pronounced Empire Furnishings 'no good any more' so Toby wasn't expecting the place to be too full tonight.

He was right, there was a little more room, but those who came had the time of their lives.

The fickle nature of clubbers, of course, works both ways, so the following week the place was rammed, and Toby wondered what on earth he would do if Frank ever decided to take another night off.

Frank, exhausted from the night's activities, was still asleep at nine o'clock the following morning. His mobile woke him. Probably Joe Hennessy with his first job of the day. 'Hello?'

'Hi, it's me.' There was urgency is Sarah's tone.

'What's the matter?' he asked

'Well, do you want the good news or the bad news?'

'The good news.'

'Howard Miller has offered me that job in New York.'

'And what's the bad news?'

'Howard Miller has offered me that job in New York.'

37

It was good news because Sarah was being offered more than twice her salary. It was bad news because she was being forced to make a decision. Fear of the unknown had started to creep through her, making the familiarity of her old routine seem comfortingly attractive. She was very happy in Fulham and at Collins, Davies & Pearce where, to be fair, the ghastly Jane Steele hadn't done anything wrong.

The huge upheaval of emigration frightened her: having to find an apartment in New York, selling the flat in Fulham, or maybe renting it out in case they didn't like it out there. And what if they didn't? Their marriage was still in its infancy. Shouldn't they let it grow and develop before taking it off to an unfamiliar environment and putting it under such strain?

What about Frank? After a cataclysmic change in his circumstances, he was only just finding his feet. Was it fair to knock him off them again?

And the job was undoubtedly a great challenge, with a lot of responsibility, but to Sarah these weren't necessarily plus points. New York might have much in common with London but it was still a very different place. They both loved it, but they'd been lucky enough to view it with the wide-eyed wonder of tourists. Living there would be a different story. They would not spend every day up the Empire State Building, having dinner at Peter Luger's or staying at the W. She and Frank weighed up the pros and cons over endless takeaways and bottles of wine, going round and round, ironically enough, just like the New York Circle line.

Frank was careful not to apply any pressure on her either way.

They were considering moving to New York because of her talents, not his. Also, he was ambivalent. He loved his life in London, but he could love it equally, possibly even more, in New York. Unable to come down conclusively on one side or the other, Sarah was increasingly hoping that he would make up her mind for her. In the end, he asked her the question he always asked himself when an important choice had to be made.

'Give your answer to this question immediately, with no thought at all,' he said. 'How would you feel if Howard Miller suddenly changed his mind and withdrew the offer?'

'Oh, gutted.'

'There you are, then,' said Frank. 'Take it.'

'Well, I don't have to let Howard Miller know until the end of the month.'

'So leave it for a week or two. Then it looks like it wasn't a decision you took lightly. He'll appreciate you all the more for it.'

Sarah laughed. 'Just an extension of your old twelve-minutes-late trick.'

'I suppose so.'

Two weeks later, on a Monday morning, Sarah prepared to hand in her notice. Frank, after his Sunday-night session, was still asleep, but by seven o'clock Sarah's jittery tummy had got her up and she was pacing uneasily around the flat working out what to say. This had been her first and only job. She'd never given notice to anyone and it was making her feel sick. Why? New York was a great opportunity, which she'd be mad to turn down. She'd been unswervingly loyal to the agency, she'd done nothing wrong, so why was she feeling queasy? She wasn't frightened of Jane Steele and couldn't have cared less what her new boss thought about her resignation. So why the churning in the stomach and the dry, metallic, battery-like taste in her mouth?

Frank was still deeply asleep. This was a man who had shared a house with Father Michael Lynam, whose legendary snoring could shake the putty out of his bedroom windows. Frank had slept peacefully through it, but even he was stirred from the depths of unconsciousness by the violent chundering from the bathroom. He sprang out of bed to find Sarah not looking her best. She turned to him, deathly pale, rheumy-eyed with a long globule of saliva hanging from her chin.

'Christ,' he said, helping her to her feet. 'Are you all right?'

She managed a wan smile. 'Top of the world,' she breathed, 'and don't call me Christ.'

Frank led her back to the bedroom, bunched up the pillows, put her back into bed and got her a glass of water. 'What happened? I thought you might be nervous but . . .'

'No, that's just it. I'm not nervous at all.'

'Well, perhaps it's food poisoning. What did you eat last night?'

'Only a bit of toast,' she replied, sipping the water and taking a deep breath.

'I wonder what it is.'

Sarah shrugged her shoulders as a tinge of colour returned to her cheeks. She looked so vulnerable that Frank's first instinct was to give her a gentle hug. As he did so, she winced and drew away, tenderly touching her left breast. 'What's the matter?' he asked. This was the first time she had ever pulled away from a hug.

'I'm not nervous,' she said slowly, as the penny dropped with a deafening clunk. 'This isn't food poisoning and my boobs are sore.'

She paused and looked up at him. 'I think you'd better go to the chemist.'

38

Frank had never understood the human male's fabled fear of commitment. What was commitment anyway? Having a girlfriend wasn't a 'commitment'. You're both adults – you can split up any time you like. The same applied to marriage, and one in three couples did. Buying a house? You can always sell it. Even becoming a priest, in Frank's case, hadn't turned out to be a permanent commitment, but as he and Sarah stared, dumbstruck, at the Predictor, with its blue unbroken stripes of confirmation, he suddenly understood what commitment meant. Legally, emotionally, morally and practically, he was, for the first time in his life, committed.

Just as he'd asked Sarah's instinct to provide a split-second answer about her job, he asked his own instinct what it thought about becoming a father and was surprised by how happy it was. He had always assumed that he would never have children, and, as a celibate Catholic priest, this had been a fair assumption. And now, his life would never be the same again. So what? All through life things happened that ensured 'life will never be the same again'. Being born, learning to walk, going to school, leaving home, becoming a priest, getting married. If life never changed, he'd still be in his mother's womb.

True, it had scuppered his and Sarah's plans to travel. The trip to New York had triggered what he knew would have become an addiction to boarding passes. They might now have to abandon plans to sail up the Nung river into Cambodia, ride out in the Sahara on horseback and kick snow off their boots in a Mafia-run nightclub in Stalingrad but, again, so what? He drove a taxi – he changed direction for a living.

He was only half listening to Sarah, who was telling him something about switching to the mini-pill, something about oestrogen and, unlike the standard pill, you had to take them at exactly the same time . . . and what must have happened was . . .

He wasn't interested: none of that mattered now. She was almost certainly pregnant but, again, he didn't want to show how delighted he was in case she wasn't.

The dream move to a Brooklyn brownstone was now off and, in all probability, Sarah's career would never recover from this without monumental effort. The sort of effort that a man whose career is momentarily interrupted by becoming a father would never have to put in. She was ten years younger than him. Perhaps she wasn't ready yet. And, of course, he wasn't the one who'd have to go through the startling physical and hormonal changes.

He looked with sympathy and adoration at his wife, but she wasn't looking at him. She was gazing into the middle distance, but her shell-shocked expression gave nothing away. It might have been the look of someone who'd just been diagnosed with cancer or of someone who'd just won the lottery: it was impossible to tell.

At first Sarah herself couldn't tell, but as the clouds in her head began to clear, she realised it was the latter. She felt like the luck-iest woman alive.

For no particular reason, she'd always thought she'd have to 'try' for children and endure the indignity of sex without love, lust or passion, coldly and clinically premeditating what should always be the most glorious and spontaneous pleasure in the world. She'd been less than thrilled at the idea of lying on the bed afterwards for ten minutes with her legs in the air to increase her chances of fertilisation. Worse than that was the prospect of trying to conceive without any sexual activity at all, her partner standing behind a screen, buffing up the happy lantern, before the physically, emotionally and financially painful process of fertility treatment. And, worst of all, the cold, empty heartbreak if these invasive experiments failed to work.

She'd avoided all this by somehow messing up the mini-pill's strictly prescriptive routine. Although it was unplanned, this baby wasn't really an accident. It was the result of a passionate love between a man and his wife and she couldn't think of a better reason to bring a child into the world. When this thought occurred to her, she flung her arms round Frank, who she knew would make a wonderful father, and burst into floods of unstoppable tears.

Frank held her, still not sure whether these were tears of horror or joy. Her shoulders were heaving. Then he noticed that the rhythm of the heaving was getting faster and faster. He pulled her face away from his now damp T-shirt, and realised she was laughing.

Overcome with emotion, she planted at least a dozen wet, salty kisses on his lips, he swung her round and they fell back on to the bed where they remained for the next hour.

They tried to work out when conception might have taken place but it was impossible. Since Frank had regained his old prowess, they'd been at it like a pair of goats. It's often the way with the first child. The second would be different. That occasion would be simple to remember since it would almost certainly have been a one-off punctuated by a three-month barren stretch either side.

'Well, that's my decision made for me.' She sniffed.

'If you're honest,' said Frank, 'you were never really a hundred per cent about New York.'

'I wasn't, was I?'

'Why was that?'

'Well,' said Sarah, 'it would have been a hell of a lot of work. When a job pays that well, they're going to want their money's worth. I'd have been starting a new agency from scratch, early mornings, late nights. I'd never have seen you.'

'Well, I'm afraid you will now,' he said.

'And that was the other thing. We did have a vague plan to have kids one day and that job would have made it difficult. I've seen it happen to so many women in advertising – too busy to have children. They intend to get round to it but by the time they do they can't.'

Having witnessed the Jane Steeles of this world do the very opposite, Sarah had decided long ago to put her life before her career. In an insecure workplace, she had no desire to slave away for another six or seven years with every chance of then finding herself redundant so that all the hard work had been for . . . for what, exactly?

She knew she'd have to go back to work because Frank's casual earnings, though not inconsiderable, would never be enough to support three human beings. Not unless they swapped Fulham for Feltham. No, she liked her job, she'd be happy to go back. She'd have had the baby and no one could take that away from her. Everything would be fine.

Wouldn't it?

39

In his last couple of years as a priest, Frank had baptised a lot of baby girls as Lily, Molly and Daisy. Little boys were held over the font and christened Alfie, Harry or Jack. When he'd first started cleansing innocent babies of original sin, it would have been inconceivable to give them the names of Victorian parlourmaids or members of the British Legion dominoes team.

Alone in his taxi on the way to a pick-up, his thoughts often turned to what he and Sarah would call their own impending descendant. If Jack and Harry had made a spectacular comeback, would Roger and Derek ever perform the same feat? Would it ever be fashionable to revive Shirley, Marjorie or Brenda? Or would these names, like Cyril, Doris and Herbert, be destined to die with the last of their owners?

The Catholic Church had reduced the chances of its children being saddled with unfortunate handles by trying to insist on saints' names. But that still left the way clear for babies to be named after St Abbo, St Cadfan or St Elvis. Parents who had named their boys Michael might have thought they'd spared their children any chance of ridicule. How were they to know that if their surnames were Jackson, Owen or Barrymore, they'd handed a gift to playground bullies? One of Frank's dad's Irish friends from the parish was called Des O'Connor and the brightest boy in Frank's class was never taken seriously because his name was David Cassidy.

Frank had always suspected Cassidy's mother of bringing the wrong baby home from the hospital since her husband and her other two sons were brick-shithouse-sized scaffolders. It was either that or she'd had a secret affair with Bamber Gascoigne.

Unlike Frank, who had blagged his way into Oxford with lousy A-level grades through the back door marked Theology, David Cassidy had been welcomed through the main gates with three As to read English.

He was phenomenally bright but his genius was more of a curse than a blessing. That, and his naturally awkward, choleric nature, had made him question everything around him and see injustice wherever he looked. Though he and Frank had known each other at school, they hardly saw each other at university. While Frank was going to as many parties and sleeping with as many girls as possible, Cassidy was marching for the miners, the Sandinistas and CND. Frank always admired his passion, conviction and integrity. Unlike many of his contemporaries, who played at being left-wing at college before pursuing highly paid careers the moment they left, Cassidy was the real deal. He wanted to make a difference and sincerely believed that he could.

But he didn't. Despite the passion, conviction and integrity, Cassidy must have fallen by the wayside because Frank had never heard of him since the day they'd left Oxford. Like so many friendships, theirs hadn't been strong enough to survive once their lives had taken disparate paths. They hadn't kept in touch since the day they'd promised faithfully that they would. Frank had often wondered what had happened to Cassidy, and on a rainy Tuesday afternoon behind King's Cross Station, he wondered no more.

'Hackney please, mate – Fassett Square,' said a scrawny, bespectacled figure, who had just left Housmann's bookshop. Without looking at Frank, or waiting for him to reply, he climbed into the back of the cab. He wouldn't have noticed that it had neither a TAXI light at the front, or a Metropolitan Police licence plate at the back. He would only have seen what he needed to do, and that was get home to Hackney.

'Mind if I smoke?' he asked rhetorically, his sixteenth Marlboro of the day already alight.

'Burst into flames, for all I care,' said Frank. He looked at his passenger in the rear-view mirror. At first glance he seemed about twenty, but a second later he realised the man was at least twice that. With his pale crêpe-paper skin and hollow cheeks, he had the look of a compulsive blood donor.

'Oh, man,' he said, in a dry, reedy voice, before sitting back and exhaling a huge sigh of smoke and relief, 'I can't tell you what a joy this is. Most cabs have that fucking "Thank You for Not Smoking" sign.'

'Well, this isn't a proper black cab,' said Frank, as he did to anyone who hailed him off the street. 'And I'm not a proper black-cab driver, so before we set off—'

The man cut him short with a slow smile of recognition. 'I know exactly who you are.'

Frank stared at his passenger in the rear-view mirror, and smiled the same slow smile. 'Christ, Cassidy,' he said, 'how are you?'

'Get me over to Hackney,' he smiled, exhaling so much smoke that Frank thought he'd lit a bonfire, 'and I'll tell you.'

Fassett Square, where Cassidy had a small scruffy flat containing almost as many books as Frank's did records, is the square on which the BBC based Albert Square in *EastEnders*. The Queen Elizabeth, on the corner of Graham Road, is the pub on which they based the Queen Vic and, as Cassidy smoked his nineteenth and twentieth Marlboros at a small table in the corner, the two forty-year-old teenagers caught up with the last two decades of each other's lives.

'That's the joke, though,' said Cassidy, with the distinctive raspy chuckle he'd had since school. 'That programme is so unrealistic. Nobody like that lives round here any more. They couldn't afford to. They all moved out to Essex years ago. If they called it *EssexEnders*, it might ring true. It's all City types here now. Has been since the late eighties, except for a few lucky old council tenants like me. I moved in just after I came down from Oxford when I was on the dole. It was a real shithole and I've never got round to moving out.'

That figured, thought Frank. Cassidy would have been a council tenant for ideological reasons of the all-property-is-theft variety. However, as the area improved, he'd have stayed put because he was paying a modest rent for a handy flat in an increasingly desirable part of town.

'God, I can't bear that programme,' Cassidy continued, 'more than anything for its patronising depiction of black people. They'll never show a black person in a bad light. A black actor in *EastEnders* is only allowed to play a doctor, a God-fearing landlady or some sort of lovable rogue. There's a black actor who lives downstairs from me, Trevor, says it drives him mad. In *EastEnders* he'd never be allowed to play a thug, a wife-beater or a drug-dealer. He wouldn't be allowed to display the full breadth of his talents. No, only white actors are given those opportunities and, to me, that's discrimination against black people in the workplace.'

Good old Cassidy, thought Frank. The more he'd seen of life, the more he'd found to rail against. 'You say you're a journalist?'

'Yeah,' said Cassidy. 'I started off at the *New Statesman*, then went freelance. Been all over the world. All the best places – Rwanda, Bosnia, Afghanistan.'

There was sadness in the way Cassidy reeled off the places he'd visited, quite unlike the way travel bores bleated on about their 'amazing experiences' in Thailand or Goa. He had been to some of the most dangerous places on earth in the line of duty and, having written about them extensively, had no great desire to talk about them.

'Course I had to change my name,' he went on. 'I mean, you're not going to want to read a piece about the plight of Rwandan refugees by David Cassidy, are you? I've always been known by my middle name.'

Suddenly Frank found himself face to face with one of his heroes. 'You're Niall Cassidy?'

'Yeah.'

Niall Cassidy, the crusading investigative journalist, was one of a small number of people whom Frank Dempsey idolised. He held Niall Cassidy in greater esteem than he held God. Which, admittedly, wasn't saying much.

It had never occurred to him before, but now it seemed so obvious. Cassidy was a wonderful writer. His terse, brave, thought-provoking prose was a joy to behold and Frank had been reading it for years. He'd always read it because it was so easy to read, which, as Frank knew from his brief stab at autobiography, didn't mean it had been easy to write. He now appreciated what a craftsman Cassidy was. How, like any great carpenter, chef or musician, he did all the work so you didn't have to. One of the reasons Frank had abandoned the QWERTYUIOP was that he knew he'd never be able to write with the flair and fluency of Niall Cassidy.

'God,' said Frank, 'I don't believe it. I've been reading your stuff for years. I never realised it was you. But I suppose, in all that time, I've never seen an interview with you – I didn't even know what you looked like.'

'With a fucking ugly mug like mine, Dempsey, wouldn't you want to keep it a secret?' Cassidy sucked almost the entire second half of his cigarette away in one impressively long drag and screwed the butt into an ashtray. 'Besides, that's the way I wanted it. It's about what I write, not who I am.'

'And you've never made the big switch to TV.'

'Nah. Why do you think I'm still living in a council flat in Hackney?' He laughed, as Marlboro number twenty-one came out of a fresh packet. 'Anyway, you know about me, so what about you? This taxi-driving isn't your main job, is it? You're a writer, aren't you? I noticed a Dictaphone in the front of the cab. Invaluable.' He pulled his own from his jacket pocket. 'Christ, my brain's so fucked most of the time that if I didn't record my thoughts the moment they occurred to me they'd never occur to me again.'

'No, I'm not a writer,' explained Frank. 'I spent nearly twenty years as a priest.' He waited for Cassidy to choke on his Marlboro and stare at him in disbelief. After all, they had known each other at Oxford where Cassidy remembered Frank as a man with 'a very sociable penis'. And yet he nodded, accepting Frank's unlikely choice of career as though it made perfect sense. 'Good for you. At least you didn't end up as part of the big capitalist machine like most of my so-called "comrades" did. They reckoned they wanted to make the world a better place, but they didn't, did they? They did fuck-all. Most people's lives don't make a blind bit of difference to anyone else's and that's why they're so unfulfilled. I bet you made a hell of a difference to people's lives.'

Frank, taken aback by the accuracy of Cassidy's compliments, almost blushed.

'So why did you give it up?'

'Well, I met someone,' said Frank, 'and, I suppose, after a while I just wanted to feel fulfilment on a micro rather than a macro scale. I just wanted to feel loved and appreciated one to one.'

Cassidy shook his head with more than a trace of sadness. 'That's something I never managed to do.'

'You never married, then?'

'Nah. I know it's a cliché, but I've always been married to my work. I had important things to do. My flat's a slum and I was away for months on end in hell-holes all over the world. What woman in her right mind would put up with that? And even when I did get back, I'd usually have to spend the first month drying out.'

Frank had often wondered why Niall Cassidy's dispatches had been so sporadic. 'And now?'

He took another long lug on his cigarette before continuing quietly, 'I've seen too much and it was seriously screwing me up. If I witnessed any more examples of man's inhumanity to man, I'd have to be sectioned.'

Frank recalled the gruesomely simple details with which Niall had sketched atrocities from all over the world. There were several occasions when he'd used those descriptions to raise money from the pulpit, and now he told him so. 'Oh, that's great,' said Niall, 'but I just couldn't keep it up. I mean, alcohol helps numb the pain but only to a point. I was needing far too much of it just to carry on.'

Prime candidate for the Pioneers, thought Frank. Joe Hennessey would have him behind the wheel of a cab in no time. Except, as Niall explained, he'd never learned to drive. 'Can you imagine it?' He laughed. 'I couldn't be trusted to operate an electric toothbrush, let alone a car. The only time I ever want to drive is when I'm too pissed to walk.'

'You still drinking much?'

'On and off, but not as much as I used to. I'm working almost solely in the UK now and, believe me, there's plenty of shit going on here. But now that I'm not abroad, depressed and getting shot at, I'm not quite so dependent on it.'

'Well, that's good, isn't it?'

'Oh, God, yeah. I used to come back from some fucking war zone and try to go along to these AA meetings in the West End on Sunday nights. Full of celebrities. *Stars On Sunday*, they used to call it. God, the money I could have made selling their tales to the tabloids. That was the good thing about never being recognised. No one knew who I was and I was able to say, quite truthfully, "My name is David and I'm an alcoholic." Except now I don't think I was. Compared with some of those people, household names, I was a fucking amateur.'

Frank's mobile rang. Joe Hennessey. Pick-up at Canary Wharf.

'Well,' said Frank, getting up, 'fantastic seeing you again. I still can't believe you're Niall Cassidy.'

And he couldn't. He'd always imagined the great Niall Cassidy as a strong, handsome man in flak jacket and combats, striding fearlessly into the world's most dangerous places. Instead he was shaking the bony hand of a pallid emphysemic wreck who, if you'd given him a crutch, could have passed for Tiny Tim in *A Christmas Carol*. Sometimes it's best not to meet your heroes.

They said goodbye, exchanged phone numbers and promised to meet up again soon. And, like the last time they'd promised to do that, they knew they almost certainly wouldn't.

40

Sarah's mother was fond of saying that there were three stages in any pregnancy: weary, cheery and dreary. In that order. Sarah was still in the weary stage. *God*, she was weary. Sleep would suddenly ambush her at the most inopportune moments – in the middle of eating one of Frank's takeaways, for example, forkful of Singapore noodles raised half-way to her mouth. She had never found client meetings particularly inspiring but now had to dig her nails into her thigh until she almost drew blood to stop herself lolling face first into the client's lap. She found the most effective way was to keep talking, keep contributing and keep feigning fascination with the mind-numbing minutiae of a quarterly budget review.

Frank would pick up her up in the evenings, and when he looked at her in the rear-view mirror five minutes later she would no longer be there, having slumped sideways on the seat, fast asleep.

She managed to stay awake long enough to get to Sadler's Wells to see Nessie, as promised, on the opening night of *La Bohème*. Once there, though, the combination of darkness, comfortable seats and extreme fatigue had sent her to sleep within five minutes. The combination of darkness, comfortable seats and extreme boredom had sent Frank to sleep within ten. When he woke to discover a fat lady singing, he knew that meant it was all over and nudged Sarah.

They went backstage, Sarah still half asleep, panicking about what she could say to her friend about a performance through which she had slept like the dead.

Frank, however, suddenly wide awake, fixed Nessie with

practised, priestly sincerity and delivered a masterclass in bluffing. He rhapsodised about how he'd loved this particular opera since he'd first heard the music in *A Room With A View*. With mock self-deprecation, he confessed that he hadn't understood a word but was amazed to discover how little that had mattered. Italian, he went on, was such a romantic language, and Nessie's movement, her phrasing, the way she was able to convey her emotions had held his attention throughout. Artists simply live for praise, and Frank knew that if he deluged Nessie with enough of it, she wouldn't ask him questions about specific parts of the plot that he wouldn't be able to answer.

When it was Sarah's turn to give her opinion, all she had to do was hug her friend and kiss her on both cheeks, as though words couldn't do justice to such a magnificent performance. 'Thank you, thank you, thank you!' she wanted to scream, after Frank's eloquent extemporisation. At the moment she loved him more than ever for saving her from having to tell Nessie the truth – 'I fell asleep and missed your fabulous performance because, guess what, I'm pregnant' – thus topping her friend's moment of glory.

She'd decided not to tell anyone yet – although plain old-fashioned vanity had made her desperate to tell certain people at work. She'd seen the way they'd been looking her up and down with that 'Hmm, put on a bit of weight, haven't you?' glimmer of *Schadenfreude* in their eyes. She found that the most irritating part of early pregnancy – the fact that nobody knew so they couldn't make allowances. They could be forgiven for thinking she'd been overdoing the double chocolate cheesecake when she hadn't. Still, she'd rather this than have people look at her thickening midriff and congratulating her on being pregnant when she wasn't.

She was bursting to tell everyone she'd ever met. The initial shock was over and she had to remember that the tiredness, sore boobs and colleagues' curious glances were just confirmation of the most wonderful thing that had ever happened to her. But she wanted to wait until after the twelve-week scan before she told anyone. So far, only two other people knew: Carole Kendall and Howard Miller, for obvious reasons.

However, one morning around ten o'clock she was gripped by the cruel hand of morning sickness right in the middle of a client meeting. As she got up to speak, it turned her upside-down, round and round and inside-out. Those around the table noticed the colour drain from her cheeks as she tried gamely to carry on with the presentation, but soon, mumbling excuses, she had to sprint to the loo where she remained slumped in the cubicle for ten minutes. Five minutes later, Jane Steele went to see if she was all right. Head still over the porcelain, Sarah realised the number of people who knew her secret would have to be increased to three.

41

Carole Kendall had set up as a headhunter shortly after the birth of her first child. Like Sarah, she had been an account director, but as soon as she announced she was pregnant, she knew she had no future in an advertising agency. The industry she'd always loved, the one in which she'd flourished, the one where more than 50 per cent of employees are female, many in very senior positions, revealed a side she'd never seen before. It lost interest in her and became a heartless bastion of misogyny where compassion was outweighted by commission.

When Sarah told her why she was unable to accept the job in New York, Carole warned her of what would happen. 'Overnight, I'm afraid, you'll become damaged goods, no longer a serious player. The industry will know that your priorities will be split. Obviously you won't be sacked – only because that's illegal – but you'll find yourself subtly sidelined.' Carole continued, 'If you make the choice to have a baby, return to work, then try to "juggle" your responsibilities, you'll get very little sympathy from male colleagues, but even less from childless female ones. You see, women like Jane Steele have made a conscious decision not to have children. And, the way they look at it, why should they, having forfeited their right to reproduce, have to provide constant cover just because you've decided you "want it all"? And they do have a point. Anyway, it doesn't matter who's right or wrong. That's the way it is and always has been, though nowadays it has to be a lot more cunningly concealed.'

Jane was delighted that Sarah had 'fallen pregnant' – 'fallen' being the operative word – because this was the excuse she had been looking for to make sure Sarah's career fell to pieces. The first thing she did was invite Sarah into her office to 'congratulate' her.

Jane Steele was one of those rare people who look even less attractive when they smile. And, boy, was she smiling now. 'Sarah,' she said, oozing false sincerity, 'what's most important is your well-being and that of the baby. The last thing you need is the stress and strain of working on big, important accounts. Clients need continuity. If you're going to be off on maternity leave for three, maybe even six months, it's best to get a new account director bedded in as soon as possible so that by the time you have to take your break there will already have been a nice, smooth hand-over.'

Jane always felt undermined by Sarah and uncomfortable about being her boss. She knew she didn't have Sarah's respect and possessed neither the talent nor the charm to earn it. As long as Sarah handled her accounts with efficiency, intelligence and aplomb, she would have had to go on feeling uncomfortable, but the pregnancy had changed all that. By being outwardly kind and accommodating, she knew she could start making Sarah feel surplus to requirements. It's a scenario played out regularly at football clubs all over the world. The gifted midfield maestro, the fans' favourite, is suddenly left rotting in the reserves when a new manager arrives: this manager, dour and pragmatic, isn't confident enough in his own talent to make the best use of his star player's.

Sarah found herself shunted into the reserves, moved off accounts on which she had worked for years and that were central to the agency's creative reputation. Instead, she was given less important ones, those with the worst kind of cautious, pedestrian clients who wanted meeting after meeting before they could be persuaded to part with the peanuts necessary to run a couple of little press ads in a local newspaper.

With no faith in their own judgement, combined with a

pathological terror of taking any kind of risk, these dullards would insist on every idea being researched by focus groups. Sarah began to wonder whether they asked others to sleep with their fiancées before they married them.

During one particularly soul-destroying meeting, twelve adults had spent three hours discussing the launch of a new-shaped teabag.

'So,' said Sarah, 'who are you aiming them at?'

The client's reply was delivered without a trace of irony. 'Flat-bag loyalists.'

This time Sarah couldn't help herself: she put her head in her hands and groaned. Flat-bag loyalists? She had nothing against the words 'flat', 'bag' or 'loyalist'. She had heard them used hundreds of times but never in this order and never in this context. She never wanted to hear anything so ridiculous again.

Yet the phrase echoed around her skull 'Flat-bag loyalists . . . Flat-bag loyalists . . .' These words were joined by others from around the table, voicing gentle echoey concern. 'Sarah? Are you all right? Sarah?'

Was she all right? No, not really.

Jane Steele was slowly and deliberately destroying her career. Like many a struggling pregnant woman, she found herself wishing she'd been fired – or that Peter Clay had made her redundant instead of himself. Most people would prefer to be put to death by quick, lethal injection than by slow, horrible torture. Sarah felt the same about her career. Even if it survived, how would it recover from this? She had to spend every day dealing with people who were acutely aware that their working lives were of little consequence. People who therefore endowed themselves with unwarranted levels of self-importance.

Sarah was bright and likeable enough to have them eating out of her hand, but she could already feel the rod she had made for her own back. As soon as she returned from maternity leave, she would be told that since she had done such a fantastic job 'turning those accounts around' she'd have to stay on them permanently.

Suddenly she resented Frank for not being rich and successful enough to allow her to tell Jane Steele to stick her job up her arse. Then suddenly un-resented him again for being such a wonderful man. A man who loved her and looked after her. A man who made her happy, made her laugh and made her mushrooms on toast at two in the morning.

She put everything into perspective. Her life outside this meeting room was important; her life inside it was not. She decided that she didn't care. And, as the old saying goes, you can't beat a man (or woman) who doesn't care. Flat-bag loyalists were to be laughed at, not groaned at. If Jane Steele had lined up these people to make her life miserable, she was going to make sure they had the opposite effect.

She heard the voices again.

'Sarah? Are you all right?'

She lifted her head out of her hands. 'Yeah,' she said, that winning smile reclaiming her features, 'I'm fine.'

42

'You know, this is the first time for weeks that you haven't fallen asleep on the way home,' said Frank.

'I know,' said Sarah. 'I must have moved on to phase two, cheery.'

'Well, you've got about three months until dreary kicks in. What do you want to do?'

'Everything,' said Sarah.

So, instead of going home that night, they went out. In fact, every night, instead of going home, they went out.

They went to jazz clubs, comedy clubs, concerts, great restaurants and cosy little pubs that only a cab driver would know. They went to the cinema, to the theatre and back to Sadler's Wells to see *La Bohème*. Nessie was thrilled that Sarah and Frank had been so moved by her performance they had both wanted to see it a second time when, in truth, they were yet to see it for a first.

At weekends, they went to markets, museums and galleries, to the top of the Monument and the London Eye, in the knowledge that soon, for them, London's many avenues of pleasure would be closed until further notice.

On the day of the twelve-week scan that they hoped would give them the green light to tell the world their good news, Frank had promised to meet Sarah at the Chelsea and Westminster Hospital at two thirty. In view of this, perhaps he should have said no to the twelve fifteen pick-up at Heathrow, but he thought he would have time to take his passengers to Twickenham, then be at the hospital for Sarah's appointment. He should have known that the flight would be delayed and, despite some truly reckless driving not seen since the last episode of *The Sweeney*, he failed to make it.

When he pushed open the swing doors, Sarah was waiting for him, silent and motionless on a hard hospital chair. Her face was ashen. Clearly she had had the most terrible shock. Frank looked at her, scared to know the answer to his question. 'What's the matter?' he said.

She gazed vacantly at him, seemingly unable to speak.

'What is it?' he almost wailed. 'What's wrong?'

Dr Murray, Sarah's consultant, had seen Frank arrive and turned to him, frowning. 'Mr Dempsey?'

'Yes.'

'If you'd like to come with me for a moment, I want you to take a look at the scan. There's something you ought to know.'

43

Frank found it hard to take in the news.

'Is there a history of this in your family?' said Dr Murray, in a tone filled with professional compassion. 'Mrs Dempsey says there isn't in hers.'

'Yes,' said Frank quietly. 'My grandmother on my father's side.'

'Why did you never mention it?' asked Sarah.

'I didn't think,' said Frank. 'Never really thought it was important.'

'Not even when you found out I was pregnant,' said Sarah in disbelief.

'No,' said Frank. 'I was so happy I completely forgot . . .'

'That your granny was a twin,' she said.

Sarah was slightly less fazed than Frank. She'd had twenty minutes longer to get used to the idea that she wasn't having a baby, she was having two.

'It's hard to explain,' said Frank, when they got home. 'Families are very important to the Irish, but then again, they're not.'

'It obviously is hard to explain,' said Sarah, confused. 'I don't know what you're talking about.'

'Well,' said Frank, 'families are important – that's why they have such big ones, but because in any Irish family there are so many people, each person only has a sliver of significance. It's hard to remember everything about each one. My mum was one of eight. My granny was one of, oh, at least twelve or thirteen but I do remember her having a twin sister.'

'And how many kids did the twin have?'

'None.'

'None?'

'She was a nun.'

Sarah shook her head and laughed. God, what on earth had she married into?

'It was almost compulsory, in those days. If you had a few daughters, it was frowned upon if you didn't donate at least one to the local convent. Even when I was little, most of the kids in Kilburn had an aunt who was a nun. It was something to be proud of, like an avocado bathroom suite.'

'What if you only had sons? Did you have to give one of them to the Church?'

'Not so often. Boys were usually needed to help on the farm. Mind you, in a big Irish family, there was usually one who became a priest to get out of helping on the farm.'

Frank had always identified with these sons of the soil, who couldn't face of a lifetime spent cutting peat and milking cows. His decision to become a priest had had a lot to do with escaping his own version of 'the farm'. Now, suddenly, with twins on the way, he was knee-deep in silage. He'd got into something he could never get out of. Not that he wanted to. He was delighted, secretly proud of the speed and ease with which Sarah had become pregnant and was now, strutting around as fathers of twins invariably do, thinking about the double strength of his sperm.

He realised that the romantic old notion about a priest's flock being his family wasn't strictly true. They weren't a real family; they were adults from whom he could walk away any time he wanted. Or any time the bishop chose to transfer him. His 'family' would just swap their allegiance to whoever was sent to replace him.

Soon he would be 'married with two kids', the epitome of the farm he'd vowed he'd never work on. They were going to need two cots, two car seats, twice as many nappies, toys and clothes. Twice as much food, twice as much love, twice as much attention. There would be twice as much joy but twice as many problems. All of which meant he'd need twice as much money. But how could he drive twice as many taxis or play twice as many records?

His old maxim was coming back to haunt him: 'Believe in Fate but lean forward where Fate can see you.' Frank wasn't just leaning forward: he was now leaping around, waving his arms in the air, wearing a fluorescent jacket and a hat with flashing lights.

Surely someone would see him; and before long, somebody did.

44

'Frank!'

That huge booming Irish voice belonged to a huge booming Irishman who, unfortunately, had seen Frank emerge from the basement flat and now knew where he lived.

'Danny,' Frank smiled, 'what are you doing round here?'

'Earning a fortune for a day's work.' He jerked his head at the other builders who had arrived to continue renovating a handsome Victorian house across the road. 'Piers, Rupert!' he boomed, words which sounded odd coming from a mouth that usually shouted 'Mick!' or 'Paddy!' 'You remember Frank, don't you?'

'Ah, yes,' said Rupert, the posh plumber, offering his hand courteously. 'We met at the old furniture shop.'

'That's right,' said Frank. 'How's it all going down there?'

'Fantastic,' said Rupert. 'I'll let you into a little secret. The night to go is Sunday. It's amazing. You really ought to come down.'

Good old Toby, thought Frank. He really had kept his word and preserved his star DJ's anonymity.

'How about you, Dan?' said Rupert teasingly. 'You'd love it.'

Oh, no. Frank held his breath but he needn't have worried.

'Ah, fuck off, would you?' said Danny. 'Me dancing around a fucking furniture shop? We've got the best parish centre in the world. Ask this man.' He pointed at Frank. 'He built it.'

Again, Frank froze at the thought of his ex-occupation becoming common knowledge. 'Helped *you* build it, Dan,' he said, staring evenly into Danny's eyes. 'We all did.' He turned to Rupert. 'Busy, then?'

'Unbelievable,' said Rupert. 'More work than we can handle. That's why we have to keep begging Danny here to help us out.'

Piers emerged from the van carrying two planks of MDF.

'Piers,' said Rupert, 'this is Frank.'

'Of course,' said Piers. 'We met once before.'

'How's it going?'

'Well,' said Piers, as unlikely a chippie as Frank was a priest, 'it's . . . sort of . . . paradoxical.'

'Oh, Jesus,' said Danny to Frank, 'don't start him off.'

But Frank was intrigued by Piers's answer. 'Paradoxical?' he asked.

'Well, yes,' said Piers, pensively. 'I'd underestimated the detrimental effect that life as a builder can have on one's feelings. People beg you to come in to their houses, then almost from the moment you arrive, they can't wait to see the back of you. These people, for instance, have made no bones about the fact that they'll be having a huge party as soon as they get rid of us. Not great for a chap's self-esteem.' With that, he drifted philosophically back into the house.

Rupert and Danny were laughing. 'See what I have to put up with?' said Danny. 'He's fucking priceless, that one.'

'Anyway,' said Rupert, 'good to see you again, Frank. Cheerio.'

'So this is where you've been hiding?' said Danny to Frank, with a wink.

No point lying. 'Yeah,' said Frank. 'And what about you? Working with this lot is getting to be a habit.' He could see from Danny's now serious expression that he'd hit some sort of nail on the head.

'Yeah,' he said, almost sadly. 'I really want to talk to you about that. I'm only here for the day. I should be finished by five. Will you be back by then?'

Frank could easily have got out of it, but he was already feeling a bit guilty about trying to avoid Danny and his ilk. He didn't want to start behaving like an egocentric rock star who wants nothing to do with his fans, the people who made him.

The priest, or maybe just the human being in him, could never ignore the plaintive call of an ex-parishioner.

'That's the good thing about this job,' he said, getting into the cab. 'I can make my own hours. See you back here about five, then?'

'Good man yourself,' said Danny, with a grateful smile.

At five past five Danny and Frank were in the Wilton Arms on Dawes Road, one of the few remaining relics of Fulham's insalubrious past, drinking Guinness and shandy respectively.

'So, what's the problem?' said Frank, putting on an imaginary dog-collar and erecting a temporary confessional box in the corner of the pub.

'Well, I'm doing fine, like,' said Danny. 'Those fellas have saved my life and I'm making a packet – but my own business has all but dried up. I think I mentioned to you a while back that we weren't getting much work from the councils, road-digging and that. Well, now we're not getting any at all and that was our bread-and-butter. They've centralised it now, streamlined it, and apparently the old arrangements have changed. You have to be very slick, very professional.'

Oh dear. Frank knew that Danny had been successful. He was straight (give or take a bit of tax 'avoidance') and his work was faultless. 'Slick', however, was not a word you would associate with Danny Power.

'Not only that,' Danny went on, 'but the really big firms are now coming in for much smaller jobs. Domestic stuff – loft conversions, extensions and that.'

'Why do you think that is?'

Danny took a huge gulp of Guinness and thought for a moment. 'Not sure, but I've been contacted by this fella called McGuire.'

'Who's he?'

'Again, I'm not sure, but the councils use him to sort out all the building tenders. To keep it centralised, simple and all above board. He's the fella you have to be in with. Now, I could never be bothered with all that arse-licking just to get work but it seems that that's what you have to do now. He phoned the other day. Seemed nice enough, said he'd heard great things about me and my lads, and would I like to have lunch with him?'

'Are you going?'

Danny suddenly looked self-conscious, almost afraid. The word 'lunch' was clearly a chink in his armour. 'Ah,' he said quietly, 'I hate anything like that. I've always avoided it. I may have made a lot of money but in here . . .' he tapped his head '. . . I've never left County Cavan. I'm not having lunch with anyone. I can't send any of the lads either – they're worse than I am. They wouldn't know which knife and fork to use.'

'How about Rupert?' said Frank. 'Public school, university, he'd know which way to pass the port.'

'That lot operate in a different world. They know a lot of wealthy people who know even more wealthy people. They have to turn work down. Mind you, they're very good but they don't have to dig roads – they don't have to go near council jobs. It's all private, all word-of-mouth. I was just wondering . . .'

Oh, God.

'. . . if you'd go, as my representative, like, and have a meal with this McGuire fella. Tell him you're my site manager or something. You'll get away with it. You're a genius at that sort of thing, you know you are.'

With his closing compliment, Danny had unwittingly clinched it. Frank Dempsey, like the Jean Genie, loved to be loved. 'Of course I will, Dan.' The tension left Danny's huge shoulders. 'Anything for a free lunch.'

However, as the old saying goes, there's no such thing.

45

The arrival of a railway has always brought with it work, prosperity and investment. The relatively recent arrival of the Heathrow Express line to Paddington had brought regeneration to a seamy side of London that had lain neglected for years. The only surprise was that it had taken so long. Paddington Station and the line heading west had always been there, as had the Westway, and yet, between the two, there had been acres of wasteland. Not any more. Towering office blocks and waterside apartments had replaced the blowing sprigs of tumble-weed – a big boon to Sacred Heart Cabs, serendipitously placed about a mile up the road.

Not a day of Frank's working life went by without a trip to Paddington and today was no exception, although for this particular task he'd left the taxi at home. Steam-cleaned and crisply attired in the black linen suit that Sarah had made him buy at Banana Republic on Fifth Avenue, he arrived at the Hilton Hotel by the station. It had originally been known as the Great Western, a huge Victorian masterpiece that, over recent decades, had fallen into decline. Frank remembered it as a sad, crumbling anachronism, one up from the seedy hostels around Norfolk Square where rooms were rented by the hour. A £60 million refurbishment had restored the famous old hotel to its former glory and cleared away all the working girls. The Hilton's well-heeled guests had no need for the smacked-out have-it-away-day hookers who arrived every evening on the 125 from Cardiff. These new clients would probably demand a better class of adultery, preferring to phone down to the concierge and ask for an 'extra pillow'.

Frank entered the Hilton's shiny new brasserie, described in its brochure as 'the ideal venue for that all-important business lunch'. Twelve minutes late, he asked for the table for two booked in the name of McGuire.

'Frank,' said his host, welcoming him to a table in the corner, 'Tim McGuire. How are you?'

'Fine, thank you,' said Frank, shaking a hand that was almost shockingly soft. 'Sorry I'm late.'

'That's fine, Frank, just fine,' said McGuire, who had clearly already had an aperitif. 'What are you drinking?'

'Glass of house white would open the old appetite nicely.'

'Ah, come on,' said McGuire, 'we can do a bit better than that – the Château d'Yquem is sensational.'

That remark told Frank all he needed to know. When the fiendishly expensive bottle arrived McGuire, as expected, made a great spectacle of swinging his connoisseur's nose back and forth across the glass, then slowly tasting it and solemnly pronouncing it fit for consumption. The wine waiter probably walked away from the table thinking, What a prat.

Frank's father-in-law, a wine merchant, would never have behaved like that: he would have assumed that the wine he'd ordered was fine, but if not, a discreet word with the waiter would sort it out.

Frank could also see more obvious clues to the sort of man he was about to have lunch with. He didn't, for a moment, think that all Irishmen should be raucous, stout-swilling navvies who sang rebel songs in the pubs of Kilburn until way after closing time, but he had a far greater affection for that sort of Irishman than he had for the newer, smoother breed, as typified by Tim McGuire.

He was about the same age as Frank but there the similarity ended. McGuire was plump and pale-skinned with dark hair already on the road to recession. He was expensively but tastelessly dressed. The fawn suit was too light, the blue shirt too bright, and the loud, orange tie just too loud and orange. Also, there was something slightly repellent about the dark hairs on his wrist that were poking through the gold bracelet of his new TAG-Heuer.

Although Frank could see that they had nothing in common, it was crucial that McGuire thought otherwise, so he slid into the appropriate persona – honest, intelligent, wide-eyed, with a few Irish expressions peppering his speech to help McGuire relax and reveal.

'Danny sends his apologies,' said Frank, 'but he's happiest on site, getting his hands dirty. Trouble was, the business had got so big he had to get me in to run it for him. I'd known him for years. Now, at last, I seem to have got it sorted.'

'What did you do before you worked for Danny Power?' His beady little eyes weren't quite brave enough to look straight into Frank's.

'Quantity surveyor.' This was a path down which Frank was not going to be led. He knew nothing about quantity surveying so, taking a sip of the Château d'Yquem he changed the subject. 'Mmm, you're right,' he said. 'This wine is fantastic.' He didn't know if it was good or not: he knew even less about wine than he did about quantity surveying. The Château d'Yquem might just as well have been a three-quid bottle of screw-top tramp fuel.

'Frank Dempsey wasn't a name with which I was familiar—' said McGuire.

'Sorry,' said Frank, cutting him short and shuffling uncomfortably in his seat. 'I have this little hobby – don't laugh. I work Sunday nights in this sort of nightclub and, well, it was extremely loud last night and I think I've done something to my ear. What were you saying?'

'Um, that yours wasn't a name I'd heard before,' said McGuire, raising his voice slightly.

'Well,' said Frank, 'Danny's such a big character and it's very much his firm. I prefer to stay in the background, making sure everything runs smoothly. I think of myself as a facilitator.'

'Me too,' said McGuire evenly.

'Exactly,' said Frank. 'Now I *have* heard your name mentioned but I'm not quite sure what it is you do.'

'Well, basically I'm a solicitor. I spent many years working for local councils, specialising in planning applications, building regs, that sort of thing, and then I set up on my own.'

McGuire was either being cleverly cagy or more likely, Frank suspected, he was trying to create an aura of mystery. Best just to play along. 'Really?' he said. 'Doing the same sort of thing?'

'Basically, yes,' said McGuire. 'As you know, more and more council services have now been outsourced to the private sector. Having worked for them for so long, I saw a window of opportunity.'

Yeah, thought Frank, I bet you fucking did.

McGuire, horribly pleased with himself, was ready to explain, but Frank wasn't quite ready to listen. Fortunately the waiter intervened, so Frank was able to change tack. First he got McGuire talking about football, then films, music, house prices, TAG Heuer watches, New York, *Coronation Street* and papal infallibility. He moved on to how much Dublin had changed, with the unwelcome visits of stag parties from Surrey, the Northern Ireland peace process, his impending fatherhood, the Jaguar X-type and whether the *Daily Mail*'s constant scaremongering was fostering a climate of fear.

Frank was a fantastic lunch companion, wonderful company. He could see that McGuire thought that he was a man after his own heart, a man he could trust and in whom he could confide. Another bottle of wine later, Frank was ready to hear his confession. 'I'm so sorry,' he said, over coffee and brandy, 'you didn't come in here to listen to me blathering on. What can I do to help you?'

'Well,' said McGuire, 'it's more what *I* can do to help *you*. Let me tell you about local councils . . .'

Here we go.

'They are the last great bastions of corruption.'

Frank had guessed before the starters had arrived that someone somewhere would be paying for this extravagant lunch.

'The people who work there get paid fuck-all yet they wield a huge amount of power. More and more of them are starting to realise that, which is why I set up on my own.'

Frank didn't want to look too innocent or he might lose the trust he'd worked so hard to acquire. 'Well,' he said, 'backhanders between builders and councils are nothing new.'

'Ah,' said McGuire, 'but it was always so crass and disorganised. There's too much money at stake now, which is where I come in.'

'Where you come in?' said Frank, pretending he didn't understand.

'Now it's all done very discreetly. I negotiate a price between, say, a developer, or a builder who wants a piece of the action, and the council official who can grant the permission he needs to go ahead. They're not all corrupt. In fact, it's only a small minority who are, but when you add up all the boroughs in London, there's enough of them to make a lot of people a lot of money.'

So far, so totally expected. McGuire was after an 'arrangement fee' to put council work Danny Power's way. Frank wanted McGuire to tell him something that wasn't so blatantly obvious. He had a feeling that one innocuous observation might start to open things up. 'I have noticed,' he remarked, 'that there seem to be far more roadworks than there used to be.'

'Funny, that,' said McGuire, with a plump, greedy grin. 'Once you understand the scale of the corruption, it all starts to make sense. Speed humps, unnecessary traffic-lights, chicanes, road-narrowing schemes, what we like to call "pinch points". That's where your money goes, I'm afraid. Local councils, especially in London, have the most enormous budgets yet they're subject to virtually no scrutiny. Government departments are answerable to all sorts of independent review bodies, but with councils, things just go through on the nod. Especially anything to do with "making the roads safer for our children". And we're talking millions and millions of pounds.'

'But surely that's not right,' said Frank, raising a feeble objection so that McGuire could brush it aside. 'All that money being spent on things that nobody wants when schools are running out of books and special-needs centres are closing down?' He sensed that McGuire was both proud and ashamed of what he was doing. He seemed to want to unburden himself. He'd come to the right place.

'I suppose you're right – in fact, you *are* right,' he said. 'And if you want my honest opinion, local councils are to blame for just about everything. It's a terrible combination – stupid people, huge budgets, no accountability. It's the worst of all possible worlds.'

'Or, from your point of view,' said Frank, 'the best of all possible worlds.'

'Exactly,' said McGuire, the avaricious smile returning to his face. 'Unfortunately schools and old people's homes offer no scope for this sort of activity, but anything to do with "road safety" is instantly seen to be a good thing and local councillors and their friends in the building trade all know this. The situation isn't going to change so you might as well make a profit out of it. If I wasn't doing this, someone else would be.'

'But you thought of it first,' said Frank, mock-flatteringly.

'I did, and now I'm reaping the benefits. Benefits that are there for you to share.'

'But surely it can't go on for ever,' said Frank. 'What are they going to do – put speed humps all the way up the M1?'

'On the contrary,' said McGuire, with a laugh. 'Councils have now started ripping them out. People hate them so much that nobody's going to object. Think of the money that's going to cost. And I don't suppose you've heard of the Zebra Pelican and Puffin Pedestrian Crossing Regulations and General Directive?'

Frank shook his head.

'Well, it's a brilliant council initiative that has decreed that those zigzag lines you get on all pedestrian crossings have to be repainted so that instead of going zig-zag they go zag-zig.'

'Why?'

'Well,' said McGuire, with a sickening wink, which made Frank want to close his fucking eye permanently, 'why do you think? Lot of work for a lot of contractors. They'll be spending millions. We're doing it in dribs and drabs, of course, otherwise it'd be too obvious.'

'But it sounds like you've done practically everything you can do already,' said Frank. 'Surely my company would be arriving at the table just as all the plates have been cleared away.'

'Are you joking?' McGuire chortled. 'We haven't even got on to what they like to call Environmental Improvements.'

'Which are?'

'You know,' said McGuire, with a cackle, 'those pointless iron railings and pretty little red-brick pavements. All very lucrative.' He rubbed his fat, soft thumb and forefinger together. 'Each department,' he explained, 'is desperate to spend its budget, because if they don't they won't get as much the following year. They won't be able to justify their little "teams". It's all to keep themselves in a job. It's a fucking scandal but, hey, do I look like I'm complaining?' He laughed again.

Frank laughed too, although inside he wanted to roar with indignation and use McGuire's fat face as a punch-bag. Somehow he managed to stay calm.

'Lately we've been finding cash a bit crude, a bit obvious, so in return for these favours, the contractors involved have opted to do private work on council employees' houses for nothing. Anything from a bit of decorating to a full-blown extension or loft conversion. Some of them are very big firms who normally build office blocks and underpasses.'

Puffed up with his own importance and spurred on by Frank's deliberately fawning disbelief, McGuire then got sloppy. In a fantastic four minutes of indiscretion, he named the companies, their employees, the sums of money involved and the borough councillors whose houses had been so generously extended.

Frank's shock and incredulity this time were genuine. McGuire had finally made the impression he'd been so keen to make. He liked Frank Dempsey, he wanted to be his mate, and if that was what it took to impress him, fine. McGuire's own business was expanding faster than his waistline. He might need a fellow 'facilitator' to help him run it. He finished by saying, 'You ought to see my house. Jesus, it's a palace. You and your good lady must come over for dinner. Here, let me give you my number.'

A sudden glance at the gold TAG told McGuire that the meeting he'd enjoyed so much had overrun and that he was late for the next one. He signed the bill and apologised for having to rush off. Frank was relieved to be left alone at the table.

While McGuire was making such a show of tasting the wine, he hadn't noticed the Dictaphone that Frank had dropped carefully from his sleeve on to the seat next to him, where it had remained for the entire meal.

He knew he'd find a use for it one day.

46

Outside, Frank pressed rewind, then play. Not exactly broadcast quality, but all McGuire's boasts and confessions were clearly audible.

Now what?

The one part of the priesthood that Frank had taken seriously was the confidentiality of confession. He had never been a grass at school and was finding it very hard to contemplate becoming one now. McGuire had trusted him, bought him lunch, filled his glass with Château d'Yquem. Was this any way to repay him?

He thought about that dilemma for all of ten seconds, then made his decision.

Despite his generosity and practised civility, Tim McGuire was rotten to the core. Morally and legally, Frank would be failing in his duty as a human being if he turned a blind eye. He wasn't a priest any more, he was no longer bound by his vows and, anyway, McGuire hadn't made these admissions in a confessional box.

But was it fair to try to exact revenge?

In a word, yes. Frank had never seen anything wrong with the concept of revenge. It's the very thing that separates humans from animals. A cat can torture a defenceless mouse then leave it to die and nothing will be done about it; humans on the other hand live with the knowledge that if they do something wrong they may well get clobbered for it.

With that thought, he pulled out his mobile and dialled a number he'd never thought he'd dial.

'Mr Cassidy? Mr Dempsey . . . Yeah, fine, thanks . . . Listen, can we meet up? As soon as possible. Boy, have I got something for you!'

47

Jane Steele had done Sarah a favour. Had she left her to work with clients she liked on accounts she cared about, Sarah's life would have been very difficult. Her professional integrity would never have allowed her to slack. As she had been instrumental in building up their businesses and producing award-winning ads for them, she would have felt rather shabby about having to abandon them. Instead with only dreary, indecisive clients, she felt less guilty about taking her foot off the gas. She knew she could have six months' maternity leave and return to find them poring over the same research findings, still wondering whether it was prudent to sign off a tiny portion of the budget that they'd promised to spend.

She therefore had no compunction about taking an inordinate amount of time off for scans and obstetrical appointments. Now people knew that she was expecting twice the normal number of babies, she was afforded twice the normal level of latitude. If Frank wasn't stuck waiting for a late arrival at terminal four, he would pick her up from the Chelsea and Westminster and, if it was warm and sunny, they'd go for a picnic in St James's Park.

The mobile phone was a wonderful invention, and Sarah used it to pacify her clients with regular, reassuring, just-catching-up phone calls as she sat in the sunshine, eating for three. During the first three months, she'd lost her appetite – nausea seized her at the whiff of a bacon sandwich – and by now she was celebrating its return.

Her priority now was to relax and enjoy the last precious weeks of her life when she wouldn't be somebody's mother. Nobody minded. Nobody cared. That was the good thing about being sidelined and Sarah thought she might as well take advantage of it. If she ran around like a dervish, desperate to prove that pregnancy made no difference to her professional commitment, she would only end up in hospital with high blood pressure, being told to do what she was doing now.

Confident of her ability, Sarah knew she could let things slide for a while, then get everything back on track when she returned to work.

She wasn't sure whether to be impressed or alarmed by Frank's attitude: perhaps he was in denial, but he was carrying on as though nothing had happened. However, as he explained to her, what was he supposed to do? Over the years, he'd noticed how most expectant or recent fathers had fallen into two camps, both of which he was keen to avoid. One was the 'traditional' man who spent all week at the office and all weekend on the golf course, leaving his wife to get on with what he considered to be 'women's work'. The other was the role-reversed liberal ninny who wanted to wear a strap-on tummy and experience contractions so that he could 'really empathise' with what his 'life partner' was going through. Frank just concerned himself with taking care of his wife and making it as easy as possible for her to grow two human beings inside her.

His always voracious consumption of magazines now included articles he had hitherto ignored. Articles about fatherhood by various 'media fathers' whom he dubbed the 'Laddy Daddies'. The archetypal 'Laddy Daddy' was in his late thirties. When presented in the delivery room with his offspring, he saw not just a baby but a career opportunity too. Frank was well aware of the old maxim that 'all experience is copy', but when that experience is first-time fatherhood, it's not particularly interesting copy. People have been procreating since time began yet the Laddy Daddy believes that his 'take' on the experience will be much more illuminating than anyone else's.

First, he's 'gobsmacked' at the sudden demands and unexpected crises of parenthood: 'And there I was, just about to go to this launch party at Soho House, when Josh suddenly threw up all over my new Commes des Garçons suit.' Then comes the mock-moaning about how his Stolly-drinking, charlie-snorting, babe-bedding lifestyle has been cruelly curtailed by a very different sort of babe. And the horror of discovering that his partner's breasts were not created solely for his carnal gratification.

What he's trying to convey, of course, is not how rich and fulfilling his new life is, but how enviably chic and hedonistic his old one was. He just wants everyone to know that although he's, like, you know, cool about warming bottles and changing nappies, hey, he's still a party animal. He wasn't quite ready to let go.

This was the bit that Frank found almost poignant: Laddy Daddy had obviously never been 'laddy' at all. Frank had met his type many times at Oxford, the boy who had acquired his confidence rather late in life, then spent the next few years desperately trying to catch up. Having reluctantly accepted that it's time to settle down, Laddy Daddy feels he might as well throw himself into it. He worked hard for his degree, so he treats fatherhood as some sort of post-grad humanities course. He writes magazine articles and offers volumes of unwanted advice on raising children 'in the new millennium', as though it is somehow different from the old one. Quite often, he'll undergo a cloyingly sincere Saul-on-the-Road-to-Damascus conversion: he suddenly sobers up to realise that his little 'miracle' is the world's most perfect creation. He looks for the reader's sympathy as he tries to combine the pressures of his dazzling career with trying to find a window in his diary for the school sports day. Tips are proffered on remaining a good father while retaining those all-important laddy credentials.

It was the whingeing ingratitude of these pieces that stuck in Frank's craw. He felt sad when he thought of his own father and the millions like him who adored and cherished their children. They would have loved to be 'more involved' but lacked the luxury of laptops, mobile phones and flexible working arrangements that make modern fatherhood so easy.

'Laddy Daddies' was one way of describing these media fathers but Frank still preferred the other one:

Wankers.

48

Like most nightclubs, Empire Furnishings had a disabled loo. Unlike most nightclubs, theirs was hardly used. It wasn't that those with disabilities were not welcome, far from it, but in Clubland disabled loos seldom contain disabled people. More spacious than normal cubicles, they are much in demand from cokeheads, who disappear inside three or four at a time to bring new meaning to the phrase 'powdering your nose'.

The success of Frank's residency had been phenomenal. When Toby had asked him to think of a name for the one-nighter, he had decided, in a private joke with himself, to call it Benediction, since that was what he used to do on Sunday evenings. Someone had misheard this and it was now known as Addiction, with music played by Ben. This was even better for Frank since, if people thought his name was Ben, there was less chance of them discovering it wasn't. Addiction was also apt since that was how its regulars felt about their Sunday-night fix.

It had become the place where clubbers went when they weren't clubbing. At Addiction, there was no attitude and, astonishingly, no real drug culture. Even for systems that were habitually abused, Sunday had become a day of rest, hence the almost permanently 'vacant' sign on the door of the disabled loo.

Sacred Heart Cabs were much in evidence. At least half a dozen of their abstemious drivers would be sitting at the bar every Sunday night, Occasionally they would look across at the indoor taxi rank that Frank had set up by the DJ booth. If anyone was waiting there, one of them would put down his lime and soda, take the customer wherever they wanted to go, then return to the club to collect his next fare.

Still, no one knew who the DJ was. A rival club-owner had left a brown envelope with £2000 in cash as a 'signing-on fee' if Ben wanted to swap venues. Frank had been tempted when he ran the thick wad of notes through his fingers, but left a message on the number he'd been given that the envelope and its contents were ready for collection.

He now had another flock depending on him, but this time he also depended on them. They were the ones who ensured that he returned home every Sunday night weighed down with 'pennies for Pampers'. How else would he provide for his family? But how much longer could he remain on a treadmill that was going ever faster, watched by more and more people?

One group of people had been watching him very closely and, in the time-honoured fashion, intended to make him an offer he couldn't refuse.

49

Niall Cassidy was a drunk, a scruffy, bone-idle, couldn't-give-a-fuck wastrel. Until he got the bit between his teeth. Until something triggered his ire and his over-developed sense of justice. It was then that Clark Kent stumbled into the phone-box and emerged looking exactly the same. Except for the fanatical glint in his eye, which meant that his formidable brain power, determination and cunning would be ceaselessly employed until somebody's lies, cant or corruption were brought to the world's attention.

Frank hadn't heard from him for weeks because Niall had been busy. That Dictaphone alone would have been enough for less dedicated journalists, but Niall Cassidy had made his reputation by wanting more. He wanted those allegations to be watertight: he wanted irrefutable answers to any excuses that McGuire and his sleazy council cronies might try to put up.

He had a network of narks and grasses that would have been the envy of Scotland Yard. The numbers stored in his mobile had been backed up and printed out several times because without them, he'd never get hold of these people again.

Early on in his career he'd discovered a lopsided moral code among his shady associates that forbade them to talk to the Old Bill but allowed them to spill all sorts of stories to an engaging, principled journalist. He followed up leads to civic centres and town halls all over London. The vast majority of people who worked there were honest. They knew what was going on and were only too relieved to help put an anonymous stop to it.

Only when he was completely happy, only when he had every shred of evidence he could possibly require, and more, only when he had drawn on that evidence to write a piece of such elegant and damning conclusiveness, did he approach the editors of all the national newspapers. And only when they were falling over themselves to print what they had long suspected but had never been able to prove, and Niall knew his job was done, did he remember who had first set him off on this trail.

It was Sunday night and he'd procured early editions of all Monday's papers. He kept trying Frank's mobile but in Empire Furnishings' DJ booth, the ringtones had been drowned by Fatback's 'Yum Yum' and 'I Got It' by the New York Port Authority. Undeterred, he had Frank's address and his taxi arrived there at around half past midnight, five minutes after Frank's.

Sarah, who had now entered the 'dreary' phase and felt too heavy and cumbersome to go out much, was still up. It was Nessie's night off and they had spent the evening eating, talking, eating, watching a bit of TV and eating.

Nessie, who loved the new, temporarily gluttonous Sarah, had waited to say hello to Frank, who was about to give her a lift home when the buzzer sounded. Unannounced and unexpected, Niall Cassidy came running into the sitting room. Too elated to speak, he dropped the early editions of Monday morning's newspapers on the sofa, brandished a bottle of champagne and opened it, almost demolishing the ceiling. 'We did it! Dempsey, we fucking did it!'

'Who is this?' Nessie murmured to Sarah.

Sarah shrugged, and Niall suddenly realised there were two other people in the room. 'Sorry,' he said. 'I'm Niall. I'm . . . er . . . the paper-boy.'

Frank got four glasses, made the introductions and tried to forget how tired he was. Sarah was too tired to be tired, but Niall and Nessie were wide awake. After the tale of McGuire had been related, they took their conversation on to a plane where Sarah and Frank, through fatigue and ignorance, were unable to join in.

Nessie's histrionic manner concealed a depth of knowledge

that even Sarah, who had known her for years, hadn't known she possessed. Niall was enthralled to find someone else who shared his passion for Walt Whitman and J.H. Prynne. Nessie was delighted to discover a man whose passion for opera predated the 1990 World Cup.

Frank had been playing records all evening and didn't want to play any more, but since the flat was never without some sort of soundtrack, he put on an old John Coltrane album and let that smooth, smoky sax provide the backdrop, as it must have done countless times, for a slowly burgeoning romance. He watched Nessie and Niall become more and more interested in each other, and less and less in their hosts. Their conversation had moved on to Strauss versus Strauss; Niall was in Johann's corner, batting for *Die Fledermaus* while Nessie favoured Richard and insisted that *Der Rosenkavalier* was more complete as an opera. Then they both agreed that *The Magus* was Fowles's finest work, despite the execrable film adaptation.

'But have you read the revised edition?' said Nessie.

'Yeah, but when you put it side by side with the original, it's not that different.'

'Except,' she said, 'for a lot more sex.'

And they both burst out laughing.

Frank looked on with a warm feeling of empathy. He remembered how he'd felt when he'd first met Sarah. Tortured. As a Catholic priest, he'd known that the friendship they were developing was inappropriate yet neither of them could stop themselves. Niall, Nessie and 99 per cent of couples suffered none of that angst. Their relationship, if they chose to have one, could blossom untrammelled by vows of celibacy.

He felt that good-natured envy again. Not that he found Nessie attractive – he liked her enormously but, within minutes, she'd have driven him mad. She wouldn't drive Niall mad. How can you drive a man to where he is already?

He looked across at Sarah, now the size of a caravan, her dark hair and smooth complexion robbed of their usual lustre by the little parasites inside her, who, like all unborn babies, take the nutrients they need from their mother, leaving her to survive on what's left. Frank nudged her gently, heaved her out of the sofa and led her, in her XXXL T-shirt, to bed.

When he returned, Niall and Nessie hadn't even noticed his dis- and reappearance. They were now discussing the tragic sensitivity in the work of Thom Gunn. 'So neglected in his own country,' said Niall ruefully.

'I know, I know,' nodded Nessie. 'Apart from anything else, I've always loved the idea of a poet wearing a leather jacket.'

Frank felt like a green and prickly fruit, but he also felt as though he and Sarah had really made it now. No longer the giggling about-to-be-lovers revelling in the early throes of infatuation, they were married, established and expecting twins. Yet, watching Niall and Nessie, he liked to think that his and Sarah's love might prove an inspiration to them. It was as though they had passed on the baton in the romantic relay race. He just hoped that Niall Cassidy, in a drunken fug, didn't drop it.

Cassidy was a hard-bitten journalist. He was used to bluntness and plain speaking. So, at twenty to three in the morning, Frank had no qualms about yawning, stretching, and saying, 'Well, I'm at home. I wish everyone else was.'

50

It was hard to say what the clients thought about attending a presentation given by an account director who was wearing a fluffy white bathrobe and a towel on her head. But it was a novelty and they seemed to enjoy it. Sarah began by apologising for her attire but explained that if she'd waited until she'd got dressed, she'd never have made it for nine thirty. Still, she said, did it really matter what she was wearing? She carried the meeting along with wit, grace and charm, and since everybody knew she was about to have twins, they were impressed she'd made it at all.

As her satisfied clients trooped out of the meeting room, she couldn't help thinking, Thank God for conference calls.

She waited until noon before giving Nessie the 'Well-how-did-it-go?' call: she knew that her friend's night would have been even later than hers.

'Darling, he was amazing,' was the gushing verdict. 'Simply amazing. As you know, I'm no stranger to men, but he is without question the best. I can't begin to tell you.'

But Nessie did 'begin to tell' Sarah and carried on telling her. 'Darling, after we left yours he took me to this little Portuguese bar just the other side of Vauxhall Bridge. You'd never know it was there. We danced to this Portuguese music and drank Agua Ardente. I know he's not the most handsome man I've ever met, but he's by far the most attractive. It's all behind the eyes. He's seen so much, done so much and knows so much. Such a contrast with those pointlessly good-looking men who have nothing behind their eyes.'

As Nessie went on, Sarah realised that it was Niall's cerebral rather than sexual prowess with which her friend was so enraptured. They hadn't slept together. In fact, they hadn't slept at all. 'We talked all night. Can you believe that?'

'Quite easily.'

'Then we had breakfast over in Smithfield.'

'Where is he now?'

'He says he's gone into hiding because every councillor in London will be after him.'

'When are you going to see him again?'

'Well, I'm working six nights a week but we're meeting up tomorrow afternoon and going to the Eva Hesse exhibition at Tate Modern. Anyway, darling, I've got to get some sleep before the show tonight otherwise I'm going to sound like Barry White.'

Niall was 'hiding' in the Queen Elizabeth, where he'd arranged to meet Frank at twelve o'clock. As a long-time member of the 11.01 club, he'd already been there for an hour – just enough time for three pints and who-knows-how-many Marlboros.

'What a result, eh?' said Niall, as they clinked glasses.

'As we speak,' said Frank, 'McGuire will be making plans to fake his own death.'

Niall looked at him quizzically. That job was done and dusted. On to the next thing. 'Oh, I couldn't care less about him. I was talking about Nessie.' His smile was so wide and his gappy teeth so visible that his tongue looked like it was in jail. 'Oh, she's amazing. After you slung us out, she wanted to come back to mine but . . .'

'But what?'

'Well, you know that scene in *Withnail and I*?'

'Not the bit in the kitchen?'

Niall nodded. 'That's why I'm here. A team of industrial cleaners are in there right now. It's going to be like mucking out the Augean stables. I don't envy them. So, anyway, I took her to Cavalho's, this little bar I know just off South Lambeth Road, the one place guaranteed to be packed at three in the morning, and we got smashed on a Portuguese liqueur. She even had me dancing. I've never danced in my life. Oh, what a girl . . .'

'Is it serious?'

'I hope so. I'll try not to fuck it up this time. I always had trouble with women. No sisters, you see. I think that was the problem. Two brothers, then an all-boys' school, an all-male college, then a very male working environment. I tended to fall in love *at* girls rather than *with* them. I never really knew what to do.'

'Just be yourself,' said Frank.

'Well, I don't suppose I was particularly keen on myself so I didn't see why anyone else should be. I wouldn't want to go out with me.'

'Well, Nessie obviously does.'

'Yeah,' said Niall, seemingly more proud of this than any of his journalistic achievements. 'I now know exactly what happened to you. You spend your life trying to make a difference to other people's lives . . .' He let out a long lungful of smoke. '. . . and there comes a time when you just want to make a difference to your own.'

51

After Niall's lengthy eulogy on love, Frank was almost dead from passive smoking and had about twenty minutes to fill his lungs with fresh air in Victoria Park before resmoking them again on the other side of London. Danny Power had called. He was working in Maida Vale, close to the Sacred Heart Cabs office. Could Frank meet him around five, this time in the Truscott Arms?

When Frank arrived, Danny's big, ruddy face was more flushed than usual. 'I don't know what you did,' he said, knocking him bandy with a slap on the back that was heavy with gratitude and awe, 'I don't know how you did it, but I know all that stuff in the papers about that bastard McGuire was something to do with you.'

Frank raised a non-committal eyebrow.

'Well, all right, you don't have to tell me but since I've been proved to be "clean", the phone hasn't stopped ringing. I'm suddenly getting more work than I'm going to know what to do with. I'm going make a packet out of this, so it's only right that you do too.' He slid a brown envelope across the table, bigger and thicker than the one that Frank had only recently returned-to-sender.

Frank looked at it longingly, then at Danny. He couldn't possibly accept it. If he did, he'd be no better than McGuire, taking money from a builder in return for council contracts. 'Danny, I couldn't,' he said quietly, and slid the envelope back across the table.

Then, for the first time, he saw the less affable side of Danny Power. 'Yes, you fucking can,' he growled. 'What's the matter with you? You're not a priest any more. When are you going to wake up? This is the real world. You did some work for me, for every straight builder in London, and now I want to pay you for it. Don't insult me by giving it back. Don't insult your wife, don't insult those twins you're expecting. They need you and you need money, otherwise you wouldn't be driving a taxi. Now, take it. You've earned it.'

Danny was right. Frank was no longer a priest, he was a free-lance human being, having to earn money any way he could. He hadn't broken the law. Quite the contrary, he'd called a halt to some nasty illegal activities. He hadn't sought a reward, which was why he deserved one. Slowly he took back the money he'd earned. Danny reached over and got him in the old bear-hug. 'C'mere, you great bollix,' he said. 'You saved my business. I'll never be able to thank you enough.'

52

They knew what flavour they were and they knew they wouldn't be identical. Well, since Sarah's last scan had clearly shown a boy and a girl, they hoped they wouldn't be.

She and Frank had always insisted they didn't want to know, but as soon as they were offered the opportunity to find out, they'd jumped at it. Now they were looking forward to meeting two distinct human beings, rather than two nondescript 'babies'.

Had they both been boys, Frank would have been tempted to call them Ronnie and Reggie, just to see the look on Effy Baker's face. Even that would have been preferable to the names given to two little boys he had christened in Harlow just a few years previously. Their mother could not be dissuaded from calling them Robson and Jerome.

Sarah wanted to call the little girl Holly, since her romance with Frank had begun at Christmas. Frank had nodded and said, 'Yeah, but what are we going to call the boy – Santa?'

They were still no nearer finding two names; Nessie's latest, rather unhelpful New Age suggestion had been Yin and Yang.

Sarah was at her desk with a list of names and another of celebrities. Jane Steele's latest cruel move was to ask her if she'd mind 'doing a bit of fire-fighting' on MakeSure, the worst account in the agency. They were a horrible insurance company who, like many others, had seized on 9/11 as an excuse to double their customers' domestic-contents premiums. Feeding on the pernicious new compensation culture, they had opened a legal division for greedy, self-pitying individuals who wanted to sue their employers because they had tripped and nearly fallen on a loose carpet tile. MakeSure took half of whatever sum they acquired and were proud of their finger-pointing slogan: 'Get the name, fix the blame.' They also insisted on some sort of celebrity endorsement to hammer home their message, even though that celebrity would have no connection with either suing people or tripping over carpet tiles. Sarah wondered whether they adopted the same attitude to everything. Plumbing, for instance? 'Oh, it's going to be fine – Posh Spice is coming round to fix the stopcock.'

She tried to be sanguine and retain the insouciance that had kept her going but the camel's back was close to breaking and MakeSure might be the last straw. The one that would send her storming into Jane's office in a huge, hormonal huff and storm out again for ever.

'Fire-fighting' was a phrase much loved in the advertising industry but Sarah loathed it. As if helping some greedy insurance company make more money was akin to rescuing people from burning buildings. So, when she picked up the phone and heard a friendly voice she couldn't quite place from the past, she was at a particularly low ebb and at her most receptive. She felt like one of those depressed and aimless loners who fall into the hands of the Moonies.

'Sarah?'

'Yes?

'How's the greatest account director in the world?'

'Hungry,' she said, still not sure who it was.

'Good. Because, basically, I was just about to ask you out to lunch.'

The gratuitous use of the word 'basically' had given it away: it was Mike Babcock, the ex-client whom she thought she despised more than any other, and he now sounded almost human.

'Mike,' she said, relieved it wasn't the odious little man from MakeSure whose fire she was supposed to be fighting. 'How are you?'

'I'm good,' he replied.

Oh, God, Americanisms had found their way into his

vocabulary. If she accepted his invitation to lunch, he would no doubt say to the waiter, 'Could I get . . .' rather than 'May I have . . .'

'Basically, I'm involved in something very exciting,' he continued, 'and, Sarah, I think you could form a key part of my team.'

That put the smile back on her face. Lunch with Mike Babcock was always fun. However, since he was the joke he could never be in on it. Mike took himself incredibly seriously, which was why others tended not to. He'd always fancied Sarah but would never do anything about it. Even he didn't take himself seriously enough to think he stood a chance but, like most people, he still enjoyed close contact with those he found attractive.

When Sarah's huge protuberance entered the restaurant about ten minutes before she did, it was hard to say which was bigger: her belly or his disappointment.

Sarah had gone along largely to see the look on his face. She'd seen it, it had been a picture, and now she wanted to be back to her desk with a sandwich.

'Sarah,' he managed, 'you're – you're pregnant.'

'Nothing gets past you, does it, Mike?'

'Well, I – I never knew . . .'

'Yeah, I must have got married not long after I last saw you and, well, I got pregnant rather more quickly that I'd intended to – twins.'

'Um . . . right. Well, congratulations.'

'Thank you.'

Mike had no time for small-talk. He regarded himself as an all-conquering captain of industry who liked to 'cut to the chase'. The truth was, he simply couldn't do small-talk. He had no sense of humour or irony and no idea how to talk about anything other than his latest 'project'.

The waiter arrived to take the drinks order. They ordered a bottle of water, Sarah because she was seven months' pregn and Mike because he was far too important to 'lose focus' over lunch.

'Still or sparkling?'

'Still, please,' said Sarah. 'Fizzy water always reminds me of an itchy jumper,' she said to Mike.

He didn't really get it. He didn't get humour. 'Sarah,' he said, with his usual misplaced solemnity, 'let's cut to the chase. The old Mike Babcock is dead, long live the new one. Sure, I've made a few mistakes in the past. Basically, at the end of the day, who hasn't? But, in the final analysis, you know what the key thing is?'

Tell me, O font of all wisdom.

'To learn from them. Basically, I've been doing a lot of thinking and I'm not the sort of guy who can play to someone else's rules. I'm far better cutting my own swathe, thinking outside the box. I've always been too much of a wild card, too much of a loose cannon. Big organisations never appreciate true mavericks.'

From where Sarah was sitting, the new Mike Babcock seemed exactly like the old one. Possibly even more full of self-regarding piffle. She looked at the 'wild card' in his ironed shirt and neatly pressed slacks that had 'dress-down Friday' written all over them.

'At the end of the day, I had to go my own way. The old Mike was too constrained.'

'So, what has the new Mike been up to?' she asked, knowing he wouldn't notice the smirk in her voice.

'Well, basically, this may surprise you, but I've started going to church.'

'Church?' This really did surprise her. Someone with a sense of humour would have squeezed a little more juice out of it but, of course, Mike had to jump in immediately with the punch-line.

'Hey, not in some religious sense, no. Christ, I've been around the block too many times to fall for any of that crap.'

'So why have you been going to church?'

'Basically,' he said, as though a drum roll were going off beside him, 'because a church will be the basis for this secret project I might want to get you on board with. I've got a team of backers and we've come up with the most amazing idea.'

'Which is?'

Mike could hardly contain himself. 'We're going to open a nightclub in a church.'

Sarah had to be honest. 'It's not exactly an original idea, Mike. The Limelight opened in an old church on Charing Cross Road twenty-odd years ago and they were doing it in New York long before that.'

'Sure, sure,' said Mike, dismissively, 'but this place will be different. Bigger, more spectacular than anything this city has ever seen. Basically, we've looked at a number of key sites but they haven't been right. And there's all sorts of problems with deconsecrating.'

'Then getting the music and liquor licences,' added Sarah, 'plus the planning permission.'

'Not if you know the right people on the council.' He winked, tapping the side of his nose.

News of Cassidy, the Caped Crusader, plainly hadn't reached his ears.

'But at least we've got our DJ in place. I don't suppose you've heard of a place called Addiction. Why would you?'

Mike was too soaked in self-importance to see the look of momentary alarm on Sarah's face that she had banished within a second. 'You're right, Mike,' she said. 'Why would I?'

'Well, there's a DJ down there called Ben. Apparently he plays the most amazing music. Not really my zone but the guys who've seen him say he's awesome. Very odd bloke, though. Only works Sundays, never speaks, never gives interviews, never promotes himself. Almost unheard-of in this game, but I know what he's up to.'

'Really?' said Sarah, intrigued to see just how wide of the mark Mike's theory would be.

'Oh, yeah,' said Mike, with a condescending, man-of-the-world sigh. 'He's just trying to create a bit of mystique, push up his market value. It's an old trick that I'm too smart to fall for and I'll be the one negotiating with this Ben, whoever he is.'

Poor Mike. He really believed that the whole world was like him, pathologically obsessed with the 'bottom line'. He could hardly have been more wrong about 'Ben'.

'We've been watching this guy very closely,' he explained. 'When we find the right venue, we'll invite him down. He'll be overawed. Typical DJ, probably never seen the inside of a church before. He'll be desperate to be part of the action. That's why when we make him this offer there's no way he'll refuse.'

Sarah wasn't quite sure how to react. She was hiding her shock and amusement behind her napkin while thinking, Dream on, sucker, dream on.

But a tiny part of her was desperate to set fire to 'fire-fighting' and give up work for ever so she kept quiet. Maybe, just maybe, 'Ben' should hear what he was about to be offered.

53

When Prince Charles arrived in the world, the Duke of Edinburgh was playing squash. Frank's father hadn't been present at the birth of any of his children. Neither had Sarah's. Neither had most fathers before about 1970. The closest they'd got was the hospital corridor where they could pace up and down, chain-smoking. Yet now it was considered *de rigueur* for the father to witness the pushing, screaming, swearing and anguish that his moment of pleasure had resulted in.

For Frank, there would be none of this. The twins were to be released into the world by Caesarean section. It was abdominal surgery, but he would be expected to get Quincy'd up in mask, hat, gown and those ridiculous clogs so he could stand, rather impotently, holding Sarah's hand and offering support in the form of clichéd platitudes. He didn't really want to be there, any more than he would if she were having her appendix out, but he assumed she wanted him beside her so he wouldn't have considered refusing.

Sarah didn't really want him there. She knew how useless and in-the-way he would feel, but she assumed he wanted to be there so she wouldn't have considered refusing him.

So there he stood, squeezing her hand, making sure his eyes didn't stray over the screen. He didn't know whether or not he was squeamish but this wasn't the time or place to find out. He resisted the feeble joke cracked countless times before Caesareans about the woman looking just like John Hurt in *Alien* and repeatedly told her instead how brave she was, how wonderful she was and how much he loved her.

He saw very little blood so he remained upright and, on receipt of his son and daughter, he was surprised by how surprised he

PAUL BURKE

was. That Sarah had given birth should not have come as a shock. The gigantic stomach had been a bit of a clue. And yet, somehow, he couldn't equate it with the sudden existence of Joe and Holly Dempsey, now tightly swaddled and snuggled in his arms.

Ten minutes earlier, he'd had no children, now he had two and he still couldn't work out where they'd come from.

Only then did it dawn on him that their births were the beginning, not the end. Only then did it truly sink in that he was married, he was no longer a priest and that his life, as he'd always known it, was gone.

He looked down at them and felt a depth of adoration he hadn't known he was capable of. They were perfect – the greatest gifts he had ever received. Greater than his taxi, greater than all his records and even (though only just) greater than the second-hand Raleigh Chopper he'd been given for passing his eleven-plus.

He was overcome by a compulsion to thank someone but he didn't know who. His first instinct was to thank God, but he still didn't believe in Him. So he decided to 'thank God' using 'God' as a metaphor for everyone and everything *but* God: for nature, for Fate, for the surgeon, for the nurses, for Sarah, for the universe and for anyone else who had helped put these beautiful babies into his arms.

He wanted to celebrate this happiness and mark their arrivals and, to his horror, realised that there was only one way to do this. Although he had vowed that no child of his would ever be baptised, he was now undergoing that most uncomfortable of emotions: a change of mind.

The twins were enjoying their first night's sleep, lulling their parents into a false sense of security, making them think that it would always be like this. Joe was in his cot on one side of Sarah's bed, Holly was in hers on the other. Frank kept walking from one side of the bed to the other, then back, so he could keep gazing in wonder at each of them.

What he really wanted was to be dangled Barnum-style from the ceiling of the ward so he could look down at all three of them at the same time.

'Um . . . you know I said that no child of mine would ever be baptised . . .' he began.

Sarah raised a weary eyelid. 'Yes . . .'

'Well, I just think that they might like to have silver christening mugs too. No religious significance, mind.'

Sarah opened the other eye and grinned. 'No, no, of course not.'

'I just think,' said Frank, 'that not having a baptism is even more of a silly religious statement than just going ahead with one.'

'Whatever you say,' said Sarah, both eyes closed.

'I mean,' he continued, 'I do think that, viewed rationally, the whole idea of baptism is nonsense.'

'But then, so's Christmas,' said Sarah, eyes open again, 'and I can't imagine you refusing the gifts and goodwill just because you know, theologically, it probably isn't true.'

'You're right. And, well, although people may have accepted my reasons for leaving the priesthood . . .'

'I should hope so too.'

'. . . I'm not sure they'd be quite so understanding about not giving the children a christening.'

'And supposing,' said Sarah, 'just supposing the Catholic Church is right. Can you imagine getting up to heaven only to find that your children would never be allowed to join you?'

'Well,' said Frank, still bursting with besotted naïvety, and horrified at such a hypothesis, 'how could heaven be heaven without them?'

'Good,' said Sarah. 'Now, what about godparents?'

'Well, Nessie obviously,' said Frank. 'She's Bohemian, theatrical, generous, she's one of life's "eccentric aunts" and every child needs one of those.'

'And Niall?'

'Are you out of your mind?'

'He'd be great.'

'No,' said Frank. 'It would be too much like responsibility for him.'

'Well, ring him,' said Sarah. 'You see if I'm not right.'

Frank went outside and phoned Niall's mobile.

'Cassidy,' came the terse reply. Clearly Niall thought it was one of his narks.

'Niall, it's Frank.'

'Dempsey!'

'Where are you?' said Frank.

'In prison.'

Oh, God, maybe he wouldn't be such an ideal guardian of the twins' moral welfare.

'Prison?'

'Yeah. Nessie's here in the cell with me.'

'What?'

'Oh, don't worry. We're in Stockholm in this hotel called the Langholmen. It used to be a jail . . . What? Godparents? This prison must have done its job. My rehabilitation is complete. We'd be delighted.'

Like Frank had been a year earlier, Niall was keen to rejoin the human race.

Frank returned to the ward, but his family's six eyes were all shut so he went outside to phone another pair of godparents. It was a bit of a left-field idea. Frank hardly knew the potential godfather and had never even met the woman he was about to ask to be godmother. Sarah had never met them either, but the more Frank thought of it the more he thought they would be perfect.

When he rang, the response was as he'd expected.

'Fucking hell? You're having a laugh, ain't you? Me? Godfather to your two chavvies? I ain't been inside a church for thirty-seven years and look what happened to me then.'

'Effy,' said Frank, trying to cut through his old friend's throaty

chuckle, 'I'm serious. But if you're not up for it, I quite understand. I can always ask someone else.'

'Don't you fucking dare,' said Effy, deadly serious. 'I've never
been so up for anything in my life.'

54

'The christening's on Sunday the twenty-third,' said Frank. 'Means I won't be able to work that night. Mind you, neither will you.'

'Wonderful,' said Toby. 'Do you want to have the party here?'

'That's very kind of you,' said Frank, 'but the service is at the Church of the Sacred Heart in Quex Road.'

'Kilburn?' said Toby.

'Yeah, then afterwards in the parish centre next door.'

'Great,' said Toby. 'But isn't that the big Catholic church? I never really had you down as religious.'

'No, well, I'm not but . . . er . . . brace yourself,' said Frank, with a big sigh. 'I've got something to tell you.'

And he told him.

'You?' said Toby, for the eighth time. 'A Catholic priest?'

'Until recently, yes.'

'But you always said . . .'

'I didn't say anything.'

'Yes, you did. You said that your past life was something you didn't want to talk about.'

'Well, that's true.'

'And that you'd made a bit of a mistake when you were too young to know any better.'

'That's true as well.'

'And you were trying to rebuild your life.'

'And I have. I've got two children.'

'But I thought . . .'

'I know what you thought. You thought I was a villain. Charming.'

'I could hardly have been more wrong, could I?' said Toby, still staring at Frank incredulously. 'But why did you never say? There's nothing wrong with being a priest. Actually, priest-turned-DJ is pretty cool.'

'No, it isn't,' said Frank, shaking his head. 'You think it is now because I've sort of proved myself, but if you'd known I was a priest from the off, you'd never have given me a go, would you?'

Toby was about to say yes, but thought for a second and said, 'No.'

'Anyway, I've left it all behind. I don't want to come on like some trendy vicar who's now into drum'n'bass, sitting on the sofa telling Richard and Judy all about it. That's why I wanted to remain anonymous. Which, incidentally, I still do.'

'Absolutely,' said Toby.

'I'm only telling you now because you're a good mate,' said Frank. 'I want you to come to the christening and you'd have found out within two minutes of getting there. Anyway, I'm sorry.'

'What for?' said Toby. 'You never lied to me.'

'Yeah, but I deliberately deceived you.'

'Well, I'm bloody glad you did.' Toby smiled. 'We've got the biggest one-nighter in London. Long may it continue.'

And who knows how much longer it might have continued if Frank hadn't taken his usual afternoon trip to the steam room?

55

Frank had never been so happy, or so unhappy, at exactly the same time for exactly the same reason. Though his love for the twins increased exponentially by the day, nothing could have prepared him for the depths of physical fatigue into which he would be plunged. He had always intended to do his share of nocturnal feeds and nappy-changes but, like any father of twins, he had no choice. When four tiny lungs were yelling for a feed, what else could he do? When they finally went to sleep and were eerily silent, Frank would go to check that they were still breathing, wake them up and have to spend the next two hours getting them back to sleep again.

It was no wonder that, when he was getting himself ready for work in the morning, he found that even his hair and eyebrows were aching. Unable even to contemplate physical exercise, he still trundled along to the Go For It! Health and Fitness Club, but the steam room was now the only 'it' he was going for.

The ten minutes he spent in there were his only chance to relax, reflect and recharge, the only time he had on his own, which was why he was always disappointed if anyone else joined him. On this occasion, two men in their late thirties were chatting excitedly. He couldn't see their faces through the steam but from their voices, he'd decided instinctively that one was called Simon and the other almost certainly Martin.

On second thoughts make that Martyn. With a Y.

Martyn was busy telling Simon all about his 'new hobby'.
'Oh, it's fantastic,' said Martyn. 'I should have done it years ago.'

'Yeah, but you couldn't, could you?' said Simon. 'Not without the Internet.'

'No, I suppose not, but it's so easy now. There isn't a track you can't download from somewhere.'

The word 'track' made Frank's ears prick up and he was dismayed to discover that Martyn's new hobby was DJ-ing.

'Well, everyone's doing it now,' said Simon.

'Aha,' said Martyn, with a smug chuckle, 'but they're not doing it like me. I've got this new software that basically means I don't even use CDs. I can download everything on to my hard drive so all I have to bring to a gig is a laptop.'

There and then Frank decided he no longer wanted to be a DJ. At his age, he could easily be mistaken for a Martyn who had taken it up in his thirties in a belated attempt to be hip. Martyn probably had little interest in music. He wouldn't have been a regular at Auntie Jean's, or at Bluebird or City Sounds, waiting for the latest imports to arrive, yet he and his laptop could set themselves up as DJs.

Martyn wasn't doing anything wrong, and perhaps the world had moved on. Perhaps Frank, with his crateloads of vinyl, was no more than a Luddite, reacting the way bandleaders must have done when Jimmy Savile first started playing records at dances.

Whatever. The game was up. Frank was going to quit while he was ahead. But how would he, Sarah and the twins avoid the inevitable slide towards the breadline? He had no idea.

He'd worry about that after the christening.

56

Effy's suit didn't fit properly. It had come back from the dry-cleaner's slightly tighter, pressed in the wrong places with that unwelcome ridge at the back of the neck. Still, he was delighted to be wearing it and took his duties very seriously. Mrs Effy was a handsome East End matriarch named Elaine, pronounced 'Eeelaine' by her husband, who clearly did as she told him. Frank had been slightly concerned that Effy would start effing during the service, but he needn't have been. Like many a foul-mouthed man of a certain vintage, he didn't like 'swearing in front of ladies', and Frank had a suspicion that Eeelaine would have boxed his ears if he'd stepped out of line.

The ill-fitting suit meant that Effy himself was far from ill-fitting. The place was a catwalk of ill-fitting suits. Those worn by Joe Hennessey, by Frank's dad, by his Uncle Eddie and by most of the other guests were every bit as bad.

In Kilburn the Irish community had shrunk considerably over the years as the older residents moved back to Ireland or out to the suburbs. But for one night only they were back, many still wearing the suits they had worn to mass thirty years before. Planeloads from Shannon and Cork, carloads from Wembley and Wealdstone, the same faces, albeit much older, who had danced and drunk the night away at Frank's christening at this same venue, their lust for both activities undiminished by the years.

Nessie had given a beautiful rendition of 'Ave Maria' to lend a little panache to the service, but once inside the parish centre, once the caeli band had struck up in the corner, ill-fitting jackets were thrown to one side as ancient legs defied arthritis to dance the 'Walls of Limerick'.

Toby, who thought he'd seen some 'serious partying' over the years, had never seen anything like this. There were no spritzers, cranberry juice, mineral water or freshly squeezed orange. These people drank properly and brought with them the heavy aroma of Guinness, brown ale and Irish whiskey to prove it. And, once the Cellophane was removed from the buffet, that aroma was augmented by the smells of white bread sandwiches, greasy sausage rolls and weighty slabs of pork and egg pie.

Toby had been foolish to believe he could come to this party as a polite, casual observer. Within minutes, he had been grabbed by one of Frank's many aunts and corralled into dancing frenetically around the hall. He didn't know any of the steps but that didn't matter – neither did anyone else.

Sarah thought she was hallucinating when she saw her mother, usually so politely and Englishly inhibited, reeling wildly with Jimmy the Wardrobe.

Frank made the shortest speech of his life. He bowed to pressure and took to the stage, taking Sarah and the twins with him. 'What can I say?' he asked. 'What do I need to say but [*eyes to the left*] thank you [*eyes to the middle*], thank you [*eyes to the right*], thank you. And may I ask you to raise your glasses to the late Father Jack Dore.'

The very mention of this name brought tears to some of the older eyes. Back in the sixties, this charismatic Irish priest had made Quex Road the liveliest parish in Britain.

'Father Dore,' said Frank, 'as you hardly need reminding, was an inspiration to us all. He was the catalyst for so many friendships that began in this hall and are still in evidence today. It was because of him that I wanted to become a priest. It was because I was a priest that I met my wife. It's because I met her that we have two beautiful children, so if it wasn't for Father Dore, none of us would be here today. Ladies and gentlemen, Father Dore.'

Frank looked on as Toby and Effy Baker repeated, 'Father Dore,' and raised their glasses to a man they deeply admired but, until thirty seconds earlier, had never heard of.

Fired up by warmth and nostalgia, the party revved up to new heights and Toby, now wet with sweat, could see that if this was what Frank had been brought up on, no wonder he could wind up a crowd.

Sarah was tired, and the twins, who had been passed around the hall like a pair of parcels, needed to be tucked up in their cots. The party was well and truly alight, would blaze on for hours, so the Dempseys could slip away practically unnoticed.

On the way home, Frank thought for a moment about what he had just done. He'd returned to Kilburn, to the church where he had been baptised, where he'd received the sacraments of confession, Holy Communion, confirmation and Holy Orders. He'd proposed a toast to his former parish priest and had danced 'O'Sullivan's March' with dozens of Irish people. He was now married with two kids, whom he'd just had baptised as Catholics.

So far, the Great Escape wasn't going terribly well.

57

Frank had to work. If he didn't work he didn't get paid, so although – prompted by 'Martyn' – he had decided to give it up, the lucrative Sunday night at Addiction was the one thing he couldn't afford to miss.

He felt guilty about leaving Sarah, now a hollow-eyed zombie and a shell of her former self, but what could he do? What had started off as a bit of fun was now the only way he could feed his family.

It was way past midnight when he staggered back to find three people crying instead of two. Sarah had a screaming child in each arm and tears of fatigue and frustration cascading down her cheeks, so when Frank put down his records and picked up his children, it was as if he had given her Harry Winston's entire stock of diamonds. He hadn't seen the twins all evening and, despite the ear-splitting noise they were making, he'd missed them. He clipped them into their little car seats, then fastened them into the back of the cab.

Frank headed out on to the Fulham Road and slotted his 'Get Them To Sleep' tape into the machine. The Beatles were first to lend a hand with 'Here There And Everywhere', followed by Brook Benton, who got their little eyelids drooping with 'A Rainy Night In Georgia'. By the time Johnny Hartman turned up to croon 'I See Your Face Before Me', which, apparently, surgeons have been known to use as a general anaesthetic, the job was done.

With his rear-view mirror trained on two tiny, sleeping faces, he was about to turn round and take them home but they seemed quite happy so he carried on. Up past the Michelin building, the

Brompton Oratory, Harrods and round Hyde Park Corner towards Buckingham Palace. Unlike the legions of 'Laddy Daddies', Frank refused to display a 'Baby on Board' sticker on his rear window. How were other motorists supposed to react? 'Oh, sorry, I *was* going to crash into the back of you but since you have a "Baby on Board", I won't'? What point were the parents trying to make? Initially Frank had found 'Baby on Board' stickers stupid but harmless, until he realised the upset they caused to ex-parishioners who had come to him for counselling, having suffered the heartbreak of a miscarriage. He now wanted to make those smug little stickers illegal.

Tonight, because he hadn't seen any and because the light was good, the night was mild and the streets were almost deserted, Frank felt wonderfully content. He took the twins on their first excursion to the Houses of Parliament, the London Eye, St Paul's Cathedral and Canary Wharf. He drove them through the Blackwall Tunnel, past the Royal Observatory and the *Cutty Sark* for a rare glimpse of Greenwich unchoked with traffic. Back over Tower Bridge they cruised, through the almost silent City, along Fleet Street, the Strand and back around Trafalgar Square, Frank thinking of the memories each landmark held for him.

His contentment, however, was like a two-tone tonic suit. Viewed from a different angle, the discontent that formed part of its fabric was easy to see.

This taxi was supposed to have dropped him off by now, at a sensible and lucrative career. Yet he was still looking out of the window, unable to find anywhere he wanted to get out. As he went through the City he'd shuddered at the thought of working there, or of working anywhere that had a water-cooler.

He had spent his life running away from reality but now, with his two latest passengers, he was firmly entrenched in it.

He thought of Sarah, and of another thing he'd remembered from his time as a counsellor: the three ways of being good to someone – physically, emotionally and financially. A good husband, the husband he wanted to be, was all three. The first two, he hoped, would never be a problem, but the third was proving a lot more difficult.

By the time he got home, he'd had an idea. A few weeks earlier, a suggestion had been made, in a note left beside the DJ booth, about how 'Ben' could make a fortune. It would have meant leaving Empire Furnishings so he'd turned the offer down.

However, just before he threw away the piece of paper, he'd flattened it out and logged the number into his mobile.

Something must have told him that, one day, he might have to change his mind.

58

'Hi, Sarah, it's Mike. How are you?'

'Fine, thanks.'

'And the twins?'

'Just divine.'

'Good, good,' he replied briskly.

Sarah felt she could have said, 'Well, I've just had both my legs amputated and I'm afraid the twins are dead,' and she'd have got the same brisk, uninterested response.

'Listen, we've found the venue. Basically, it's awesome. Why don't you pop down and take a look?'

Mike, loathsome as he was, had an unerring ability to catch Sarah at a weak moment. This time he'd caught her wishing she was Elsa the lioness in *Born Free*. Elsa didn't get torn away from her cubs just as they were building a beautiful bond. Elsa didn't get sent off to work in an advertising agency. Sarah's return to her desk was imminent and although she had initially been desperate to get back, now she was dreading it. Some well-paid freelance consultancy work for Mike Babcock and his 'team', with whom she knew she'd only be a minor 'player', might be a way of delaying that return and eking out a little more time with Frank and the twins. 'Yeah, okay. When?' she said.

'Tomorrow – about twelve? It's called St Gabriel's – huge church in Chelsea, Cadogan Square, you can't miss it.'

'Yeah, fine,' she said. 'See you there.'

It was a gorgeous morning – reminiscent of the one she and Frank had enjoyed in New York, which now seemed like several lifetimes ago. She decided to walk and chose a pair of shoes from the collection filed under 'Comfortable almost Sapphic'. It felt strange at first to be without a double buggy, but she had to admit that it was a glorious feeling to stroll unencumbered along the Kings Road. When she got to the church, Mike was waiting outside and, to her surprise, he hadn't been exaggerating – the place was stunning. An exquisite Gothic interior with a high nave culminating in a huge round stained-glass window and a soaring spire.

'This is St Gabriel's,' said Mike, 'or, as it will soon be universally known, Gabrielle's, the most famous nightclub in the world. Of course, the residents are opposed to our plans but, basically, at the end of the day, they've only got themselves to blame. It's all very well bleating on about this beautiful church but no one goes to it. You know what they say, "Use it or lose it," and I'm afraid they're about to lose it. That's just the way things crumble, cookie-wise.'

Sarah had never noticed St Gabriel's before, even though it was right between Harvey Nichols and Peter Jones, two emporia where she'd spent many happy hours so, in that respect, much as she was loth to admit it, Mike was right. She was as much to blame as anyone else. People simply didn't go to church any more. She was married to an ex-priest, and even he didn't go to church any more. But the thought of turning this beautiful, holy, consecrated place into a tacky nightclub filled her with disgust. Mike was still talking.

'Basically, we're saving St Gabriel's. We're not tearing it down. We're going to keep as much of the interior as we can. Hey, let's face it, we'd be mad not to. Don't you think it will make the most unbelievable venue?'

'Yes, it would,' she said. Meaning, in somebody else's hands. Any consortium that had Mike Babcock 'on board' would be devoid of any semblance of taste or style. This club would certainly be unbelievable, but in the worst sense of the word.

'Now, we don't intend to hand this project to an ad agency. Basically, I'll be suggesting to the rest of the team that we put it all through you. I'm sure, with your contacts, you can source the talent you need. This is going to be a hell of a launch, we're spending serious dosh and we'd pay you very well. What do you say?'

It was tempting but Sarah's gut instinct was to turn it down. Mike Babcock was involved, it had to end in disaster – but what an easy way to make some cash and extend her maternity leave.

'I'll need to think about it, Mike,' she said. 'I'm due back at work on Monday week.'

'Okay, but let me know ASAP,' said Mike. 'It's absolutely key that we start the ball rolling. Next step is to find this guy Ben and get him on board.'

Unknown to Mike, 'Ben' was sitting just yards away, waiting in a taxi with a double buggy in the back.

59

From St Gabriel's Church, Sarah and Frank had driven up to Kensington Gardens to take the twins for a stroll into Hyde Park and let the combination of sunshine, fresh air and perpetual motion rock them to sleep. When they reached the south side of the Serpentine, they were able to park the now silent buggy and lie down on the grass next to it. Sarah lay at right angles to Frank with her head on his chest. They were both strangely subdued, with their own mixture of joy and despair. Sarah felt like a soldier in the First World War, allowed to snatch a moment of happiness before being sent off to the trenches. Frank felt an ever-increasing burden of guilt at being unable to keep her where she so obviously wanted to be.

At around four, he took them all home, knowing he'd better go out and earn some money so the kids wouldn't have to be sold into slavery. He kissed them all goodbye and said he'd be back by ten. 'Any problems, just ring me and I'll come straight back.'

But that was the problem. There weren't any problems. Now and again, of course, but after the unmitigated hell that had been the first ten weeks, she and Frank had got it down to a fine art. The bathing, drying, feeding and dressing process was like a mini-production line. They'd done the hard bit, they'd finally got the hang of it, and now Sarah would have to hand over the most precious things in her life to a child-minder for eight hours a day, five days a week.

The bond she'd only just formed would be broken, and she couldn't bear the thought of missing out, as she no doubt would, on the first time they sat up, the first time they crawled, their first steps, their first words, all of which were likely to happen when she was in some dreary client meeting.

She'd always believed that she could polish her fading career back to its former effulgence, and no doubt she could. But did she really want to? It would take a phenomenal effort. She would have to double her work rate just to prove she was still half as good as she had been. Was it really worth it? Did she truly want to give all those units of Sarah Dempsey to her job, leaving almost none for her children?

She was now horrified at the impending prospect of 'juggling' while Jane Steele sat in the front row, arms folded, waiting for her to drop the balls.

The pressures and problems faced by working mothers had been well documented, but until now Sarah had never empathised with them. As dusk fell on Fulham, she got the twins ready for bed, pressing her nose into their little towelling sleepsuits and breathing in the delicious scent of fabric-conditioner and baby. She put Joe into his cot first. As Holly was gently and adoringly placed into hers, she opened one eye and gave her mummy a beautiful little smile, never knowing the damage it would do.

It hit Sarah like a vicious blow with a blunt instrument, and she felt the searing pain of having her babies wrenched away from her on Monday week. She sank to her knees and sobbed.

She didn't want to go back to work with those dreadful clients, she never wanted to see Jane Steele again or Mike Babcock and his revolting plans for St Gabriel's Church. She lay there, sobbing, for the best part of an hour, but luckily Frank hadn't had time to phone and check that they were all okay. One of them was far from okay but she couldn't tell him why. He already had two jobs and did everything he could to help her. Her brave face would have to be applied, with her makeup, on Monday week. Even Frank was powerless this time. What on earth, realistically, could he do to save her?

60

A few years ago Frank had realised that a lot of people didn't buy records any more, they bought compilation CDs, often with tracks chosen and mixed by superstar DJs. They were now too busy or too lazy to go out vinyl-hunting, preferring to trust their favourite DJs to do it for them. The note left at the Empire Furnishings DJ booth had suggested that a CD featuring tracks chosen by Ben at Addiction would outsell anything put out by Fabric, Cream or Ministry of Sound.

Frank decided he would only do this if he was about to bid farewell for ever to the club. The double CD would be bought by thousands of people as an everlasting reminder of the best club they had ever been to, and by thousands more who'd never been to Empire Furnishings but wanted to pretend they had.

He was forty-one with two small children. His career as a DJ had been given a second lap of the track but he didn't want to hang around to witness its inevitable decline. Now was the time to cash in his chips.

Typically charitable, Frank was motivated not just by making money for himself but by providing royalties for semi-obscure artists who had probably been paid a pittance the first time round. Just like UB40 had done so commendably for all those forgotten reggae artists, whose work they had unearthed and covered.

He was paying even more attention to the music now, and the club's popularity, as expected, was reaching Himalayan heights: he was testing out what would and wouldn't work on the compilation CDs, and starting to play like a musician, making sure rhythms and melodies fitted together and that sour key clashes were always avoided. One eye, as always, was on the dance-floor.

These people, and thousands like them, were going to be his pension. Before he made his final choice of tunes, he had to be certain that every one was a belter. John Handy's 'Hard Work' and Johnny 'Guitar' Watson's 'I Need It' were definitely in: they always seemed to persuade those who had just been thinking about dancing to start moving a limb or two.

Maybe because he was concentrating so hard, Frank failed to take much notice of the man standing by the DJ booth, watching him intently. He'd seen him out of the corner of his eye, and when he turned round again, five tunes later, the man was still there.

What did he want? Addiction regulars never made requests, knowing that what Frank served up would be far better than whatever they'd had in mind. Eventually he caught Frank's eye.

'Hello, Frank. Fancy meeting you here.'

This was not a man Frank had ever expected to see again, let alone in a DJ bar. 'Fancy meeting *you* here,' was the only reply he could think of.

'Well, I've had a marvellous evening,' he replied, in his rich, cultured baritone. 'I haven't enjoyed myself so much in years.'

'Good,' said Frank, with a slightly awkward smile. 'Glad to be of service.'

The man continued staring at Frank. 'Look,' he said, 'I'm glad I've bumped into you here, of all places. There's something I want to discuss with you. Now's not really the time. I can see you're busy.' He handed Frank his card. 'Here's my number. Will you call me tomorrow? Really, the sooner the better.'

'Yeah, fine.' Frank was still almost dumbstruck. 'I'll call you in the morning.'

'There's a good a chap. I'll look forward to it. Anyway, cheerio and well done. Splendid music, absolutely splendid.'

Frank watched him go. New Jersey Connection's 'Love Don't Come Easy' had ended and he was jolted back into the real world by the sight of people standing still on the dance-floor covering their ears in agony at the gruesome sound of a stylus with a thousand watts of power behind it going round and round and round.

Such was his shock at seeing William Chambers that, for the first time in his life, Frank had left one turntable empty. His mind had gone blank. He couldn't think straight. He certainly couldn't think what to put on next so he plonked the stylus back at the beginning and played 'Love Don't Come Easy' again. The regulars didn't mind: they thought he was being 'like, really, really ironic'.

He wasn't. He could only think about William Chambers. And how different he looked without his mitre.

61

Bishop William Chambers was always called William. Appellations like Will, Bill or Billy would, even in his youth, have been wholly inappropriate. Even then, he'd been a committed young fogey, wearing a three-piece Harris tweed suit before he was twenty, but now, at sixty-four, the learned cleric had finally grown into his age.

Frank had known him for more than twenty years, dating back to when he was just the Reverend Chambers, lecturer in theology at Oxford University. They had arranged to meet in the morning room of the Oxford and Cambridge Club on Pall Mall, where Bishop Chambers blended perfectly into his surroundings as though he, too, were made of oak panelling, old leather and vintage claret.

Frank had felt compelled to go along, if only to find out what on earth this most unlikely of clubbers had been doing enjoying soul, funk and reggae the previous night. 'Oh,' he chuckled, 'it was my daughter's birthday. I was going to take the family out to dinner but she insisted on going to this discothèque. She assured me that I wouldn't be the only one over sixty and that I'd have a jolly good time and she was right. It was marvellous. I couldn't believe it when I saw you playing the records. I must apologise for staring but I didn't have my glasses and I had to be absolutely certain it was you.'

'Well, I'm afraid it was,' said Frank, with a smile.

'So, how are you, old chap? I hear you've left the priesthood and got married.'

'That's right,' said Frank.

The heavy ticking of the old grandfather clock in the corner punctuated the first pause between them. Tick, tock, tick, tock.

Frank knew that Bishop Chambers knew more than he was letting on. And the bishop knew he knew. Both men were shrewd, perspicacious and an extremely good judge of character. Like that classic game of chess between Fischer and Spassky, this was going to be an interesting encounter.

'Shame,' sighed the bishop, shaking his head. 'Damned shame.'

Frank said nothing.

'No, no,' he added apologetically, 'not for you, my dear chap, or for your lady wife. Goodness me, no. But for all your parishioners, for the Archdiocese of Westminster and for the Catholic Church. You were such a wonderful priest.'

Still Frank said nothing.

Tick, tock, tick, tock.

'Which is why . . .' said the bishop, slowly and deliberately.

Tick, tock, tick, tock.

'. . . I think you'd make a wonderful vicar.'

Still Frank said nothing, but this time the bishop matched his silence with silence. The grandfather clock was now almost deafening. Somebody had to speak first, and courtesy dictated that it was Frank. He shook his head. 'Me? A vicar?' he said, too shocked to put any power into his voice.

'Well, why not? You've proved you can do it,' said the bishop, suddenly adopting the furtive tone of a character in a John le Carré novel. 'Don't tell me you've never thought about crossing over to the other side.'

'No, I haven't,' said Frank. 'I've given all that up and, anyway, I never liked that Tory MP.'

'What Tory MP?'

'Shaun Woodward – the one who defected to Labour. If he wants to change parties, that's fine but he should have stood down and contested a by-election. Most people vote for a party, not for a person. Usually they don't even know the candidate's name. No, I couldn't do it, I wouldn't want to behave like Shaun Woodward.'

'But you wouldn't be,' said the bishop. 'I mean, you've already stood down.'

'And one of the reasons I did,' said Frank, pausing for his usual dramatic effect, 'is that I don't believe in God.'

To his surprise, this revelation had no effect at all.

'You don't say,' said the bishop, with a friendly, sardonic shrug. 'I could see that when you were at Oxford. You were probably the most sceptical student I've ever taught. I couldn't believe it when you became a priest and I'm amazed you lasted so long.'

'Exactly,' said Frank. 'At last I can be honest with myself. I'm an agnostic. I want to live a secular life. I know it's an old cliché but most of the trouble in the world is caused by religion. When do you ever hear of dangerous agnostic fundamentalists?'

'About as often as you hear about dangerous Church of England fundamentalists,' said the bishop. 'You know as well as I do, it's a very easy-going creed. Think of it as . . . well . . . Catholicism Lite.'

He could see that Frank was, indeed, thinking about it and gently started to play his advantage.

'I hear you're now the proud father of twins.'

Frank smiled. The very mention of his progeny brought a swift flush of pleasure to his cheeks. 'Yeah, Joe and Holly,' he said. 'Three and half months.'

'Congratulations,' said the bishop, with his most benevolent clergyman's smile. He, too, was a master of the rhetorical pause. He paused. 'Lot of responsibility, though. Have you thought about that?'

'I've thought about nothing else,' said Frank, beginning to weaken.

'Now, don't get me wrong,' said the bishop, 'if you want to drive a taxi and play records in a disco for the rest of your life that's entirely up to you, but you have an exceptional talent as a Christian clergyman. A talent that, in my view, is going to waste. You were truly brilliant. You say you don't believe in God but you were damned good at making other people believe in Him.'

'But is that right?' said Frank.

'Well, believing in the Church of England version of God is fairly harmless. In fact, I think it's a good thing. Wasn't it G.K. Chesterton who said that the trouble with not believing in God isn't that people will believe in nothing . . .'

'. . . it's that they'll believe in anything,' said Frank, with a smile, remembering the bishop's Oxford theology lectures.

'And I think he had a point,' said the bishop. 'Christianity is fundamentally a good creed. A creed based on love, compassion and forgiveness. There are a lot worse places to put your faith. And you were always so good at emphasising these tenets. Far too good not to do it again.'

'But, as I said, my life has moved on,' Frank insisted. 'I don't want to do it again.'

'Don't you?' said the bishop, affecting bewilderment. 'You surprise me.'

Tick, tock. Tick, tock.

'Don't you miss the good you always did for other people?' the bishop continued. 'Don't you miss the happiness you brought them, the difference you made to their lives? I used to joke with Cardinal Hayes that I'd offer him a ten-million-pound transfer fee to sign you for the other side.'

'Ten million quid?' said Frank, trying to joke his way off the hook. 'If you'd told me that, I'd have signed immediately.'

The bishop, with only a polite smile to acknowledge Frank's levity, kept him right there on the hook. 'But now you're married with children, you can never play for your old team again.'

Pause.

'But you can come and play for us.'

'But I don't believe in God,' Frank insisted.

Now it was the bishop's turn to joke. 'This is the Church of England, old boy.' He chuckled. 'Most of the congregations don't either. And, anyway, how many people did you tell about your little secret? Let me guess. None. You're too good a man to want to disappoint them.'

'Or to show myself up as a phoney.'

Bishop Chambers looked delighted with Frank's last remark, as well he might. It was the first time since their conversation opened that he hadn't protested or disagreed. He stayed silent and let Frank's tight objections start to unravel. He took a sip of his sherry and let the grandfather clock do its work.

Frank was thinking, and the more he thought about it the more ideal a solution the bishop's idea seemed. Not just for him but for Sarah. He wasn't stupid, he knew she didn't want to go back to work, he knew she often cried in the afternoons and he knew why. Empire Furnishings, no matter how good it was, wouldn't last for ever. Clubbers would stop going there simply because it wasn't new any more, so as a source of income it would eventually dry up. And he'd already decided to quit. The wily old boy's timing had been impeccable.

'Frank, your energy and sense of fun would be perfect for the Church of England. It desperately needs a shot of Catholic passion and community spirit, and I can think of no better person than you to provide it. All right, so you only get a basic stipend but everything you'd spend your money on is already taken care of.'

Frank got that queasy feeling that told him the change he was contemplating was worth making. He'd had it when he was offered the chance to go to Oxford, he'd had it when he'd decided to become a priest and he'd had it more powerfully than ever when he'd decided to give up being a priest and marry the girl of his dreams. Once the queasiness arrived, he knew that whatever he was considering was a good idea. The queasiness intensified when he thought how his stipend might soon be augmented by nice fat royalty cheques from his nearly compiled CD.

The bishop was watching him carefully. 'I have a parish in mind that would be perfect for you,' he said. 'Oh, you should see it, you'd love it. I'm sure your wife would too. Historic church, lovely setting, beautiful old vicarage.'

Suddenly the queasiness stopped. Beautiful old vicarage? Frank went stone cold at the thought of moving out to the country. Now he wasn't so sure. Yes, he could always motivate people from the pulpit, wherever that pulpit happened to be, but he was a metropolitan animal. He liked lamp-posts, he liked pavements. He didn't want to be stuck out in the middle of nowhere, 'beautiful old vicarage' or not.

'Well,' he said cautiously, 'it depends where this parish is.'

'Oh, don't worry about that,' said the bishop. 'You've spent your whole life in London, I wouldn't send you out to the sticks. No, this parish has fantastic potential but it's in dire need of funds so you really would have to get out in that taxi of yours and raise some.'

'So, where exactly is it?' said Frank.

'Well,' replied the bishop, 'Chelsea – Cadogan Square. It's called St Gabriel's, do you know it?'

PAUL BURKE

Father Frank

Father Frank Dempsey is a Roman Catholic priest who harbours an almighty secret: he doesn't believe in God.

Despite this, or maybe because of it, he is brilliant and hugely successful as a priest. His unconventional methods, which include driving a taxi to raise funds, bring his flock together and transform what was once a drab North London parish.

It's all going beautifully until Sarah Marshall hops into his taxi and into his life, slowly putting his vows under incredible strain.

Untorn Tickets

Two friends, one scam, heroic possibilities . . .

Notting Hill – 1978. Dave Kelly and Andy Zymanczyk are classmates at a strict Catholic school. Both, desperate to escape their stifling backgrounds, get part-time work in their local cinema.

Here they form a binding friendship and embark on a voyage of discovery. Dave falls in love with Rachel, a Jewish girl who also wants to escape from her strict background, while Andy falls for a girl he knows he can never have.

When the cinema is threatened with closure, the boys realise that more than their new-found freedom is at risk.

PRAISE FOR PAUL BURKE:

'A dazzling first novel – funny, thoughtful and original' STEPHEN FRY

'Refreshing' ADELE PARKS

'A warm, funny, blisteringly good read' TONY PARSONS

HODDER